PHILLY FICTION

PHILLY FICTION

**A Collection of Short Stories Highlighting
Philadelphia as a City of Literary Inspiration**

edited by

**Josh McIlvain
Christopher Munden
Greg November
Tracy Parker**

**DON RON BOOKS
Philadelphia, Pennsylvania**

Published by Don Ron Books
P. O. Box 39861
Philadelphia, Pa. 19106

Printed in the United States in the Commonwealth of Pennsylvania.

Cover art and design: Theron C. Warren
Layout: Christopher Munden
Layout assistance: Jeff McKay

ISBN: 0-9774772-0-7
Library of Congress Control Number: 2005937298

TABLE OF CONTENTS

INTRODUCTION

These stories, all by writers affiliated with Philadelphia, draw upon the city for inspiration, showing it in all its grit and glory. Our deepest gratitude goes to the writers who contributed to *Philly Fiction*, both those whose works are featured within and those whose stories we were unable to publish. We would also like to thank you, reader. We hope you enjoy this book.

—The Editors.

Elise Juska
The Stoop-Sitters

The women head on out like always, in that hour when the day goes from light to dark and their kids crowd into the street to play halfball and their teenagers take off in loud cars and tight clothes and their men, if they've still got them, settle into the couch in front of the Phillies game and the lightning bugs fire up all over and the smells of dinners still hang like glue in the sweat-thick Philly June air.

They come out slow. Mrs. Johnson pushing her bug-eyed sunglasses on her nose, even though it's too dark out to need them. Mrs. Donohue opening up her mailbox even though there's no way she's won Publishers Clearinghouse since last time she checked. Mrs. O'Hanlan turning on the rainbow Christmas lights she keeps blinking around her front door all year long.

The women stand in their doorways a minute, taking in the sky, the street. West Fifth Street is crammed full of rowhouses. Windows yanked open to air out cramped kitchens, curtains squirming in hot damp breezes. Patches of lawn burned brown by the sun, some with pinwheels or plastic animals jammed in them. Rita Carroll's got a PIERSON SECURITY eyeball she picked off a rich person's lawn to scare away robbers.

Then the women sigh the sigh. It's the sigh that goes, *What the hell, why not sit for awhile? Nothing better going on tonight.* Thing is, they never do anything different. But I think it's that pausing and looking around and pretending to make an actual decision about it that helps them feel like maybe their world is a little bigger than a row of skinny houses, a row of concrete stoops, and a row of sweaty, barefoot women lined up on them.

I watch them take their seats. With my legs bent up to my chest, I can still just fit inside my upstairs window. The old ones drag out lawn chairs and wave paper fans or rolled-up tabloids in their faces. They wear tent shorts that cover half their legs, all blue veins and cottage cheese fat. They wear T-shirts with no bras, but they've always got a word stamped across their saggy chests: *Temple U* or *76ers* or, if they have kids who take vacations, *Sea World* or *Greetings from Nashville, Tennessee.*

Younger ones like Mom sit on the stoop directly. Mom's little as a kid, only five foot three. She wears cut-off jean shorts and tank tops and no bra, which is funny because she works at Sears in the Department of Intimate Apparel. When I was too little to stay home alone, I'd hide in the middle of them round bra racks and watch ladies' hands picking through them, feeling all the lace and silk like fruit at the Acme.

The stoop-sitters drop their flip-flops. They crack their can lids, lean their heads back. Mrs. Stingel next door drinks Michelob Lights. Pat Johnson drinks gin and tonics out of a gift glass from the Sunoco on Rhawn Street, where her husband's a pumper. Mom smokes Virginia Slims and flexes her tan toes and flips her hair like she's flirting with a man in her mind.

But when Lisa Stingel walks out on her stoop, everything stops for a minute. Lisa's the prettiest girl on West Fifth, hands down. She's seventeen, four years older than me. I know Mom's hoping that soon I start acting like Lisa. I know she wants me wearing tight skirts and candy pink lipstick and going to school dances. That way, the women will head over to our stoop on prom night. When Lisa went, in May, all the stoop-sitters came around to see her in her crunchy red dress with shiny straps. Lisa flipped her hair and flashed her teeth like she took lessons in it. "She could be on TV," Mrs. Donohue breathed. "She looks just like that girl who plays on *Ryan's Hope.*" All the couples stood in a line, and I felt bad for the other girls, sized up next to Lisa. The stoop-sitters snapped pictures on the throwaway paper cameras they bought down at Willy's Super Discount Drug, and waved and waved as the limo pulled away, like they all took a little credit for how Lisa turned out.

But tonight, Lisa's back is slumped, like whatever used to hold her up straight split in half. She takes a seat on the bottom step by her mother's feet and bends her long legs to her chin. Mrs. Stingel smoothes Lisa's long hair with the flat of her palm, once, then picks up her beer. Lisa wipes a finger of sweat from the crook of her knee. The stoop-sitters each lift a hand in a wave, light a cigarette, squint skyward.

The stoop-sitters share walls. On West Fifth Street, one skinny house runs straight into the next one. On our left is the McGillicuddys, two parents and four grown boys. The boys are always banging in late and have big arms, big feet, big green mesh Eagles jerseys, and crewcuts that look like they'd cut you if you touched them. They wear gold crosses that jiggle around their necks like nervous tics. When Danny McGillicuddy was over in the Gulf War, the whole mess of them crowded on their stoop one night and those big boys sang "Danny Boy" so gentle and sweet it made the whole street cry.

On the other side is the Stingels. Mrs. Stingel is little and hard and Mr. Stingel is big and fat, and I can't for the life of me figure out how those two bodies made Lisa. Mr. Stingel's a cop who Mom says stays behind a desk cause he's too soft to be on the street. Mrs. Stingel and Mom are best friends. Sometimes, after the rest of the women head inside, the two of them sit on our back porch, giggling and whispering like girls at a sleepover party.

On the other side of my bedroom wall is Lisa. I can hear the sounds of her living in there, door slamming, phone ringing, hairdryer blowing. She's always yelling at her mother—"I said just a minute!" or "Leave me alone!" or even "I hate you!" bouncing off our walls like some kind of dare. Then I'll hear the slam of her bedroom door and Mrs. Stingel hollering up from downstairs and Lisa's music getting louder, drowning her out. If I hold a hand against the wall between us, I can feel it shake.

In our house it's quiet. Mom keeps to herself. I keep to mine. We live in the same house Mom grew up in with her parents, who died one after the other from smoking too much. Since it's summer, I get the run of the place in the daytime. I pretend it's my house that I live in with my pretend family. I get their names from the *Little Golden Book of Baby Names* I picked up for 99 cents off the rack next to the candy bars and condoms down Willy's.

In the book, I mark off names I like. Lately, I'm into M's. Mirabelle: *beautiful looking one.* Miranda: *extraordinary.* I pick fancy names, ones that sound like they're from someplace far away. In the afternoons I watch soaps, checking out the way the couples' lips fit. I'm practicing for when I meet my husband, who these days I'm calling Dylan (*from the sea*) or Thad (*courageous*), or sometimes Roy.

Roy, that's my dad, lives in California. He picked out my name: Robin. It doesn't have a meaning. It means just what it is. I like to think it's because I'm supposed to fly away from West Fifth, but that's not how the story goes. Roy used to tell me he got the idea because the morning I was born, he walked outside and saw a crowd of baby robins. Mom says she doesn't remember the robins. All she remembers is the heat.

"Wasn't that hot," Mrs. McGillicuddy told me, hanging boys' boxers on her clothesline. "She just wanted Roy waiting on her. Fanning her face, fixing her rootbeer floats. Hell, she had him sitting on the stoop like a woman." She shook her head, poked a couple pins between her lips. "Margie was crazy to think she could keep a man like that on a street like this."

This summer, August first, I'll be turning thirteen. I know Mom's counting on big things from me. Out on the stoop, having a teenager, especially a girl, gives you a certain amount of clout. You can sigh about them. You can worry. You can bitch and complain about their clothes and boyfriends and bad mouths. You can stretch your legs out and throw your head back and say,

3

"Lord, why me?" Mrs. Johnson might mix you gin in a Sunoco glass. Old Edith Mills will throw in a prayer for you, thumbing away at the rosary her son got her from a genuine church in Ireland. If it's real bad, Mrs. O'Hanlan might lend you the super-deluxe personal massager I've heard people talk about but I've never seen.

Then, when the conversation's moved on, you can let out a little smile. Because even though you know your daughter's bad, you're glad she's bad, 'cause you were bad, and that's the way teenage daughters should be, and one day your life will be like a coffee commercial when you and her bump into each other in the kitchen at midnight and heat up some French Vienna vanilla mocha and sit around with your robes and mugs and talk and laugh all night.

The stoop-sitters swap things. Recipes, hand-me-downs, leftover hunks of birthday cake with the icing all chalky and hard. They swap complaints about their aches and pains. They swap the insides of their houses. If one of them throws together a stoop sale, the others tiptoe over the hot sidewalk to pick through somebody else's old vases and lamps and Nancy Drews. You have to buy something. It's rude not to. You pay your quarter, pick up your bluebird coasters, and head on home.

Tonight after everybody goes inside, Mrs. Stingel and Mom sit in our kitchen talking. I know enough to stay upstairs. I sit in my window, check on the street. Even though it's dark and all the chairs are folded and cans tossed and the women are inside poking at their husbands' tired feet and Sunoco hands, something's still awake out there. Curtains are blowing, pinwheels flapping. The stoops are restless.

I hear a cough from the other side of my wall. Lisa's in there. I wonder what she's doing. There's no music playing, no phone ringing. I can't for the life of me imagine Lisa Stingel alone. I get down from the window and press my ear against the wall, like it's a shell from a California beach. I'm not a hundred percent, but I think I hear her crying. Not your usual screechy teenage girl variety. This is soft. Quiet.

Our back door slams. Then the Stingels' slams a little quieter, so I know Mom is alone. I creep down to the living room and sit on our sheet-covered sofa. In the summer we cover our furniture with white sheets to keep cool, so it looks like a bunch of short fat ghosts. I turn on an old *Newlywed Game*, the part where the lady says how ugly her date was from the minute she saw him and Chuck Woolery laughs so hard he cries.

I hear chair legs scrape against the kitchen floor and the slow suck of the fridge door. Mom walks in holding two cans of root beer, one in each fist. She hands me one and sits down in a ghost chair.

4

"Lisa's having a baby."

She doesn't say it upset. She says it plain. I remember the sounds of Lisa crying and it makes me scared, how plain Mom says it. She looks like she's about to say something else, then stops, closes her mouth, kind of firms up her face and nods.

Mom cracks her root beer. I crack mine. She takes a sip. I sip mine. We sit there without saying a word, the two of us on the sheets in the heat, pressing the cans to the insides of our wrists to get the cool into our bloodstreams.

When I was five, Roy made me an apple bird. I remember sitting in the kitchen watching that apple become wings, a neck, two raisin eyes jammed on a toothpick. Roy was magic like that. He could take our boring, ordinary life and make something of it. Mom acted mad that he was wasting fruit, but she was smiling when she scooped the apple scraps in her hand. She put the bird on our windowsill and it sat there for weeks while we waited for Roy to come back, its apple wings getting all hot and bright and finally brown in the sun.

When Roy was gone, Mom bought me a plastic kitchen with little rubber foods. Rubber hamburger, rubber crisscrossed pie, rubber drumstick. I hated the feel of it, all hard and fake. So she got me a makeup kit with peel-off nailpolish and a Barbie that winked if you poked her in the back. I wasn't into them either. I knew Roy would have picked something better. When I started sitting in my window, Mom left me alone. She stopped saying much when I was around, but her hands were always moving, twisting, little birds with white palms and brown backs. She'd pick things up, put them down, smoke her Virginias, crush them dead. Whenever she caught me watching her, she'd look at me like she wondered where in hell I came from.

The day I turned twelve, Mom left a Sears bra on my bed. *The Blossoming Woman*, the tag said. It had a little pink bow like a cat's mouth. It made me want to puke. I didn't want to be any blossoming woman, sitting on the stoops in a Sears bra waiting for a man to come along and scoop me up. I cut off the bow with nail scissors but stuffed the bra in the back of my dresser, just in case. I know Mom wants me to be like Lisa Stingel, going on dates and having screaming fights, but I'm with Roy. I don't belong here.

Roy (meaning *king*) makes art in California. Mom and Roy got married when I was one, and when I was five Roy left to go find himself. *I realized I just didn't belong there*, is what he wrote me on a postcard when I was nine. *I needed to find myself, I needed a different kind of space.* The front of the card showed a pink sunset and a sweep of beach, but it didn't have a return address. Roy's mail never does. I'd close my eyes and listen to the rise and fall of the cars rolling up and down West Fifth, pretending they were waves on a California beach.

Mom never found out about my postcard and I'll never tell. Roy still sends me presents on my birthday, so I should be lined up for something soon, long as I get to the mail before Mom does. It'll be cool, like a necklace made of beads. A chunk of rock that means "insight" or "serenity." Last year, this book called *Lighting Your Way* that I polished off in one night. Next day, when I found Mom tapping out a cigarette, I told her to "breathe in the white light, breathe out the black smoke," just to make her mad. But she didn't get mad. She gave me this slow, sad look, like she felt sorry for me, and when she went to touch my face with her empty hand, I jumped back just in time.

Mom doesn't talk about Roy. But he's around, if you know where to look for him. In the back of Mom's underwear drawer, there's a picture of the two of them sitting on the stoop. Roy's got blond hair in a ponytail, a big blond beard, silver glasses. His hand's hanging down over Mom's shoulder, almost touching her left breast. Mom's hair is done up in two loose brown braids and she's smiling with more teeth than I knew she had. If you peel back the wallpaper around my floor, you'll find pictures Roy painted underneath: roses and butterflies and birds and the long curly words *Peace* and *Love* and *Amen*.

The stoop-sitters swap stories. Mostly about men. Past men, present and future men. Goddamn tired husbands, goddamn no-good exes. From my window I can hear every goddamn word of it, floating up on lazy curls of cigarette smoke and the smells of fish sticks from toaster ovens.

Mom doesn't say much. She doesn't have anything to talk about. I don't have any boyfriends, she doesn't either. She could have Glenn the hairy mailman if she wanted, but always says, "No thank you, Glenn," when he asks her to go out sometime. She just keeps sitting, night after night, flip-flop dangling off the tip of her toe, like Roy's going to come riding down West Fifth any minute. She doesn't talk about Roy, though. He's been gone nine years, too long for anybody to be talked about out loud.

Mrs. O'Hanlan rips on Al, who got his ear pierced at the mall just to get the piercer girl's hands on him. "Now it's all swelled up and he thinks I'm going fix it!" she screeches, slapping her knees. Mrs. Johnson says Bill couldn't get no girl to touch his ears, the way he stinks like Sunoco. Mrs. McGillicuddy moans, "They're eating me alive," after her boys bake themselves a Betty Crocker marble cake and eat the whole thing in one sitting.

But if one of their men strolls up from work, the stoop-sitters' voices go soft. Mrs. Johnson wraps her skinny arms around oily Bill, gives him a sip of gin, tells him to go get a shower. Mrs. O'Hanlan yells inside to Al to turn the TV down, then tacks a sweet "honey" on the end. When the McGillicuddy boys kiss their mother on the cheek, she blushes like she's seventeen.

6

Before Lisa Stingel started sitting, the women watched her go on dates. Most nights, around seven or eight, some boy would come driving down West Fifth. Their cars looked different but sounded the same, full of loud rap music and rotten mufflers. "CAR!" the kids would yell, stopping their half-ball game and stepping backwards. The women would sit up straighter, touch their hair, eyes following the boy like hawks. He'd sit outside 14B, engine chugging, music blasting, horn honking once, twice. Then Lisa would come out and hop in. The stoop-sitters would watch after them till the music faded, the exhaust melted, and there was a choir of lighters snapping and cigarettes blazing like fireflies and a feeling in the air that was kind of sad.

The stoop-sitters swap baby clothes. Baby jackets, baby shoes, onesies, and booties. High chairs and placemats and cups that won't tip over. They swap baby toys. Blocks and bears and mobiles. Poked-up Lite Brite sheets and teething biscuits sprinkled with fake salt, half-done coloring books and stuffed animals with metal keys in their butts.

By the first week in July, the Stingels' front lawn is piled like a fort. Four strollers, two playpens, three carseats. The pile grows until it rains, then Mr. Stingel comes out and clears it, sweaty-faced, nightstick knocking against his soft knees. After the ground dries, the pile starts up again. A wind-up swing, Sesame Street videos, a baggieful of rubber nipples. Even Mrs. O'Hanlan's super-deluxe personal massager.

I never see boys come around anymore for Lisa. Girls stop sometimes, and they all sit out on the stoop with their Diet Cokes, pressing dents in the cans with their thumbnails. Lisa looks different from them now. She isn't big, but she's wearing her clothes baggy, like she's leaving room to grow. The other girls wear halter tops and spandex shorts that pinch where the elastic hits the skin. They wear their hair big, crimped and sticky. When they leave, they hug Lisa without hardly touching her at all.

*   *   *

July 31, day before my thirteenth birthday, it's so hot out you can see it. Heat wiggles on the street like steam. The living room chairs burn right through the sheets. Weatherman says it's ninety-nine. Too hot to move. I hang out in my window, but there's nothing to look at. Everybody's inside with their Breeze Machines cranking. Lisa hasn't been out for more than a week. I wonder what she does inside all day. I press my ear against our bedroom wall, but it doesn't shake anymore. I miss feeling it shake.

I open up the *Little Golden Book of Baby Names* and start on the N's. Naida: *water or river nymph.* Naomi: *the pleasant one.* Napea: *she of the*

7

valleys. But I can't get into it. It doesn't feel right, picking out names for fake babies while Lisa's over there having a real one. Outside, one of the McGillicuddy boys fires up the mower, and he isn't wearing a shirt and the muscles in his back flex like wings under his sweaty skin and everything feels too close.

I go downstairs and open up our front door. The pile at the Stingels is getting big again. I tuck the book in my hand and check to see if anyone's watching, but the stoops are empty. The McGillicuddy boy has his headphones on and his back facing me. I run down our front steps and over to the Stingels, where I drop my baby book on the pile, right on top of my old plastic kitchen.

I turn back to my house, then stop. I don't want to be back inside. It's too hot in there, too empty. I wander on down to the stoop and poke my toe at it, like testing pool water. *What the hell. Why not?* I look around again. Nobody watching. So I sit.

From the stoop, the street looks different. Houses are taller. Long, loose strips of bark peel off the trees like dogs' tongues. A barrel of fake flowers is tipped over on Mrs. Carroll's lawn. ("Calls it lawn art," Mrs. McGillicuddy told me.) Down the block, a bunch of kids have the hydrant going, splashing cars with hollowed-out Sanka cans. The chips of mica in the sidewalk look like diamonds.

I stretch my legs out, lean my head back. Hydrant water comes sloshing down the street, mixing with the rainbow puddles in front of the Johnsons'. A dirty white Buick is rolling toward me, right side dripping. Maybe it's a boy coming around for Lisa. I let my sandals drop to the sidewalk and flex my toes, wishing for a second I had some pink polish. But when the Buick gets closer, I see it's just a little old lady trying to get her wipers on.

I hear footsteps behind me and straighten up. It's just Glenn the mailman, climbing over the fort next door. Glenn isn't ugly, but he's hairy. Even the backs of his hands are covered in fur. He must be dying in this heat.

"Hey kiddo," he says. "Got something for you."

I was so busy sitting I almost forgot—my birthday present from Roy. I stand up and grab the envelope, the puffy tan kind they sell at the post office. The writing on it is crunched, small, not loose like the words swirling under my bedroom wallpaper. There's no return address on this one either.

"Say hi to your mom for me," Glenn says, but I'm already halfway inside. I run to my room, shut the door, tear the envelope open and pull out my present. I go slow with the wrapping paper, trying not to rush it. I picture Roy's hands folding those same corners and slicking those same pieces of Scotch tape. Inside is a box that says *Incense* on top in curly gold letters. I've never seen anything like what's in it. They look like shrunk-down cattails, but when I put my face close and breathe, they smell real, like smoke, and wood, and spices, and all the places I dream about going.

*   *   *

The stoop-sitters swap hope. They swap two-for-one coupons and lottery numbers. They swap pasts and futures and what-could-have-beens. One day a front yard is a patch of burned grass with a pinwheel stuck in it, and the next it is a fort of baby toys and the life you thought was yours just got emptied into someone else's.

When things are getting too slow on the stoops, or too sad, or the air's feeling a little too heavy with what's real, the stoop-sitters swap crushes.

"Know who I think's cute?"

It doesn't matter who says it. Doesn't matter who they say. Usually they're men off TV. Actors, shortstops, weathermen. "Know who I think's cute?" is all it takes, and everybody drops what they're doing. A held breath one whole hot city-block long.

The speaker drags out the magic answer, milking that minute for all it's worth. "Stoooone Phillips," she might say, while the sitters all start nodding, agreeing, picturing old Stone's slick black hair and tanned skin and deep buttery voice reeling off the news like he has the answer to everything.

It's nighttime and I'm watching. The stoop-sitters head on out like always. They stand in their doorways. They sigh the sigh. Mrs. McGillicuddy walks slow, testing her mowed lawn under her bare feet. Mrs. Johnson stirs her gin and tonic. The Christmas lights start blinking around Mrs. O'Hanlan's front door. Mrs. Stingel and Lisa head out together. They crack their can lids, lean their heads back. Mrs. Stingel on the top step, Lisa on the bottom step, a Diet Coke and a Michelob Light and Lisa's blond head resting against her mother's hard knees.

Our back door slaps shut, and I hear Mom taking the stairs two at a time. Mrs. Donohue is heading out now, checking her mail again. I hear Mom heading down the hall. She walks into my room, holding a big green garbage bag.

"Here," she says, dropping it in the middle of the floor. The air collapses and the plastic sinks, clinging like skin to whatever's inside.

"You got yourself some new clothes," Mom says. "Hand-me-downs. From Lisa."

My eyes jump to her face. She looks excited, and a little nervous, like a kid who's getting away with something. Her bangs are clumping up and sticking to her forehead, blue makeup starting to smear in the heat. She picks at the little white threads hanging off the bottoms of her shorts' cuffs.

9

"Cause of the baby," Mom says, which doesn't make a whole lot of sense, since Lisa isn't big yet. Maybe it's a thank you for the *Little Golden Book of Baby Names*. Or maybe somebody figured these were the kinds of clothes that got Lisa in trouble in the first place.

"Go ahead." Mom digs in her back shorts pocket and comes up with a lighter and mashed pack of Virginias. "Try them on."

"Now?"

"Just see if they fit." She lights one and blows a mouthful of smoke over her shoulder. "Be right back."

She walks off and I climb down and open up the bag. The smell inside is like perfume covering up sweat. I pull the clothes out one by one, recognizing everything. Halter tops, cut-off shorts, short skirts Lisa wore on dates. Even the red prom dress with shiny straps is flattened in the bottom. I picture these clothes on the other side of my wall, tossed around Lisa's bedroom floor, and it seems all wrong that they're in here with me.

Mom's coming back down the hall. "Ready?"

I kick off my jean shorts and yank up this short black spandex dress with little daisies around the neck, and wiggle into the armholes. Suddenly I can feel my skin.

"How's it look?" Mom says. I turn around and she looks me up and down. "Cute," she says, nodding like she does at the ladies in the Sears dressing rooms. "Fits you just right." I know what she's thinking now: finally, I'll have my teenage girl. There'll be screaming and slamming doors and dates and proms and so much to bitch and sigh about she won't know where to start.

I check myself out in the closet mirror. The dress is big, but I can see where I'm supposed to fill it. The spandex is all stretched where Lisa's chest and hips used to be. I picture how I'd look with candy-pink lipstick and my crimped hair. Pretty damn good, I have to say. It's like some of Lisa Stingel is rubbing off on me, making me look pretty but feel guilty at the same time.

"What the hell is this?"

In the mirror, I see Mom standing behind me holding my box of incense. I whip around.

"Son of a bitch," she says.

I feel sick, seeing Roy's present in her hand. The hand's shaking and I think for a minute she's going to toss my incense all over the room. "When did you get these?"

I don't answer. I'm not saying a damn word to make trouble for Roy.

"When?" Mom yells, tossing them on the bed. "Answer me!" She takes a step and then her eyes land on my wall, and I know with an even sicker feeling she's looking at Roy's old peeled-away birds and *peaces* and *loves*.

Mom's empty hand flies out toward my face, like she's really about to hit my face. Then she stops and the hand just hangs, shaking, so close I can see the chewed skin around her nails. "You think you know him," she says, and her voice is shaking too.

"I know him better than you do." My voice feels good, it's got a cool new edge to it. "He couldn't *find himself* here," I add, sticking one hand on my hip. "You never should have tried to keep him on this street."

"Oh, is that it?" Her face is getting red. "That's the reason he left?"

"Yes." The "s" fries under my teeth.

"Cause I wanted to stay on this street?"

"Yeah."

We're really acting like mother and daughter now. She looks me up and down, then drops her shaky hand. She drags on her cigarette and her face goes loose, like all the angry lines got ironed out.

"Truth is," she says, and it's the same plain voice she used to tell me Lisa was pregnant. "I couldn't wait to get off this street. But have a baby you don't want and your plans change quick."

The room freezes. I can't move. I can't breathe. Mom lifts one hand and touches her face, hair, cheek, making sure everything's still where it's supposed to be. But nothing is. Something's crawled out in the air, something terrible. Mom's eyes are the wide they get when she's watching a sad thing on Action News. Except now the sad thing is me.

I take a step backward and my heel hits the mirror. I don't feel it. Down on the street, I hear Mrs. O'Hanlan laughing, probably Al's ear again. Those women don't know what's going on in this house, and I wish I didn't either. I want to be alone in my window, down on the street, anywhere but here.

Mom runs a hand through her bangs, then covers her mouth, like she's checking to see what words she let out and what ones she didn't. I want to hit her then. I want to hit my mother with her chewed-up nails and her blurry blue shadow. But suddenly, standing in the middle of my floor, she looks too big to hit. She's filling up my room. Even that little hand looks like it could squash me if it wanted to. For once it's not moving, like whatever was living in those shaky fingers all my life just up and flew away.

Mom drops her hand. Her lips look twisted, she's trying not to cry. "Come here, baby," she says, reaching out her hand. But I'm too scared to move. I'm scared of my mother, of what else is inside her, of all that she knows that I don't.

Her hand drops by her side. She looks at the floor, then back at the wall, at the ripped edges of my wallpaper. "You don't know him at all," she says, and her voice is soft and sorry, but both of us know it would have hurt me less to be hit.

Mom's eyes fall back to the incense sticks. Slowly she starts picking them out of the box, one at a time, pushing them down in her fist like she's arranging flowers. I want to yell at her to stop, but I can't get my new teenage voice back. She empties the box, chokes the sticks up tight, then turns and walks off downstairs with my birthday present in her hand.

Soon as I hear the bottom step creak, I get myself out of that dress. Kick it off, drop it back in the garbage bag, shove the whole thing in the back of my closet. I put my old T-shirt and shorts back on and curl up in the window. But tonight, the window feels like it's too small. Tonight I can't shake the feeling that the rest of the world is watching me.

Everybody's out by now. It's too hot, too quiet. Lisa has her chin in her hands and her elbows on her knees. When Mom slams our front door, they all turn to look. She stands there for a long minute, taking in the sky, the street. Then she takes one of my incense sticks and, carefully, pushes it down in our lawn. Nobody says a word. Their eyes follow her as she goes walking down the sidewalk, slow as Miss America, stopping off at every one of the stoop-sitters, angry young ones, baggy old ones, handing my sticks away.

I watch my dream get shoved in every patch of dried-up grass on West Fifth Street. Mrs. Donohue kneels over hers and sniffs it. Mrs. McGillicuddy backs up and checks to make sure hers is screwed in straight. Mrs. Carroll jams hers next to the upturned pot of flowers. Mrs. Stingel mounds a little dirt around hers like a tree.

The stoop-sitters don't need talk to figure out what happens next. They swap lighters. They swap matchbooks. They light the tips and the smoke reaches for the sky, filling West Fifth with a smell it's never smelled before, something ticklish and faraway. The kids in the street stop playing, hanging onto their bats and balls. Lisa Stingel bends down to light her stick and the smoke winds past her pretty face. And in that moment, something relaxes on our street. Like whatever was restless calmed down and let its breath out. There's something about the silence and the stillness and the look of those lights burning and smoke rising that feels close to holy.

Sounds start up slow. Can tops cracking, lighters clicking, flip-flops dropping to the sidewalk, breathing and smoking and sighing so close and known it feels like my own skin. Mom's sitting back on our stoop now. A hot breeze is blowing the smell somewhere up and away from the street, past the thick trees and skinny houses and telephone wires hung heavy with sneakers and into the night sky. Mom rests back on her elbows. She stretches her legs out, leans her head back. But instead of flirting with nothing, she closes her eyes and breathes and smiles.

Tim Keppel
Urban Renewal

When your marriage falls apart, move to a big city. New York, Boston, Philadelphia. Try Philadelphia, it's cheaper. You won't know anyone, but that's the point.

Rent an efficiency in the barrio; be a Spartan. You won't need the things you thought you needed before: a car, a house, a wife. You were weak and indulgent then. It's time for lean and mean.

Choose an apartment above a jewelry store called The Golden Miracle. Watch kids play in the vacant lot. They make games of discarded objects, shouting in gleeful Spanish on warm summer nights, bashing TV sets with baseball bats. One day watch them pitch six bowling pins onto a tin roof, one after the other. Assume they're saving them up there for later.

Go to a bar where women dress in black—makeup, hair dye, nail polish. You'll find this appealing, mysterious, repulsive. Go early and get a stool. Assume an expression midway between content and morose. Order dark beer. Don't eat pork rinds. This is critical. Women find pork rinds a turn-off. But it won't matter; you'll go home frustrated, inebriated, alone. Turn on music that reminds you of your wife. Turn it off. Unplug your phone and stuff it in the closet.

Take long walks around your block. Inspect the grime, the graffiti, the broken glass. Hear the cacophony of car horns, trolley brakes, drunken laughter. Watch a one-eyed doomsday prophet shout at the sky. Walk past pawn shops, strip joints, and storefront churches, everyone loaded or recovering or both. Spare change, spare change, spare change. Entrepreneurs with their car wash/drug emporiums. The trolley screeches by, metal scraping metal, past a boarded-up fire-bombed building that reads "North Philadelphia Redevelopment Project."

Decide your apartment is a bit too Spartan. What you need is a comfortable sofa. Preferably one to share.

A sign down the street says "must sell." A man is being evicted. He has a sofa for thirty-five dollars and a van to help you move it.

He's a burly Slovak with thick, coily chest hair, shirtless and sweating profusely, lighting one cigarette off the other. Friendly guy with a thick accent. "You're new in ze neighborhood? I hope for you more luck than I."

Heaving the sofa into his van, lavender with a smiling sun stenciled on the side, he says, "I've had a rough time. My daughter died, then my girlfriend left." His rapid, breathy laugh invites you to join in. Think better of it. On the steering wheel his fingers are stained orange-brown, nails bitten to the quick. "I'm going to live in the van," he says.

Lugging the sofa up your stairs, he throws out his back. You feel bad for not holding up your end. Grimacing, he gives a long, wistful look. "It's better you have it than me. When I get depressed I lie on it for days."

That's when you notice the smell: not smoke, not sweat, but something else. Something unnamable. You were vaguely aware of it at his place.

But now it's at your place.

"Looks good there," he says.

You study the sofa from where you are, then go across the room to study it from there. "You'll kill me for this," you say. "But I'm going to change my mind."

"What?" His face ages before your eyes.

Tell him it's the nicotine. You're allergic. You're lying through your teeth.

He mashes a cushion to his nose. "I don't smell anything. But I have a bad sense of smell."

"I'm sorry."

"Listen, you keep it. If the smell goes away, send me a check. If not . . . " He edges toward the door.

"But I don't have a way to move it!" You hear panic in your voice— more than you intended. Not that you intended any. "Wait," you say. The smell is all around you, clinging to your clothes. "I'll give you the thirty-five if you haul it away."

The guy looks at you. He looks at the couch. He wipes his brow and sighs. "Forty," he says.

The important thing is, don't look back. Don't think about the sound of her voice, how she slept with the arch of her foot against your calf. Avoid the spices you shared: basil, coriander, thyme. Forget the things she taught you. Forget about washing onions before cutting them so they won't make you cry. Forget how she told you to never break the spaghetti.

Go ahead and break it.

Become a minimalist. Buy small amounts of everything: toothpaste, toilet paper, salsa picante. Always buy off-brands, except for trash bags and razors. Don't be seen carrying leaky trash bags with a bloody face.

Draw strength from your asceticism. Be glad your worldly assets can fit in a shopping cart. Know that you're prepared for an evacuation of the city. Appreciate how little you'd have to leave behind.

Go to a corner market called El Bodega. The owner is Korean but speaks excellent Spanish. He tells you he's been robbed three times—once with a gun, once with a razor, and once with a spoon. "With a spoon?" you ask. Later you realize you confused *cuchara* with *cuchillo*, knife.

The shelves are spare, a mouse glides across the floor. "I like mouses," the guy says in English. "When you got mouses, you know you don't got rats."

This comment will impress you, stay in your mind.

Devise elaborate ways to mark the passage of time: haircuts, nail clippings, rings around the tub. The souring of garbage, the expiration of milk. The healing of sores.

Know that time is your enemy; it's trying to take you down. If you make it go faster than it wants, or slower, you win.

One day at El Bodega you see a woman. Slender and tall, wearing a U.S. Army jacket, combat boots, and a black leotard with a run. She's young and innocent-looking; the getup seems a disguise. For some reason this appeals to you. And that face! Hair pulled tight against a small oval head. Lacquer-black eyes and nut-brown skin, evoking lush islands, wild parrots, and crystal-blue lagoons.

She's over at the canned goods. Just as you look, she does something remarkable. She picks up a can of Spam and slips it in her jacket. You glance furtively at the Korean—he's watching wrestling on a four-inch screen. The woman seizes you with her eyes. She knows you've seen. She flashes a look of complicity and dashes out the door.

Suddenly you forget why you came. Why you're in the city. Why you exist.

You catch up with the woman at the corner, teetering near the traffic. She studies your face. "Why didn't you snitch?"

Just beneath her eye, her cheek begins to twitch.

Ask, "Why would I do that?"

She deliberates a moment, then smiles. Her teeth are crooked in a charming way.

Her fingertips peek out of too-long sleeves, producing the Spam. "Want to join me?"

The streetlight changes. You look at her, you look at the Spam. You say no thanks and then regret it.

At night you hear loud, booze-slurred voices from the tenement next door.

"Let me in the house, you slut!"

"I have a restraining order, motherfucker."

Lie sweating on your mattress, moonlight pouring in the window. It's as hot as high noon. On the power line outside, objects are illuminated: a Nike sneaker hanging by a lace, a twisted beige bra, and an angel-haired baby doll, naked from the waist down, with wide, astonished eyes.

You see homeless guys everywhere. Asleep on sidewalks, crouched by dumpsters, shadowboxing in the middle of the street. You open a newspaper box and find a stash of personal items—trousers, sneakers, a disposable razor.

From out of nowhere, the thin, tinkly notes of an ice cream truck making its rounds.

To clear your head, go sit in the park. In the daytime it's fairly safe. Busted swing sets, crumbling basketball court—no nets, no rims, no goals.

See the old, white-haired black man feeding the birds. He stares at the park as though it's a paradise. Maybe he can't see too well. Maybe he can't hear. His eyes are huge behind his paperweight glasses, his ears are enormous. He carries a tattered briefcase, removing sheaves of yellowed paper, holding them an inch from his face.

You begin to look for her. At El Bodega, the laundromat, the park. You watch for army jackets, combat boots, provocative facial tics. You buy a can of Spam.

Don't think about that foot pressed against your calf, those adjacent grave plots. Forget about having a deep experience. What you need are shallow interludes.

Develop a big city strut. Saunter down the street as if nothing fazes you. Ignore blood stains on the sidewalk and ballistic noises. Assume cars are backfiring. Pay no attention to suspicious characters lurking in doorways. Avoid eye contact. If someone looks your way, suspect they either want to rob you or have sex with you.

*   *   *

You're in the park near the old man when she sits down on your bench. She's not wearing the army jacket but you notice the twitch.

"I feel bad about the other day," she says. "I'm not like that."

Believe her. Wonder what she wants out of life. Ask her name.

Her name is Dawn. "I come from a dysfunctional family," she says dryly. "Yes, I've been to shrinks." She spent time in foster homes, she was a ward of the state. At eighteen she was emancipated. She got pregnant but lost the baby.

She wants to be a dancer. She answered an ad, but they wanted another kind of dancer.

"What about you?" she says.

Say you're between jobs.

Tell her you worked in a think tank. An institution. You were into theoretical matters, deconstruction.

Tell her you're a bum.

Tell her you're trying to put things back together, reconstruct. Say that people have more lives than they think, that you're looking for another one.

"I have an aunt in Texas who sends me money," Dawn says, then glances over to see how this plays.

The sunlight brightens, then dims. Clouds. Her facial tic accelerates. You feel you should do something, comfort her in some way.

Consider telling the story about the Slav with the sofa. Instead, tell her about the Korean with the mice.

She lets out a sharp, high laugh and puts her fingers to her lips.

You look at each other. It's your best moment yet.

The sky brightens. She says, "That's the nicest old man."

Something pierces your heart. A calm descends. Her tic subsides. Tell her, "*You're* nice." But it doesn't come out right.

Then she kisses you awkwardly. "I have to go."

Tell her she can find you above The Golden Miracle.

Observe the city at twilight. Gasoline rainbows, candy-colored crack vials, diamond-like shards of glittering glass. Scraps of paper like tinsel in the trees.

A gust of wind swoops up a plastic bag and lofts it like a kite: Superfresh! An elderly couple in lawn chairs is picnicking beneath the El bridge. A din of car horns announces a wedding procession. Cars chase the JUST MARRIEDs around corners, through red lights, up one-way streets, unwilling to let them go.

Change your attitude. Go from minimalism to abundance. Buy family packs of everything: Ziploc bags, Tupperware, Q-tips by the thousands. Stock up. Take the long view. You never know.

You're leaving El Bodega when you see her down the street. You recognize her swan-like neck, her coltish legs. Quicken your pace. Think of a line. Tell her you're a different person—your cupboard is full, you're listening to music again, you've plugged in your phone.

She rounds the corner on Leithgow Street and approaches a van. You can't see the driver, just his hairy arm. She leans in as if to tell him something, or give him a kiss. The van is lavender with a smiling sun. The sunrays extend like a lion's mane. The smile is enigmatic. She gets in the van and is gone.

Take a seat beside the white-haired man. Stare with him myopically across the park. The sun paints the windows of the sponge factory orange. The old man fumbles in his briefcase. "Let me show you something." He extracts a grainy, sepia photo. Two rows of boys in suits and ties. A graduation of some kind. A commencement.

"Can you tell which one is me?"

Of course you can—the one with the ears.

"How did you know?" He reaches back in the satchel with a mottled, shaky hand. "Can you do me a favor? Can you read me this?"

A faded letter, tearing at the creases. From a former employer, attesting to his character, his integrity, his worth.

"I've got others," the old man says. You read several more. Each one corroborates the first.

The sun is setting, the man has to go. He hobbles away on severely bowed legs. You won't see him again. He won't return to the park. But you won't worry about him. He has good references.

Go back to your apartment and sit by the window. The sunset will be brilliant. The air will be cool. The street lights will flicker on, buzzing like cicadas. Kids will be playing in the vacant lot, shrieking with delight. One wiry boy will shimmy up a drain pipe, crawl out on the roof. Then he'll start tossing the bowling pins, one after the other, down to his friends.

"Urban Renewal" was first published in *Prism International*.

Jim Zervanos
Georgie

George Starakis didn't rush to answer the knock at the door. Instead, he sipped his Bombay Sapphire and tonic and checked his watch. It was noon, springtime. He would send all this Class-of-'90 shit to Hillary Walsh McCoy after all, he thought, and tossed the folder onto the mahogany coffee table. He could still picture what she looked like at eighteen—the shallow half-moon forehead, hair pulled back stubbornly, light-brown fuzz closing in toward her eyes like fine moss. He imagined her, now, almost thirty, marching around her living room in the same saddle shoes she'd worn as a flag twirler for the high school band, sitting, finally, propping her feet up, one ankle over the other, on the white-lacquered top of a brand-new Ikea coffee table, contemplating the portable in her hands, listening to the dial tone for a minute, and letting out a frustrated bark at the stucco ceiling.

She must have smirked when she mustered the confidence to dial him so early this morning. In high school—even as far back as fifth grade, come to think of it—she had always been a strange mix of awkward and aggressive, asking boys she barely knew (some of them George's friends) to dances or running for class office and losing to George. She went about such things modestly enough, but she sure as hell didn't like losing. But then neither did he.

Hillary hadn't entered his mind for years, not since he'd got wind of unsurprising rumors of her training for the Olympics. Late in high school, after years of tennis lessons and failed basketball tryouts, she'd found her niche in long-distance running and apparently stuck with it. Predictably, he chuckled, the kind of sport that rewarded diligence more than talent or intelligence.

Whoever it was knocked again, and George headed for the door.

*   *   *

After law school George picked up an M.B.A. at Wharton. For three years he had been working in a Philadelphia law firm. He had moved into the Society Hill Towers, three thirty-two-floor concrete monoliths designed by I. M. Pei. George's twenty-fourth-floor corner condo trumpeted the architect's genius for maximizing window exposure; its giant, recessed windows extended from his city-front bedroom to the corner living room, where a wall of glass framed the Delaware River and the Ben Franklin Bridge, rising like a giant blue harp and swooping toward Camden.

Six months ago George had started dating the manager of the Burberry's store on Walnut Street. She was *a nice Greek girl*, a fact he hadn't realized at first. If he had a buck for every time he'd heard his parents say *Georgie, when are you going to find a nice Greek girl and settle down?* Now all he heard from his father was *What are you waiting for? She's beautiful, smart, college educated. She's in business. She's from restaurant people* (like George's family, who owned a diner in Paoli)—*they own—what is it, three?— restaurants in Manhattan. What more could you want? And they're Critiki*—from Crete (like George's family). *She's perfect.* The truth was George couldn't argue, but he still wasn't ready to cash in his chips. It turned out she was from a *very* Greek family in New York. They had the brownstone in Astoria, spoke Greek in the house (where the grandparents lived as well), had property in Greece, and hopped the islands all summer.

The day he'd met her, he stalled during his lunch break, trying on suits, while she was tied up with a customer in the fitting room. Finally, he went back to his office and called the store, asking if he could please speak with the gorgeous girl in the long red skirt and the straight black hair. "Who is this?" the woman replied, then whispered, "It's got *some* curl, doesn't it?" George asked, "What's your name?" and the voice, rising on the second syllable, replied, "Christie."

As their relationship ripened—in the back of his mind, he'd even thought about marrying her—he couldn't shake the suspicion that she was with him only because he was Greek or that she would drop him because he wasn't Greek enough.

*   *   *

Earlier, George had been lying in bed, his back inches from the cool windowsill, when the phone rang. It felt like the middle of the night when he picked up the phone, reaching over Erin. A deep sleeper, she mumbled into the pillow without moving.

"Hello?" he said.

"Is this Hillary?" the voice seemed to say.

"Wrong number." George hung up and lay across Erin's back, his belly snug in the curve above her ass.

The night before, he had gone straight to the Cosmopolitan after work, around eight o'clock, and stayed till after closing. "It's fucking packed," George's friend Alex said when they arrived. "No worries," George said, peering over shoulders and heads and smiling at Erin in knee-high black boots and a lavender miniskirt, making her way easily from behind the bar. "There's my girl." Erin ushered them into a curved, white-cushioned booth, which waited, empty, a *Reserved* sign propped against the candle centerpiece. George palmed her bare back, pressed his mouth to her ear, and said, "You're distracting the crowd, baby." Erin giggled and pressed her belly against George's blue shirt. "I have to come out when I see you," she said. Every half hour she returned with martinis and appetizers.

Christie was in Greece with her family, going to a cousin's wedding in Athens and then going to Crete, their home island, where they had the property. She wouldn't be back until Saturday night. She was never suspicious, though she had met Erin several times; actually, she admired George for having women friends. Of course, Erin knew of George's relationship with Christie. It excited her that her friendship with George had a secretive aspect. In fact, when George first met Christie and told Erin they would have to be just friends, Erin had rolled her eyes and reminded him they'd always been just friends.

They were eating Cap'n Crunch from a box and watching Bugs Bunny when a second call came.

"Hello?" he said.

"George, I'm so sorry I woke you earlier," the voice said.

"Christie?"

"No, is that your girlfriend?" the voice said.

"Who is this?" George said.

"I'm sorry. This is Hillary Walsh McCoy, and, yes, that is *the* McCoy from high school." She laughed.

"You married Mac?"

"Last year. We have a baby, two months old. He's still teaching, so the baby's *my* job." She paused. "What're you doing these days?"

"You and Mac? God, that's—" Mr. McCoy had been notorious for hitting on high school girls, but the stories were more pathetic than disgusting; he wasn't some balding fat guy moaning in the art-supply closet, but a twenty-two-year-old college grad asking seniors—some of them George's friends, the best-looking girls in school—for legitimate dates, straddling a classroom chair and saying, "Hey, Michelle, I was wondering if you'd be up for some ice cream this weekend." He thought nothing of it, even offered to call home and clear it with their parents, like some noble suitor. He never had any luck.

George laughed to himself and wondered who had asked the other on their first date.

"Anyways," she said. "The reason I called is we were all wondering if we were having our ten-year reunion."

"Probably," George said. "I mean, if not this year, one of these years."

"Well," she said, "that's what we were wondering. I didn't make it to the five-year, and we definitely want a ten-year."

George was silent. Who's *we*?

Erin, sitting Indian-style next to him on the couch, hushed her crunching and whispered, *What is it?*

George pointed at the phone and mouthed the words, *What the fuck?*

Erin slapped his arm, laughing, and said, *What?*

"So were you planning anything, cause I'm actually really interested in getting started on this whole thing," Hillary said.

"Well—" George said. Erin pinched George's bicep hard. He muffled an *ow* and flicked his hand at her belly. "I hadn't really thought about it much, to tell you the truth." Erin threw a handful of Cap'n Crunch at George, who stood up, covered the phone's mouthpiece and pointed at the floor. Erin curled her legs into her chest, crunched once, grinning, and gave him the finger. *Bitch*, he mouthed, picking yellow nuggets from the couch.

"Any*ways*," Hillary said, "if you have information, like addresses and a class list, could you send me all that stuff? I could start getting it all on my computer."

Five years ago he would have *paid* someone to organize the reunion, but now he didn't want to give her the satisfaction of taking over.

"Oh, my," she said, "that's my baby. She's probably wondering where her lunch went." George pictured Hillary's bloated tit. "So, listen, I'll tell Steve you said hi, and I'll get back to you." She said goodbye, and the phone clicked off.

Nestled on the couch among Cap'n Crunch kernels, Erin pulled her knees against her chest and turned her face slightly toward her shoulder, half expecting a licking from George, half inviting it with the bare underside of her thighs.

"Who is Mac?" she said.

George sat down and stared at the TV. Road Runner. "My high school tennis coach." He petulantly crushed cereal nuggets into dust with his feet.

"C'mon, I'll clean it," Erin said. "Mopey."

"She wants to take over the high school reunion," George said.

"So let her," Erin said.

"She married my tennis coach and has a kid." George stood up, cereal crunching beneath his feet. "Would you—please?" he said, looking at the floor, lifting his heels.

"Would you relax? Here." Erin spread her legs and arms like a puppet, reaching for George.

George stood above her, staring at her smooth belly. She smiled and pushed the gray waistband down to her light-brown pubic line. George plunged, gripping her thighs with both hands. He bit the lean muscle that dipped into the flesh of her ass. He dragged his tongue up to her belly and under the smooth curves of her breasts and with his right hand pushed her cut-off shirt over her head and up her extended arms.

Erin said, "Fuck me," as his face neared her neck. It was sexy, her saying fuck. Still, he wanted to think of it differently—wanted *her* to think of it differently—though he knew it was exactly what they did. She bit her lip and grunted as he descended again, pulling the silk crotch of her shorts to one side, wedging his face in, imagining Christie, quiet, with her eyes closed.

The night before Christie had left for Greece, he'd taken her to the BYOB in South Philly where they'd gone on their first date. Her face flush from the merlot, she'd smiled hopefully, reaching across the table, and said, "Next time you have to come with me." As she described the sunsets in Santorini, their fingers intertwined, he'd promised himself he would end things once and for all with Erin—or with Christie, who deserved better. "Sounds amazing," he'd said.

George lay on the couch, hands behind his head, and watched Erin sweep the hardwood floor in short penguin steps, gathering Cap'n Crunch crumbs in a V at her heels. She lifted her foot and wiped grit directly onto his chest—her heel, her arch, her toes. She was in that kind of mood, flirting, pestering. He grabbed her ankle, and she laughed and hopped, and he watched her breasts bounce and her white-blond hair cover her face. She gripped his forearm with both hands and stabilized herself.

They showered then. He lay on his back in the tub. She stood and waved her head back and forth, propping her hands against the tile wall behind his view, her feet at the sides of his waist, her face and breasts and dripping hair hovering above him. The water spray bounced off her back and over her shoulders in arcs of glittery beads. Soapsuds glided from her belly button, got caught up, and fell from her pubic hair, a foamy blur.

* * *

When George had met Alex at the Cosmopolitan the night before, he'd been preoccupied. He'd been working all week on a case that seemed too simple to warrant such attention, yet he, and every other attorney willing to take a look, had been unable to come up with a single argument that had any legal heft.

"You've got better things to think about," Alex told him, shaking his head as Erin walked back to the bar. "You think she'd ever be into a little two-on-one?"

"Not with you," George said.

"How about me and her and her mom?" Alex said.

"You've seen her mom?"

Alex raised his eyebrows, unaware. "Why?"

"She's hot," George said.

"I had no idea. She single?"

George smiled. "Divorced."

"You've thought about it, you bastard." Alex laughed.

They stayed until the place cleared. With her back to their table, Erin counted cash with the other bartenders. Alex leaned into George and said, "What's it like?" Erin's skirt was low on her hips and her back was exposed nearly to her armpits.

"What?" George said.

*   *   *

After their shower, Erin put her boots and skirt on. It was already ten o'clock, and she had brunch plans with her mother. George would be busy the rest of the morning, typing away at the computer in his kitchen, finishing the brief he hadn't started. When Erin said she might stop by later, George reminded her that Christie was returning that night but that maybe they could catch up later in the week. "If you're lucky," she said.

Erin's overnight duffel bag was on a chair tucked under the kitchen table. He didn't remember her bringing it from the restaurant last night; she must have forgotten she even had it when she left in last night's clothes. Standing on a chair in his bedroom, he put the bag next to boxes of summer clothes in a small closet space above his dresser. It was something stupid like this that Christie might see—a bag left on a chair in the kitchen.

George wondered sometimes if Erin had it in her to plant little disasters. Once, he had confronted her about a pair of red stockings he'd found in his sock drawer. She had insisted she'd never wear red stockings and suggested they might be Christie's. "Why would *Christie* have red stockings?" George had said.

Erin was insulted. "Why would *I* have red stockings? What the hell is that supposed to mean anyway?"

George could never have asked Christie, of course, so he had just thrown

24

the stockings out. He hadn't seen Erin for weeks. Then one morning as Christie got dressed for work she draped her long red skirt across her bed and muttered that she couldn't find her red stockings.

George, still under the covers, touched the dress. "This is the dress you had on the day I first saw you."

Christie said, "That's right," and touched George's fingers.

"That's amazing," he said.

"You're sweet," she said.

All morning George drafted the brief for this lingering case against Manhattan Bagel, one of the firm's biggest clients, who lately had been strong-armed by a small-time doughnut store owner, bitter about declining business. A petty nuisance suit. Three years ago the old man had scoffed at the franchise's proposal that he change his doughnuts into bagels and join one of America's fastest-growing companies. Now he was citing zoning laws, claiming that he had exclusive doughnut-sale rights within a four-mile radius of his shop.

The printer jammed while George was paging through his high school yearbook. He had thought of Mac, how despite being just over five-foot tall he'd had a powerful slicing serve that no one could touch, including George.

The phone rang, and George glanced up at the portable's cradle on the wall. He walked slowly with his head bowed toward Hillary Walsh's excessively flattering photo, her teeth aglow and acne soaked in white light. He clapped the yearbook shut and lifted the phone, leaning against the refrigerator and gazing at Philly's bleached late-morning sky.

"Hello?" he said.

It was Christie. She sounded far away. She was still in Crete.

"We're staying another week," she said. "I've had time to think."

"About what?"

"I can't do it anymore. I'm tired. I think it's over."

"You *think*?"

"I know."

"You met someone over there."

"No, I didn't meet anyone," she said quietly. "We're just not . . . not moving forward."

"It's only been six months."

After a moment, she whispered, "I'm sorry. You'll be fine," and hung up.

George turned back toward the stalled printer. He shook his head and smiled sourly. *Not moving forward.*

He dialed information for Paoli and got the number for McCoy, Stephen. He was being impulsive, he knew, but maybe he'd missed something.

"Hello?" said a man's voice.

"Mister McCoy?" *Mister* sounded absurd, but he wasn't Mac anymore.

"This is Steve."

"This is George—"

"George, hold on. She's upstairs with the baby." It was silent for a minute. George felt insulted. The guy had barely said hello.

"Hi, George," Hillary said. "I was just upstairs with the baby."

Bravo, George thought.

"So, what's up?" Hillary said. "I kinda have to get back—"

"I was just wondering, I wanted to make sure, cause this whole time I was just assuming—you know, since you called earlier—that the ten-year would be *this* summer, and then I thought about it—"

"No, no, *next* summer, obviously," she said.

"So there's plenty of time, *obviously*."

"Well, a year or so, I guess."

George pressed his palm against the kitchen window. "So why're you calling me a year and a half ahead of time?"

Her tone turned bossy: "Listen, George—"

"A year and a half?" George let out an audible breath. "I mean, seriously." He sank his hand into his pocket.

"George, I'm sorry. I don't mean to cut you off, but I have to get back to my baby."

George hesitated. "Wait a minute," he said, just as she hung up.

He planted his hands on his hips.

"What's the fucking hurry?" He turned toward the printer, still stuttering.

* * *

George tried not to think of Christie as he cleared the paper jam. *Think about other women.* He thought of Erin and considered whether there could ever be more there. He imagined bringing her home, where they already knew Christie. *Immerse yourself in work.* He would need a new assignment. He had finished the report for Manhattan Bagel in, what, two hours? Something to be said for last minute. The firm and the company would be impressed with its direct approach, how it gave altogether no credence to the old man's attention to geographical technicalities or contractual agreements. George recognized that the last line of the brief was flippant but too perfect not to use. *A doughnut is not a bagel.* The obvious statement made the whole case seem so ridiculous that even his avoidance of legal issues came across as reasonable. Hopefully, someone would be in the office later. He could walk over in a little while and get some feedback.

First he'd have a drink, to celebrate. He filled a pint-sized glass with ice, sliced a fresh lime, and opened a new bottle of Bombay Sapphire. He walked into the living room and sat on the couch. The day looked perfect. He'd call Alex in a while. They could hit the courts later on—it looked warm enough. He sipped and closed his eyes, allowing himself to picture Christie. A tiny hole in his ribs expanded like a balloon.

"No." George gulped his drink, went to the corner lamp table, and opened a drawer. Checkbooks and receipts and magazines covered a light-blue folder with his high school logo on it. Inside the folder was a stapled packet of lined yellow legal paper covered with handwritten addresses—the list he'd used to assemble the five-year reunion. He set down his drink. Samantha Booker . . . Denise Blackwell . . . Robin Grimes . . . Leslie Hanes . . . They would all have new addresses, husbands, babies. He imagined being at the ten-year reunion with Christie, who would have dazzled them all with her charm, as they tried to keep their eyes off the knuckle-sized thing sparkling magnificently.

*   *   *

When the knock came at the door, George just stood there for a minute.

Erin—she wore jean shorts and a thin sweater. Her mother was in the car across the street, she said.

"It's warm out," she said.

He nodded.

"Are you all right?" she said.

"Yeah, yeah, I was just doing some work."

"My wallet's in my bag."

Immediately George pictured himself reaching into the storage closet above his dresser while Erin watched. She followed him into the bedroom through the vestibule. The chair was still against the dresser. He climbed up and opened the square closet door, and the bag fell into his arms.

"I know why you're pissed off," she said, laughing. "Maybe I *did* leave this here on purpose. Are there any red stockings up there?"

George shook his head and handed her the bag. "She won't be coming back anyway."

"Oh." Erin put the bag on the floor and looked up at George, still on the chair. She took his hand, and he stepped down.

They stood inches apart for a moment. Their foreheads met, and they looked at their touching fingers.

"Why don't you come with us?" she said. "I'll go tell my mom."

"No, no," George said.

"C'mon, we'll wait. My mom loves you."

27

In the back seat of their old Ford, George sat behind Erin, crumpling a foil gum wrapper into a ball. Erin's mom drove and was quiet. George looked at the woman's profile, at her buttery blond hair tied back and her heavy dark lipstick. He remembered Alex's proposal. George pictured himself with Erin and her mother. They turned right onto Spruce Street, heading west, away from Society Hill. People held hands and carried bags, walking in and out of antique shops and coffee bars. Doors were propped open, and the sidewalks were white from the sun. The wind blew Erin's hair past the headrest, lifting it up like a crazy kite flapping. Her mother reached for the radio. George closed his eyes, allowing the scene to play out. The sun and streets were so bright that pink light glowed through his eyelids. The car made a few turns. The smell of Erin's strawberry shampoo drifted through the back seat, and he wondered where the three of them would go, as if it might really matter.

Walt Vail

The Red Truck

At lunchtime, after eating, the elementary school children went out to play in the schoolyard. The schoolyard was large, but the children used only half of the area, so a single teacher could walk among them to give token supervision, settle arguments, and prevent fights. At the gate—a space in the length of open, black-barred fencing—a pretzel man offered pretzels with or without mustard—popular treats for children who needed bellies full of warm, crusty dough to supplement their inadequate diet. Pretzels were three for a penny. The year was 1937.

On the fringe of the active groups of children, removed from the rope-jumping, ball-playing, tag-racing, jack-snatching, and hopscotch, a few children wandered and observed. These were the loners, shy, fearful of participation, filled with anxieties. One boy was dominated by a fear of having his head plunged into a toilet, a fate promised by some larger boys who sensed his fear and enjoyed making threats. He always waited for the bell to ring before heading for the empty boys' room. He preferred a daily reprimand for being late to line up to having his hair washed in toilet water. Despite his fear, he kept watch on his younger brother, a second grader, who dashed through the crowded yard playing tag, laughing as if he had no fear of anything.

Most of the boys in the schoolyard were dressed in corduroy knickers and knee-length socks. Their shoes were cheap and worn through at the soles, their interiors lined with cardboard or newsprint. This worked well if the cardboard was cut to fit the shoe and changed every day. Unless, of course, it rained. Regardless of shoe problems, the boys were always in motion. As they ran, their corduroy knickers rubbed together, creating an accompaniment of audible vibration. Many of them wore caps; some wore suit-type jackets and ties—small examples of threadbare gentility on the children of clerks or working-class people.

Across the street from the schoolyard, a battered red truck pulled up and parked. Lettering on the side of the truck proclaimed "Rudnick Plumbing and Heating." The truck often appeared across from the schoolyard. The boy who feared toilet water was aware of the truck, but his mother had told him never to talk to its occupant, because other children carry tales home to neighbors, and neighbors gossip. In the cab of the truck a heavyset, dark-haired workman in overalls sat and ate his paper-bagged lunch, drank from his thermos, and smoked cigarettes in a continuous chain, lighting one from the butt of another. He stared out the truck at the schoolyard, searching the moving bodies of the children for the tag-playing second grader and his older, non-participating brother. Catching a glimpse of the older boy, the man was filled with yearning and satisfaction. An overwhelming love encompassed him as he gazed proudly at the shy, serious boy who was graceful and beautiful even if he was not outgoing or anxiety free. The man wondered what this boy was thinking; he imagined that the child's thoughts were profound, that the boy was sensitive and gifted, and that he would grow up to be a man with a religious or professional calling.

When he was this boy's age, Rudnick—the man—was tough, rebellious, spoiled and mischievous. He was large-boned and muscular, big for his age, but not sensible. Had he been sensible, he would not have played with matches. He would not have suffered months in a hospital after the fire that burned him and killed his mother. He survived the pain and the multiple skin grafts because his mother's final act was to save him from death, and that act gave him courage to live.

This boy that his eyes devoured was small, frail, thoughtful, and fearful, not like Rudnick at all. In a proper family, Rudnick thought, the boy might have grown up to become a Rabbi.

So Rudnick watched, and reflected, and was satisfied and proud, and longed to go over to his son and lift him high in his powerful plumber's arms, and laugh, and love him, and give him courage. He yearned for the boy to return his love, if not now, then someday, because for now the child seemed distant to him, even during his regular Sunday visits. The school bell rang, and as the boy ran for the empty boys' room and the lines of children formed in the schoolyard, the red truck pulled away for the afternoon's work, the lunch period over.

On Sundays, the boy's mother, who never attended church herself, sent the boy and his younger brother downtown to attend chapel and Sunday school. They boarded a streetcar and traveled on their own for half an hour, and the streetcar dropped them off in front of the church. They loved the great vastness of the church's arched ceiling, the warmth, the red carpet, the wooden, cushioned pews. They loved the droning, deep voice of the pastor, although they did not understand his sermons. They loved the powerful organ, the strong voices of the small choir, and the subdued singing of the congregation. They loved the sip of wine at communion which caused their faces to flush with warmth, as if the blood of the Lord had truly entered their bodies through their stomachs. They always competed to get the largest sip of wine, but the pastor wisely lifted the silver chalice and controlled the flow. They took a special pleasure in looking deep into the chalice at the red wine moving as if it was alive. They liked that the pastor always wiped the lip of the chalice clean with a white cloth, before and after they drank.

Out of shyness the boys sat in the back of the church, but once, their curiosity got the best of them and they walked past the entire congregation to the front row. The pastor looked down from his high pulpit and smiled warmly at them. They blushed, and although they never sat in front again, for a few moments they glowed in the pastor's attention and approval.

Each week, after collection, the boys left the church and played for half an hour in the parish house. They were always on hand for Sunday school, but no one ever showed up to teach them. Because the pastor was busy in the church, he never seemed to know that there was no Sunday school, only a place to play and bang on the piano, and wait until noon, when it was time to leave.

The boys did not go home at noon. Instead, they boarded a different streetcar at a different corner, and traveled for another half hour to a street that was full of small businesses and shops and rooming houses. They got off the streetcar and walked past the stores, past a store window that was lettered "Rudnick Plumbing and Heating," and past a red truck. They turned a corner, entered a side door, and went up a flight of stairs to the room occupied by Rudnick, their father. The boys knocked before they entered the room. The room contained a bed, a chest, a desk, and several chairs. Through a bay window the boys could see up, down, and across the street. Rudnick was often asleep on the bed, although sometimes he was sitting at the desk near the window, chain-smoking cigarettes. The fingers of his right hand were stained yellow from nicotine, and his calloused skin showed burn marks from his habit of crushing the lit end of a cigarette between his fingers. Upon seeing the boys, his dark eyes flashed with mischief and warmth. He kissed each boy, gave each a bone-shattering hug, and told them he was glad to see them. He talked to them a great deal, asking them questions about school and about their mother, and telling them stories about his father and his five older sisters, and his mother, who died in the fire. He often explained the scars on his legs, and his eyes teared up when he spoke of how his mother covered him with her body to protect him from the flames. He urged the boys to love their mother and to do well in school.

31

The boys listened, but they did not talk much except to answer direct questions. They liked their father, but they were waiting for two hours to pass, for Rudnick to tell them it was time to go home and give them each a shiny dime. When he presented the allowance, Rudnick always reminded them not to tell anyone of their visit and to remember that he was their real father. He told them that their mother's husband, whom he called "The Old Man," was a violent man who kept a revolver and would shoot their mother if he knew that the boys came to visit their real father. The boys were privy to a great secret that they must never tell. The boys knew that The Old Man kept a revolver locked in his bureau drawer; they had seen it. But it was very rusty and they thought it might blow up if anyone tried to fire it, so they did not believe that The Old Man would ever shoot their mother. He was forever threatening to beat the boys if they were bad, but he had never hit them or their mother. The Old Man was ten years older than their mother—as their mother was always telling everyone—and he had tuberculosis. The boys were sure that he was too frail to hurt anyone. So they did not understand what the big secret was, but they kept it anyway, because their mother also told them never to tell anyone, ever. They liked their allowance, and once in a while The Old Man gave them some money, too. He never mentioned the dark-haired man and did not seem to know about him. The boys thought it a good idea to keep the secret and both sources of income.

On warm summer Sundays Rudnick sometimes took the boys to the park and played catch with them. The younger boy liked to climb trees, and one day he climbed a forty-foot tree, and, laughing, refused to come down. Rudnick didn't worry, because he thought his second son was a lot like himself: sturdy, fearless, and daring. He was a boy who could take risks and take care of himself, who could beat up anyone who called him a bad name, as Rudnick had done when the Christian boys had called him a dirty Jew. His second son was a boy Rudnick understood, a boy who could climb a tree and stay up there all day if he wanted to. One day this boy might join him in the plumbing business. He kept on playing catch with his first son, and soon the younger boy came down from the tree to join the game. Rudnick threw the ball to his second son, and the boy threw it back to him as hard as he could, as if he was angry at being ignored in the tree. He had climbed a tree that his older brother would never try to climb, and he received no credit or attention for it.

When their weekly visits were over, the boys returned home for Sunday dinner, the comics, and the radio. They did their homework and got ready for a new week, and then went to bed. Their mother never discussed their visits to their father, but sometimes she would slip out at night to make a telephone call on the pay phone at the corner. She called Rudnick at his plumbing business, and, to save her money, Rudnick called the pay phone back, and they talked and planned their next opportunity to be together. They talked about the day when they would be together permanently, and never admitted to each other that they both liked their present arrangement.

As each new week began, the boys forgot about their father until perhaps Wednesday, when the older boy, staying well out of the crowd in the school-yard, would catch a glimpse of the battered red truck. He did not look directly at it, but he sensed its presence; it gave him a warm feeling and it reduced his anxiety about getting his head stuck in the toilet bowl and having his hair washed in toilet water.

Amber Dorko Stopper
The Slender Nerve

He grabbed me in broad daylight as I walked home with my groceries past the Morning Glory Diner. I felt brick against my back, smelled his eggy breath, and was conscious that his grip had become a caress of my shoulders before I recognized him.

"Lonnie," I said.

"Seven years," said Lonnie. "Seven years. You wouldn't have believed it was me, right?"

His hairy belly hung from a too-small T-shirt, but he was at least forty pounds lighter than when I had last seen him, seven years before. Lonnie pulled me away from the wall. Mortar yanked at the fine hairs near my neck.

"*Look* at you," Lonnie said. "Look at *me*. *I've* changed tremendously. Can you see it?"

"Sure."

"I mean," said Lonnie, abashed at my agreement. "It's fairly obvious."

"You're still you."

"You were my best friend once. You were. And I fucked it up. Do you want to try it again?"

The bag of groceries I had purchased ten minutes before was still in my hand, the ice cream still frozen. "In some way," I told Lonnie. "In some way, of course."

"I'm HIV positive," he added hurriedly. "But no opportunistic infections. *And* I have a BMW now."

"Oh God," I said.

"I'm ready to pour everything I have into this friendship now," said Lonnie. "I've been lying in bed for two years since I've been diagnosed. Depressed. Suicidal. And now I'm ready to get on with my life, such as it is. I've missed you. I'm a different person. I'm ready to be your friend now. And I expect the same from you," he said. "Ante up."

"You got up out of bed when?" I asked. "Today?"

"What difference does it make?"

"I'm just saying, you said you had been lying in bed for two years. Now you're up. Is this the first day of this? Why'd you get up this morning?"

Lonnie looked irritated. "It's been about six months," he said. "Six months that I've been doing better. I just decided I had to get on with my life, such as it was. Don't you ever make a decision on your own, without some auspicious sign from the heavens? Ante up," Lonnie repeated, his jaw hardening. He shook my shoulders lightly.

"Yes. Great. Yes," I said. "Ante. Uncle."

I had been given no auspicious sign from the heavens. Lonnie had been my best friend, once. These things often end in inauspicious ways. When fences are mended, if only by time, there is no real opportunity for a constructive postmortem.

Why did we stop speaking to one another? The motivating moments, if not the reasons, were still clear in my mind. Petty, humiliating moments of undermining one another, familiarity breeding contempt, childishness. Things I would not let happen again, now that I was older. "I can do this," I said, feeling like I had just won a large and ungainly basket of cheer from some dollar-a-chance charity. I could not see everything in the basket, but was sure it was better than nothing and was determined to make the best of it.

"Good," said Lonnie.

I suspect Lonnie was the great love of my life and that I might have been the love of his. I thought it as soon as I had met him. I thought it seven years later when he reappeared to me. I think it now that he has been dead for five years.

He had a slippery quality of attraction/repulsion, an ugly-beauty that the French have a word for: *jolie-laide*. Sometimes I'd look at Lonnie and think "My God, he's handsome, I just didn't see it before." Then the next day I'd come to my senses and think he was unfortunate-looking by any standards. Lonnie stood hopefully at the edge of the physically attractive world, dressed and ready, waiting to be invited in, and it often seemed that he would be, but never for long.

Lonnie had unusual eyelashes. They looked as though they had fiber-optic tips, like those fuzzy half-globes of bright color-changing tendrils you see in gift shops that sell black light posters and vanilla incense. His eyelashes were like that, but they did not enhance the primitive and mean eyes they protected. Looking at Lonnie reminded me of looking at multiple photos of a schizophrenic or serial killer, where each image is almost unrecognizably different from the rest. There is no way to view all sides of a three-dimensional object at one time. Lonnie was different every time you looked at him. And repulsive was definitely on the rotation.

Seven years had gone by since I last saw him, on the day that he pushed me up against the diner wall, but the three years prior to those seven had been full of him. Then, Lonnie had lived off-campus, in a barely habitable apartment. I remember the day he decided to paint his bedroom black. An awful idea to begin with, he had quit halfway through, mid-stroke, leaving what looked like ragged tiremarks on the wall. He sighed and despaired over and regretted the project, doing nothing about it, until he was evicted for non-payment of rent. Lonnie couldn't even ruin something properly.

In those years, we held hands when walking on the street. Lonnie would sometimes hold my entire arm under his, tight across his own chest. We often had skipping contests. We frequented, with Lonnie's fine connections, the back door of an Italian restaurant in the Ninth Street Market where we could knock and pay only three dollars for a foil dish of ziti that we would eat sitting on the curb, watching a thunderstorm pull in from the west. I remember summers, feeling grimy and windblown from nomadic and cheap-living days with Lonnie on Center City streets, my hair falling hot and lankly in my face. "*Don't*," Lonnie would say when I tried to brush it back. "There can only be trouble for anyone who disturbs the rat's nest."

I went to Lonnie's place to meet him, to reestablish us with each other. The apartment wasn't quite as "overlooking the Parkway" as he had described over the phone. There was an open bottle of Laphroig and a pile of Androderm patches in sterile packets on the kitchen table. The couch was covered in thickets of dog hair although no dog was present. "What do you think of the place?" asked Lonnie. "It overlooks the Parkway. See? It's not usually such a mess, though. It's just because I've been so busy. And I'm changing so much about it."

"How did you get sick?" I asked.

Lonnie twitched disapprovingly. "For the record," he said. "Nobody really likes to be asked that question."

"But how?" I repeated. "The bathhouse?"

"No," snapped Lonnie. "That's not how I got it. I *know* how I *got* it. That's not how."

"Oh," I said.

"It's okay that you asked me," Lonnie said. "But most people wouldn't cotton to it."

"Right," I said.

"You're just the same, you know," he said. "You're just the same. It always really got to me that you were the one who ended our friendship. That *you* were the one who said 'Fuck this, I've had enough.' That had never happened to me before. *I* was always the one to do that to *other* people."

"I don't remember it happening that way," I said.

"You did it," Lonnie insisted. "It was you."

"I certainly remember *feeling* that way," I said. There had been good reasons for giving up on my friendship with Lonnie.

While at home earlier that day, I had looked through drawers for photos of Lonnie and me, in an attempt to anchor myself. Photographs from that time showed that I had been prettier than I then believed. Hair dyed black, a bold twenty pounds overweight and braless in a spaghetti strap top, I was as uncivilized and unaware of my powers as the Venus Hottentot. Wide sheets of bluish, unblemished, citified flesh, yet untattooed, greeted me from a picture in which I hunched away from the camera. Lonnie faced me in this photo. His hair was just a little thicker, just a little redder, and there was a full liquid effect to his face; not just the absence of illness, but the actual quality of Youth. I had been noticing more and more lately how it was long before a person became "older" that a person lost their Youth. Youth made a person full to bursting, corpuscles and energy, like peeling away the membrane from a grapefruit and looking only at the jeweled network of cells beneath. Neither Lonnie nor I had that now.

It was dusk. The yellow sodium lights in fashionable sconces in Lonnie's part of town glowed and buzzed.

"Let's go out," he said.

There were marks on Lonnie's face from pushing his forehead against the iron bars that locked us out of the Rodin Museum's gardens. "Closed means closed," I told him, but Lonnie insisted on lingering painfully. Our next stop, as Lonnie led the way, was a small cemetery. I groaned. "Subconscious means *sub*."

"No time for subconscious," he answered. Daffodils, arbitrary and spindly, grew along the walkways. "I hate places like this," Lonnie said, and it appeared that the intention of this destination had been to provide the setting for this rueful comment. "*This* is not a monument to your life!" He admonished a headstone, pointing and addressing the person beneath it angrily: "I WANT TO SMELL YOUR COAT."

His arms dropped to his sides. "So who do you still see?" he demanded. "Do you see Jacklyn? Missy? Any of those people we used to hang out with? Kevin? John?"

"Jacklyn moved out West," I said. "I never hung out with Missy or John. Kevin lives in New York, I still see him sometimes when he comes down."

"You hung out with Missy when *I* hung out with Missy," Lonnie corrected.

"You guys didn't get along that well. I think you had a little jealousy thing going over me."

That was a dynamic Lonnie had tried to conjure even then, even as he had introduced me to Missy for the first time, years ago. These people were in the past, and Lonnie was in the past for them. There was something about Lonnie that made you feel you had taken a step forward by outgrowing him.

"Mostly my friends now are people you wouldn't know," I said.

"Oh, of course," said Lonnie. "But you know what *I* believe."

"What?"

"I no longer believe in survival of the fittest," he said. "I believe in Survival of the Fittest Friend. I think you have to be able to say, 'I need to believe I'm the only person who exists for you right now.' I think you have to exact your pound of flesh."

"Who do you still see from those days?" I asked.

We sat in unharmonious silence, side by side on a damp slate bench. Lonnie reached for my shoulders, rubbed them. "Oooooooh," he said, his small, broad hands squeezing stubbornly against unhappy muscle. "Who lives in *there*?

"So anyway," he said. "So you hang out with a lot of professional people. You used to have a lot of male friends. Do you know any women?"

"I know women," I said.

"Do any of 'em like having sex with men with AIDS?" Lonnie snarled, in a lecherous drawl. I hesitated to come up with too quick an answer.

"It's ironic," said Lonnie, playing off of something he wished I had said, but hadn't. "Being HIV positive has forced me to work so hard on myself, and really made me someone *worth* being around, *worth* being in a relationship with. But it kind of limits my scope, so to speak."

"I guess so."

"I mean I used to be such a *mess*."

"Some people are just messy people." I excavated a small rock near my shoe. "It's incredibly damp here," I said. "This feels stupid."

"I could take you to dinner," Lonnie said. "I'm making a lot of money now."

"Doing what?"

"Voices," Lonnie said.

"What's that mean?"

"And I was a camp counselor last summer," he continued. "And I get some disability checks."

"What's 'voices?' " I asked again.

"Cartoon voices," Lonnie said. "It's no big deal. This sergeant guy on a GI Joe–knockoff cartoon. No, I'm not kidding. I haven't taped in a while. What?" he demanded.

"That's *funny*," I said. "That's great."

"Everything you say sounds very sarcastic," Lonnie snapped.

"That's because you make me feel so comfortable."

"I have a *voice*," Lonnie continued. "By nature, I can make these voices. I swear, I think the protease inhibitors helped. But like I said, I haven't done it in awhile. I get checks, though, 'cause it's on TV in the afternoons."

"That's hysterical."

He seemed to regret having told me. "It can be very physically demanding work, actually," he said. "What I really value is my work with children."

"Camp counselor," I recalled, in an effort to deflect some of his irritation.

"Yeah," he said. "Camp for boys. Young Jewish boys. Just the kind of summer camp I always got sent to and hated."

"And what do you do with the kids?"

He gave me a menacing look.

"I'm not intentionally talking you into corners, here," I said. "You told me this was important."

"I know." He sighed and held his head. "I was a camp counselor," he said. "And at night, in the cabin I was assigned to, when all the lights were out, I would do the voice of Sergeant Smash, and a few other ones I'd make up, and enact homoerotic escapades. Sometimes, there'd be a couple action figures lying around; I'd use those too. Have Sergeant Smash cruising, finding an innocent little Lego guy, offer him an amyl nitrate popper, ask him to dance . . . put on some Frankie Goes To Hollywood . . . "

I laughed.

"The kids would just crack up; they all knew the show. They loved it. Otherwise, I did pretty much what every camp counselor does. It sucked. It was buggy. It paid shit."

For the next few weeks, we saw each other every other day and talked on the phone on the days in between. Lonnie's routine of health, now that he had stopped taking the protease inhibitors, was an impromptu amalgam of "healthy eating" and exercise. He would take me to lunch a few times a week, at various cafés featuring faith-based menus of veganism or paganism or krishnaism. He would eat huge amounts of food, treating every item as though it were an elixir with benefits in direct proportion to the quantities consumed. He would pay for both our lunches with ostentatious gallantry, unable to tear his own fascinated eyes from the denominations of the bills he was laying down. "No," he would tell me angrily, when I tried to chip in or reciprocate. "I am *treating*." I had never known Lonnie to have the resources to be generous. Marked for death, this poignancy was part of every meeting we had.

After eating, we would be walking through a bookstore or shopping for CDs and Lonnie would be galvanized by the need to work out at the gym. "Come on," he would beg. "Come with me. I have guest passes you can use. I'll buy you a set of shorts and a T-shirt when we get there. We can *schvitz*." I would decline. Lonnie would insist on parting then, immediately, and would go alone to run, in jeans and sandals, on the treadmill.

"I have to go to Home Depot," he said one Sunday morning when I called to see what we were doing. "I have to buy paint. I want to paint my kitchen cabinets." When he rang the doorbell of my apartment at one thirty-five, he was dressed in a too-small sharkskin suit and was carrying a kitchen cabinet door. "I figured they could recommend an appropriate base paint for me if I brought this."

Lonnie's BMW was parked outside. It was an old one, somewhat beat up, stripped down, and painted a murky brown. It did not run smoothly. We drove east on Washington Avenue, passing vendors who sold live crabs alongside unbranded toiletries and cleaning agents. Lonnie blasted Springsteen's "Rosalita," windows down.

"I love that I have a BMW," he said, since I hadn't. "But really, sometimes it makes me depressed. Like I've sold out. I mean, would *Tom Waits* have a BMW?"

At Home Depot, Lonnie pushed an empty cart. He consulted an orange-aproned associate and the three of us stood looking at color chips. Lonnie put three gallons of primer down heavily into the cart. The sales associate wandered away. We looked at the color chips some more.

"You don't seem very interested in this," Lonnie said, with some accusation.

"Why would I be?"

"Here," he said, removing an engraved silver ring from his right ring finger and slipping it onto my left. "I want you to feel more vested in the proceedings, honey." He put rollers and trays and new porcelain knobs into the cart, and for a moment, with the warmth of his ring on my finger, I felt like we were in this together. "The custom-blended colors cost a lot more than the pre-mixed," he said. "But they're much more subtle."

I went to the ladies' room, a mildewy, sulphurous place. When I returned, Lonnie had three gallons of custom-mixed paint in the cart. The color was mossy, heathery, and Lonnie had added some natural sponges and texturing tools to his purchases. "I'm happy with all this," he said solemnly. "I want to go talk to the guy about wood. I want to build a bed."

"I have to get home soon," I said.

"Why?"

"Because I want to."

"I don't *care* about that," said Lonnie, moving very close to my face. "I'm in the *middle* of something here."

Seven years earlier, I would have walked away, not spoken to him for days. But then Lonnie had never gone anywhere that required the use of a car; I had always been within walking distance of my own dorm or apartment. Seven or eight years before, it would have been de rigueur, and viable, to ignore Lonnie when he banged on the door late at night, apologizing, vilifying, serenading. I didn't want that happening at my door now. I read a gardening magazine while Lonnie waited for a consultation in the lumber department. He made a pass at asking questions and obtaining information, but I could see his heart was no longer in it. The check-out line was long and slow. I helped bag the smaller items. Lonnie swiped his debit card to pay. It was declined.

"Fuck," Lonnie said.

I remembered when Lonnie had purchased the black paint for his bedroom years before. That paint, I remembered now, had been deeply discounted remainder paint, shelved after it was mixed for some well-meaning individual who had never picked it up, or whose credit card had been denied.

I bought a soft pretzel and sat on some bags of landscaping rocks in the enclosed space between two sets of sliding doors, next to the pay phones and soda machines. Lonnie called his bank. "Eight dollars," he yelled to me, incredulous. "*How* can my bank balance be *eight dollars*?"

I shook my head.

"I have somebody I can call," he told me, and so I sat down again, sucking salt grains from my fingers, trying not to listen. "What do you mean, '*I don't want it to be like the last time*'?" I heard Lonnie shout.

A moment later, he hung up the phone. "I have no money," he said. "And *you* have to go *home*."

I felt he was offering me a blank space in which to apologize to or contradict him. But I just wanted to go home.

"I don't even know what I'm going to eat tonight," he said glumly. "Of course, it'll all be fine by Monday. I'm expecting a check on Monday."

"Tomorrow's Monday," I said. "So that's good."

"Yeah," Lonnie said. "That's real good."

We drove home in sullen silence. We left behind the abandoned cart, the custom-mixed paint destined for the remainder shelf, the rollers. "Your cabinet door," I said to Lonnie. "Did you put it back in the car?"

He had not, and he did not acknowledge me when I got out, but drove away with an abashed lurch.

Lonnie always loved to give the impression that he was getting it together. I think that's why he burned bridges with so many people—to create the space in which he could reinvent himself for the next time he saw them. But the other shoe always dropped. It had dropped for me this time, as it had dropped years before. The reaction to Lonnie's reinvention, no matter who gave it, never satisfied Lonnie for long. He enjoyed *initial* reactions, and he burned through providers of these quickly. Now, I wondered, to whom had he turned next? Why, I wondered, had he spent so much time with me to begin with? Why, I wondered, had I given him so much of mine?

It was no longer me he was calling or treating to lunch. Greener pastures surely existed; Lonnie knew a lot of people. Instead of leaving them laughing, he wanted to leave them impressed by his transcendency. But even Lonnie's spirit was stubbornly corporeal and grounded to the Earth—almost, it seemed, as much as his body.

If Lonnie or I had seemed happy, even only one of us, the whole thing would have been more familiar. Like a tender, bitten shred of skin in the mouth, caressed by a protective tongue, our good intentions were severed from their connection—not just with life, but soon, with the pain they had treated us to, as proof of their presence.

"Long time no hear," I said, when Lonnie called two weeks later.

"I don't respond well to that kind of talk," he answered.

"I see," I said. "I don't miss you, and have had lots to do without you," I offered. "How's that?"

"I don't want to be friends with you," Lonnie said. "Anymore."

He got from me the confused moment of silence he was undoubtedly striving for. "I don't understand," I said. I wasn't surprised, but I didn't understand.

"I'm sorry," said Lonnie. "Cold feet, I guess." I heard the smile in his voice. "I don't feel . . . *tranquil* around you. And you have to admit, it's important to my *health* to feel tranquil. I've been listening to Beethoven's Sixth a lot," he said. "And thinking about you."

"Listen to the Ninth," I said. "For a new perspective."

"I don't want a new perspective. I don't want to change my mind."

"What were you trying to *do*?" I asked Lonnie. "What have you been trying to *do* to me?"

He laughed now, and unkindly. "There's you," he said. "And the whole rest of the universe is like a crossing guard. And the crossing guard is saying to you, 'Ma'am? I'm only going to ask you one more time. *Please* step away from that edge.'"

This analogy never left my mind. It did not cripple me, but I would wrestle with this pronouncement of my unrehabilitatable separateness for a long time. Married, a mother, divorced, single, re-partnered, whatever my situation was, whatever anyone's was, I was finally wounded enough to have a change of character. Being sick unto death had not yet done this for Lonnie, but Lonnie had done it to me.

I had not known that when a person says something intended to drive you away it often tethers you to them, like a nervous, pocketbook-sized dog, never still, never out of sight.

"So it was stupid of me," I said. "To ante up."

"Probably," said Lonnie. It sounded as though he had just taken a big swallow of something. He was luxuriating in this, I was positive. "But then again, I should have known *myself* that I'd reject anybody who fell for that line. And particularly anyone who considered themselves a better person for it."

I forgot the awkwardness of what was happening. If Lonnie had seen this false altruism in me, I was surprised he had never said so earlier. "But you're wrong," I said. "You're wrong. You can't do this if you're basing it on the idea that that's what I thought."

"I'm sorry," he said. "I'm sorry I couldn't give you want you needed. I wanted to give you what you needed . . . " his voice changed, and I thought that he was crying, but then realized in a split-second that he was not crying at all—he was using his Sargeant Smash voice.

"Oh God. You fucking bastard."

" . . . just not friendship," Lonnie finished. He knew I had heard him. He knew I believed him. I heard him hang up the phone. It was the last time we ever spoke.

There are little things I left out: like how I always had this ridiculous fantasy of getting up in some bar and singing X's "See How We Are" with Lonnie. Whenever I hear that song, I think it's him and me singing it. Whenever I think I am done remembering everything I need to remember about Lonnie, I think of something else worth remembering. When someone dies, no matter if they were a casual acquaintance or a close loved one, you're always stuck with one visit's worth of stuff that you never got to say to them.

I called Lonnie a few times and emailed him in the weeks following our last conversation, but he blocked me at every turn. Every few months, I imagined where he might be and how he might be. Years again went by.

I was alone in a coffee shop half-listening to the conversation of two men next to me. "Did you ever know Lonnie Emmaus?" one asked the other. I never found out what he was going to say about Lonnie, and neither did the other guy. "*I* know Lonnie!" I said. "Have you heard from Lonnie? How is he?"

"Dead," the man said, rather apologetically.

Lonnie did not die of AIDS. According to Jackson, my bearer of bad tidings, Lonnie was in Portland, scouting out apartments, looking for a place for himself and his new, HIV-positive wife to make a new start. He purchased some heroin there, and did it in a motel room with the guy he had bought it from. When Lonnie started feeling sick, the guy bailed. Lonnie got out of the motel and knocked on doors until someone took him to the hospital, where he died.

I wondered if, out of politeness to this stranger, I should express surprise at this shabby death. The last time I had seen Lonnie he had been all sprouts and Stairmasters, but it did not surprise me that he had died this way. I got the impression from Jackson that it had not surprised him either. Anyone who knew Lonnie was familiar, I now saw, with his bell curve. Nothing he purported to be was as healthy or clean or together as he wanted you to believe. The truth was always a little, or even a lot, worse than you imagined.

And yet, although I had done without him for years, I now had a reason to miss Lonnie. His reinventions were over and I had never had a chance to have a single one of my own, even if Lonnie wouldn't have noticed it.

"My wife had a dream about Lonnie," Jackson told me. "She saw him in her dream and asked him if he missed being alive. Lonnie told her yes. *'The way your skin feels against your shirt,'* he said. *'And how when you take a knife and cut a piece of cheese at a party, the sound it makes when the knife hits the plate.'*" Jackson described these corporeal joys in a voice like Lonnie's. It was something Lonnie would have said, but born of the subconscious of the sleeping wife of a stranger, and voiced, accurately and believably, through that stranger. It was like identifying the body.

Jackson and his wife, and others they knew, decided to have a wake. "An Irish wake," Jackson told me, since people who knew Lonnie had found out about his death in a scattered pattern, over a drawn-out period of time, and there had been no collective mourning. Jackson was going to run an ad in a free weekly paper so that people would know to come. He wanted me to tell people I knew, people he thought I must have known if I knew Lonnie. "If you knew Lonnie, you must know Betsy," he said. "Or Melissa. Or Cory." But I didn't.

"I only knew Lonnie," I told Jackson, and although I knew a lot of other people, there was no point mentioning them, and it was therefore no wonder that Jackson seemed to feel a little sorry for me, beholden to me, that he had orphaned me of Lonnie, and was now responsible to be a little of the company I must miss. "But I'll give you some money to run the ad in the paper."

"The ad is free," Jackson said. "I think Lonnie would have wanted something like this."

But no ad ran in the weeks prior to when Jackson said the wake would be and I did not see him in the coffee shop or on the street.

On a Thursday morning, I received an email from a woman in my own apartment building, whose plants I sometimes watered.

Jackson Kramer said to let you know that the thing for Lonnie Emmaus will be this Saturday from two to four upstairs at Fergies.

I was touched that Jackson had found a way to get this message to me, and was not curious about the chain of familiarity that had made it possible. It only told me that more people knew more people, including Lonnie himself, than I realized.

I had every intention of going. But the thought of seeing people I had never heard of and who had never heard my name reminded me: according to Lonnie, it was still only me who stood at the edge. I thrust forward, while the crossing guards, tight-lipped with distaste for my feelings, held me back. I did not think that was anything people would want to see. I did not attend the wake.

It was Jackson's wife who emailed me next, in the days after the gathering, to assure me that I had not made a mistake in failing to attend.

It was a shame that we didn't have much of a turnout, but as we told stories about him, it became clear that we were all pissed off because the last conversation we had with him was an argument. Oh, that Lonnie was an angry little man. Somehow, he convinced some of us that putting up with him was worth it.

She wanted to make me feel better. I didn't expect to hear from her again. Lonnie had died, unhappy with everybody. Everybody was unhappy with him. His death did not make him any more wise or precious to me. The shrill pain I often felt when he was near pulses even now, but only in a nearly severed part of me.

Unlike me, Jackson's wife was able to say it was worth it. And so it is to her and not me that Lonnie can appear in a dream and speak his short list of his loves on Earth.

Greg November
Dinnertime at 42B

T he hookers at 42B eat their pizza at seven. I've known this for a while. We all used to sit around and watch the pies delivered. Right at seven every evening the guy would pull up in his blue LeBaron and honk. And every evening the door would open and the madam, who looked a used forty, would stick her haggard face out, watch the guy lift three boxes from the car, and turn back into the building and holler something like "Feed time!" We were usually well-sauced by this point and Marv would pound the table and throw his head back in laughter. Tyson would insist we do another shot. It was grand stuff. Tonight, though, I'm sitting alone, sipping whiskey and trying to catch Kylie's eye. She's new, only been cocktailing here about two weeks and far as I can tell she thinks I'm disgusting.

They're my hookers, in a fashion. Sort of like this is my city. And by that all I mean is I still live here, which I guess is not much to say. But it's true. Here's something else that's true: Marv, Tyson and the rest are gone and not even the bartenders know me anymore.

The girl who used to cocktail here, Sugar, always smiled and did her flirting thing and kissed us all on the cheek when she was drunk. But she moved to Oakland earlier this year to help her one-eyed brother raise his baby. The day she left we all did a shot together and for the next hour drafts were half price.

Kylie brings my lager and places it along with a fresh napkin on the table in front of me, which is sticky with old beer and cigarette ash. She's a poor substitute for Sugar, who treated her customers like friends. Kylie, for my money, is one of the prettiest girls I've ever seen, but she never smiles. I'd be lying, though, if I said I didn't like ogling her rack when she stretched to clean the mirror behind the bar.

By 8:30 I'm drunk and decide it's time to leave. I pay what I owe and take a leak. Coming out of the bathroom, I tell Kylie I'll see her later and she looks up and says goodbye without warmth and this time I make a deliberate show of staring at her tits.

Out in the street I take a look at the wasted façade of 42B, at the dirty green curtains in the second-floor windows, at the chipped brick arch over a concrete stairway. The place is certainly dismal, but nothing about it suggests it's a whorehouse, no red light or anything. I know what it is because Tyson used to come here for oral during his lunch breaks.

A breeze starts to blow and I look up to see if it's going to rain. A hooker in a blond wig sticks her head out from one of the second-floor windows, pushes the curtains out of the way and looks at the sky, doing the same thing I think. She takes a deep breath and adjusts her wig slightly, places both hands on the sill and elevates her head up and out. For a second it looks like she might jump and I hold my breath, but she sees me and pulls herself in. I wave and she cocks her head. She looks into the room behind her and again out at me. From the street I can see her wig isn't on straight, which makes it look comical. After a moment she waves back. I open my mouth to say hello, but she draws her head in and closes the curtains. On the walk home I stop to urinate in an alley and take a couple tugs at my pecker, but decide against the idea.

At home I put on shorts. I drink a glass of water then poor a shot of bourbon. I take it down and go to brush my teeth. I look at myself in the mirror. I'm young but I feel two hundred years old. In bed I think about old friends and adjust myself under the covers. I put a hand on my pecker, but decide against the idea.

Somewhere east of Broad I realize I've been on the bus too long. I get off near a bar where Marv used to work, and grin, not really from anything that's funny, maybe just the opposite. I used to bring dates here because Marv and the rest treated me like royalty—free drinks and that sort of deal. They asked how I was doing, joked with my dates about what a bum I was. Tonight I stand across the street and look at the neon beer signs in the window. A chalkboard on the sidewalk advertises free wings until six-thirty. This is the way it feels these days, in this city. Too many places I used to know but no longer do; too many memories captured in deserted bars where staff turnover has filled old haunts with strangers. I turn away and walk south, home, and think of Marv, and how he moved back to Jersey last year, and of the guy I used to live with who nailed Marv's sister.

Twice today I fell asleep at work. This isn't anything extraordinary or new. I fall asleep most days because my job is not exciting. It isn't even dull in a romantic sense. I drive a forklift for a decorator that does most of the work at the Convention Center. I set up the large pavilions at shows that come through the city. I've been doing it for two years and in the beginning it was fun, when it was just a stepping stone, but now that it's become a destination I find it intolerable. Tyson used to work here too. But he left shortly after Marv. We all went to school together and moved here when we graduated, looking for city experience. The rest of the guys never really took a shine to me and Tyson. They called us college queers. It's not like I blame them, really. I mean this was their life, like it or not, and we were only there to mess around so we could say we slummed it for a bit after college. The people we worked with could smell an attitude like that. It made them want to kill.

Today I fell asleep in the john, and again lying on some boxes by one of the loading docks. My supervisor caught me and yelled and I just yawned, dared him in a fashion to fire me, but it's union work and so there I was. I walked back to my forklift and got through the rest of the day thinking about old girlfriends, and ranking in my head who was the best lay.

When my shift is over I catch the Seventeen east to the bar across the street from 42B and walk in, grinning at Kylie. She doesn't say hello, just moves behind the bar and deadpans, "Lager?" I nod and move to my booth, with the view out the front window.

Kylie brings my beer and I settle in to watch the hookers' pizza delivered. The way other people go to the movies or out to dinner, that's what this is for me. Maybe it's the thought of these women eating something I used to order all the time in college. I like the idea of a bunch of hookers in different colored wigs, chowing down and getting sauce on their faces, occasionally dropping a mushroom or piece of pepperoni into their cleavage.

I tell Kylie she looks dynamite and she says thank you without looking up, then flips the page of her GRE study book. Fuck her then; I hope she fails. I order a turkey club and a whiskey. There's no one else in the bar and as I watch Kylie wipe down the mirror behind the cash register I resent her for not caring whether or not I enjoy her company.

At seven, the pizza guy comes and the madam opens the door. I wonder if they have to call the pizza place every day and order, or if they have a regular set up where the guy just comes automatically. I wonder if it's the same type of pizza every time, or if there's ever a dispute over toppings.

Back when Marv and Tyson used to sit here with me, we'd always stop whatever we were talking about when the LeBaron pulled up. It was like the car was an alarm, telling us to shut up and listen. With fixed smiles we'd watch the guy get out with the pizza boxes. Sometimes a hooker held the door open while the madam grabbed the boxes. Once when it was raining, a girl in a yellow halter top came out instead. She scampered down a couple steps holding a sombrero over her head in an attempt to stay dry. When the guy handed her the pizza boxes she tossed the sombrero on top and ran back up the stairs. Marv laughed like a bastard at that one.

When the guy pulls away I order another drink. "Since there's no one here," I say to Kylie. "Would you like to join me?" This time she looks up at some point over my shoulder. She says no and moves to restock the glasses hanging above the taps. Her indifference makes my head hurt. Sugar used to sit with us and we'd laugh and do shots of bourbon and sometimes carry on until closing.

I eat my food, drink my whiskey, and leave. Another night in the books, so to speak. Maybe tomorrow I'll drive my forklift into one of the electrical rooms at the Convention Center and blow the place to the sky.

Outside I see a hooker standing on the front steps of 42B smoking a cigarette. She's dressed in a black miniskirt and a low-cut white top that shows off her ample chest. She's got a red wig on but I can tell it's the hooker from the window last night. She sees me and grins. "You again," she says.

"What?" I say, struck by the soft sound of her voice.

She takes a drag. "Didn't I see you from the window last night?"

I smile. "That's right."

"Thought so," she says and stubs out her cigarette against the brick.

I walk across the street and stop at the curb. I flash what I intend to be a disarming smile. She crosses her arms. "You're wearing a different wig," I say.

She puts another cigarette to her lips and says, "They make us do that. You know, gives the clientele variety." She exhales. "You really creeped me out last night."

"Why?" I say, taking a step back.

"You were staring at me like a lunatic."

"I thought you might jump."

The hooker laughs. "That'll be the day." She cups her breasts, adjusting them without any embarrassment. A true professional. I look away and she smiles. "Name's Tanya," she says.

"Hi Tanya," I say, looking back.

She lights another cigarette and puts a hand on her hip. "So?" she says, blowing smoke.

"What?"

"You going to tell me your name or do I have to guess?"

"Guess," I say, surprised at my answer.

Tanya scowls. "Forget it." She stubs out her second cigarette and turns to go back up the stairs. Suddenly I don't want to be left alone in the street, not again, not tonight. "My name is Danny," I say, rather loudly.

Tanya turns and stares at me and without thinking I reach into my pocket to see how much money I have. She watches my hand. "I'm taking a break, Danny," she says.

I pull my hand out and hold a wad of twenties. "I wasn't thinking, really, of buying anything from you. I mean, of the stuff you sell, really." I've never known how to talk to women. But something about holding the bills in my hand makes me feel powerful. Maybe it's the whiskey. Or the fact that Tanya turned around when I told her my name. "Would you like to have dinner with me?" I say.

"Excuse me?"

"I'll pay you." I show her my wadded twenties as proof.

"To have dinner with you?"

"Yes."

"You'll pay me for dinner?"

"Yes."

"And you're not going to ask me to give you a hand job under the table or anything?"

"No."

"Because that's extra."

"I promise I won't ask you to do anything weird."

"Anything weird," Tanya repeats to herself. Then she looks at the money in my hand. "I want the money up front, Danny."

"No problem," I say.

Tanya gives me a look and I hand her the cash. She links her arm in mine. "Alright, hard-on," she says. "I'm yours."

Eat your goddamned heart out, Kylie, I think to myself as we start down the street.

Tanya smokes two cigarettes—one per block—on the way to a martini place I know by the entrance to the interstate. She's pretty, in a street sort of way. Nice legs and an impressive chest, though it looks fake. The red wig does not fit her well. It's like a gaudy version of the things they give cancer patients. She smells like smoke and flowers.

Several months ago I would have been nervous walking next to her, like someone might see us and notice right away I was walking with a hooker. But tonight I don't care who sees. No one I know is around anymore. I look over at Tanya and grab her hand. I swing our arms. Tanya pulls up short and stares at me. "Is this a set up?" she says.

I let go of her hand. "What do you mean?"

"I mean is this a set up? Are you the kind of guy who lures prostitutes into alleys with promises of dinner and nothing weird, and then bludgeons them with a flashlight or heavy rubber dick or some shit?"

"No," I say. "I'm not that type of guy."

Tanya looks at me for a moment. "I don't see why we can't do this the old fashioned way," she says.

The martini place is fairly packed for this early on a week night and Tanya seems uncomfortable in the midst of all these people, as if she didn't expect to see them here. When we sit down, she leans forward. "Look," she says. "I don't know what you have planned here, but eighty buys you no more than a half hour, even if it is just dinner. Got it?"

"Yes," I say.

"Okay, then." She leans back and exhales loudly and I call over the waitress.

"Anything you want, dear," I say.

Tanya looks at me without smiling and turns to the waitress, a little thing with acne. "Kettle One and water," she says. I order a whiskey neat. The waitress nods and scoots away. "Couple a serious drinkers, we are," Tanya says, stubbing out her cigarette.

The waitress comes back with our drinks and sets them on the table. I thank her and take a sip of whiskey. Tanya drinks her glass down in one swallow and looks at me. I call the waitress back. "My lady friend will have another, please, and make it a double." Tanya spreads her arms along the back of the booth. I smile at her. She shakes her head. "What are we doing here?" she says.

"We're having some drinks."

"That's all?"

"Maybe some food."

"God, you must be desperate."

When the waitress asks if we're ready to order food, Tanya raises her eyebrows at me. *Are we really going to do this?* they say. I shrug. Tanya shakes her head. "I'll have the steak," she says. I order a tuna melt. Tanya takes a sip from her second drink and brushes a strand of wig hair from her eyes. The girlish gesture makes her appear momentarily less threatening. But when she sees me staring, her eyes narrow.

"Okay, Danny," she says, wiping her mouth with the back of her hand. "I keep waiting for the other shoe, know what I mean?"

"It's not like that."

"I mean, shit, you tell me you'll pay me to have dinner with you and in my head I think, he couldn't really be talking about dinner, but here we are."

"This isn't nice?"

"Nice? Up until a minute ago I thought you were going to ask me to get on my knees under the table. But now I see you're just some lonely dude, which is sad, man, because you're not that old."

51

"No, I'm not."

"So what's your story?"

"Okay. If you want the truth, I have no one else to eat with."

Tanya nods and lights a smoke. "Well, now we're getting somewhere."

Before they left, Marv, Tyson and I went to a show at the TLA. We ate at Lorenzo's beforehand and got drunk at some dump on South Street and sauntered into the show halfway through the opening band's set. Tyson accidentally spilled beer on some guy trying to maneuver closer to the bar. The guy, a big, tattooed monster, turned and started yelling at Tyson, who didn't back down although he probably should have. He called the guy a punk and the guy hit him in the face. Marv and I rushed in and the whole scene turned ugly, with people pushing and shoving and yelling and the band had to stop its set. Someone's nose was broken and the cops showed up and we ducked out in the commotion. We ran up South Street, through the crowd of teenagers and stylized emo kids on dates. We shouted at each other and laughed and a month later Marv moved back to Jersey and Tyson got married and I haven't seen either one since my last birthday, although sometimes I'll call Marv and leave a voicemail which he doesn't return.

Tanya lifts a forkful of steak to her mouth. "This is shit," she says, swallowing. "Tastes like dead ass."

We continue eating in silence and I think about what my eighty has just purchased: the unexcited company of a hooker at a popular martini bar in a popular part of the city where the food's not so good and the servers have acne. As Tanya forks the last of her overcooked steak between chapped lips, I think about running out on her. I feel overwhelmed and insulted. Why am I spending so much money for her company? I go so far as to lift my napkin out of my lap and place it on the table. Tanya looks up. I hold her glance. Then I think about what I'd be leaving her for and as twisted and insulting as this dinner is, it doesn't compare to another night alone at my apartment. I put the napkin back in my lap and take a sip of whiskey.

Tanya calls the waitress over and orders another round for both of us. "Hope you don't mind," she says to me, playfully. It's almost like a date, I think. I could as easily be just some guy out with his girl as I could be a pathetic john who lacked the discretion to carry out his perversions in private. Either one is possible, I tell myself.

Tanya swigs from her new drink and says, "Where were you headed when we ran into each other?"

I take a sip as well. "Home," I say.

Tanya lights her umpteenth cigarette and adjusts her red wig, for the umpteenth time. Her lipstick is smudged and after several rounds of vodka she's starting to look her part. "Why me?"

"I don't know," I say, smirking. "I figured you'd be good company."

Tanya leans forward and points her lit cigarette at me. "So let me get this straight. You walk out of the bar intent on heading home for another lonely night by yourself, maybe a couple rounds of jerking off before you fall asleep in your pants. But before you make it two steps you see me and you think to yourself: 'Here's someone more up shits creek than I am. Here's a poor damned soul who has obviously made worse decisions than I have. Maybe I'll take her to dinner and it'll make me feel a little better about my own bad decisions.'" She raises her eyebrows. "Is that it?"

I try to hold her look. "Not at all," I say.

"Sure," she says.

I open my mouth to say something, maybe that it isn't her I think is up shit's creek, that I don't know why I asked her to dinner because I hadn't really thought about it, but it sure wasn't because I felt sorry for her, or because I wanted to save her. But before I can say anything Tanya leans across the table and grips my hand. Our eyes lock. It's the type of moment where had we been the guy and girl on a real date we might have kissed. Instead Tanya holds my hand in hers and says, "Look, if you want me to stay you'll have to pay up again."

I look at my watch. Not even eight o'clock. If I go home now, it'd be to do pretty much what Tanya said. If I'm lucky I'll pass out before I decide to call Marv. But I think if I can keep this evening going a bit longer I'll be okay. If I have company—professional company, but company nonetheless— I can stave off loneliness for one night. I tell Tanya I have to hit an ATM but would love to spend more time with her, because it's not how she thinks it is. "How much do I need to keep you until closing?"

"Five hundred, no bargaining," she says, smiling for the first time in a while, in a good mood again.

I smile back. "Don't go anywhere," I say. She grips the table in a mock show of obedience. What a doll.

The nearest ATM is around the corner outside a convenience store. The night air sobers me up a bit. I realize the chances of Tanya being there when I get back are fairly slim, but seeing as I had agreed to pick up the tab for the night, it wouldn't make any difference if she ran out and stiffed me. But I want her to be there. I want her to be there so I can say certain things to her, not profess my love or anything, just things. I want to tell her about Marv and Tyson and how I miss them, how the cold faces of strangers on the Seventeen fill me with dread. There are things I haven't been able to say to anyone in a while, not to Kylie or my boss or the people who ride my bus; things about

Marv and Tyson and the girls we used to meet; about the guy I roomed with who nailed Marv's sister; about how Marv didn't believe me when I said I knew nothing about it; about how Tyson punched my roommate in the eye and told me to fuck off; about how Tyson's fiancée screamed at him to clean his act up; about the messages I started to leave a month later that were never returned; about how almost a year later Kylie's indifference gives me a headache.

I get my money and head back to the martini place, excited that now I have a captive audience, that now I have company.

I step inside. Tanya is sitting at our booth, right where I left her. She nods as I sit down. "The waitress was concerned you'd stiffed me, and I must admit for a second I was too."

"What did you tell her?"

"I told her you were paying me to have dinner with you."

I laugh.

"Do you have the money?" she says.

I hand her the bills and she stuffs them in her pocket. "Okay Danny," she says, her eyes sparking. "Where were we?"

An hour later, fully drunk, I ask Tanya about the pizza. "I mean, is it always the same thing?"

She shakes her head. "What do you, watch our fucking dinner delivered?"

"We all used to," I say.

There's a moment of silence and suddenly I feel like Tanya might get up and leave. "Spend the night with me," I say.

She raises her eyebrows. "Are we finally getting down to it?"

"I want you to see my place. I want to show you some pictures."

She finishes her drink. "Danny, I'll come to your place but you have to pay me."

I slap the table with both hands. "No problem. How much?"

"Well, what's the maximum you're aloud to withdraw in one day?"

She says she has to make a phone call first and I step outside to wait for her. I can't stop laughing. For the first time in weeks I don't feel like I'm in a haze. If Kylie walked by right now I'd tell her to go straight to hell. What do I need with her emotional unavailability? I've met someone who listens.

Tanya walks out and links her arm in mine. "Let's do this and hop in a cab," she says. "I'm freezing in this getup."

I turn and kiss her on the lips. She kisses back and grabs my hair in her fist. Her mouth is ashy and wet, her tongue a bit like sandpaper. When she pulls away she grins and puts her hand on my cheek. "Come on, let's go back to your place, I'm freezing." I insert my card and punch in my PIN. I hear

54

Tanya hopping up and down behind me. As the machine dispenses my money I hear another sound, footsteps, and I turn. Standing next to Tanya is a big guy in a Donovan McNabb jersey. "I think you have my money, nutbag," he says. I look at Tanya and she frowns impatiently. "Come on, cocksucker," she says. My first thought is to protect her from the guy. But as I take a step toward the guy, I feel Tanya jab me in the chest with a fake-tipped finger. I look at her and something drops within me. Then the guy hits me square in the jaw and I crash against the ATM and collapse to the ground. He leans over and yanks my fifteen hundred from the ATM without so much as looking down at me. Then he walks off into the night.

I look up and see Tanya, her expression all resentment. She says, "You couldn't just pay for some simple shit, like a regular fucking asshole." Then she spins and follows the guy down the street in the direction of 42B. She doesn't turn when I call her name, when I call it again louder or when a woman coming out of the convenience store stoops to ask if I need help.

Michael Aronovitz
The Big Picture

The other day, my son asked me if there was really a Santa Claus. "I'm serious, Dad."

He'd just turned seven and our conversations were getting quite adult-like. Though the subject matter was often limited to fantasy weaponry or video game strategies, he was starting to analyze things with an eerie sort of depth. The other day he explained to me, kind of up on his toes like a ballerina, "Dad? Did you know? There's a difference between Flame Thrower and Fire Wheel? Flame Thrower makes a ring and continues until you miss, but the Fire Wheel goes, 'shoooo!' through your body, around and around and around and then back to the first player like a boom-rang!"

Max also had a sense of humor. He liked to sit in his car seat, spot old ladies walking down the street, lower the window and shout, "Who cut the cheese?" He would give himself a wedgie, turn his back to you, stick out his butt and say, "Shake your booty!"

My Max. He had an angel's smile, a killer wit, and brown eyes that still held a lot of that virgin trust when it came to his father's word.

I'd already screwed up the tooth fairy. When his first one came out, I was so psyched I left ten bucks under his pillow. His friend Danny's dad heard and was mildly annoyed. He said I'd driven up the price for the whole neighborhood. Max, of course, overheard the conversation and couldn't get it out of his head how funny I must have looked prancing about his room wearing a pink tutu and waving a magic wand. Now his eyes said, "I still trust you Dad, but don't mess with Santa. Come clean. The tooth fairy is for girls anyway, but Santa is big time. Does he exist or doesn't he?"

I dropped open my mouth in one of those obvious gestures of delay and was thankfully interrupted by a creak on the stairs. Both Max and I looked up from our positions in front of the television on the living room floor.

"Ta-dah!" Kim said. It was early for her, considering it was Sunday. She was posing, beaming. Her hair was up in a temporary bun stuck through by a black comb with a long, pointy handle. Max tensed a bit beside me.

"Mom! I'm asking Dad a *question*."

"Good morning to you too." She winked at me. "Boy's club?"

"You've got it."

"Well, when you're done, bring up the paper. And while you're at it, haul along the boy. I want to pinch his cheeks."

"Ma!"

"Ok, I'm going." She gave me one last look glittering with mischief, and it reminded me of the candlelight that had danced across her eyes on our first date, the tears that made them sparkle as we exchanged wedding vows, the sweet and desperate pain they revealed during Max's birth. Her eyes were unafraid to directly reflect what was written on her soul, so unlike those of my mother, whose gaze had slowly hardened as she became the ghost at the top of the stairs, robe collar curled in her fist up by her throat. Dad was the statue at the desk, fiddling papers into the night, the dark prisoner at the edge of the lamplight. They had both tiptoed through life in a way that made the day-to-day grind seem like it was all there was to the big picture, and I suppose that's why I opted for cartoons on Sunday mornings with Max. The inner child only dies if you let it.

"Oh, before I forget," Kim said. "Ben called. He wanted to know how it went with the ninth graders on Friday."

She turned up the stairs and my face colored, not because there had been anything wrong with the way I had handled the problem with the ninth graders, but because it was then that I knew I was going to tell Max the truth about Santa. Could I erase the very heart of the inner child and still preserve its spirit? I was about to find out.

Though I had always been a dreamer of sorts, I was a practicing realist. I never did that baby-talk stuff with Max, and never took parenting advice from psychology books boasting the latest theories by the newest Ph.D.s. I was on a mission, building my own big picture one high school student at a time and trying my best to keep all of these kids from fading to the edge of the lamplight, outsiders looking in at their own hands as they blindly worked the machinery. I wanted to make things right and show them that there was a chance to discover beauty in the world through school, through literature, through creative writing,. And if that meant doling out a hard lesson or two in the process, so be it.

Last Friday I was the new face in school, on my first lunch duty, and these particular freshmen played around as I stood a foot from their table. They pretended to listen when I casually explained acceptable dining room behavior, but then went back to tossing rolled up sheets of tin foil, flicking rice and corn off plastic forks, snapping bottle caps, spilling plates on each other, and turning away when I put an eye on them. Pull one out of the crowd and you got complaints of others doing it first, hardheaded denials, a blame ring with no end. If you tried to pin anything on a specific individual, the whole room seemed to erode before your eyes.

I used my own psychology. I held the entire ninth grade after lunch and stuck a sword right where they thought a stranger couldn't reach—their scholastics. I handed out pencils and paper while every twenty seconds or so the maintenance guys pushed those long brown tables to upright positions. BOOM! All around us like bombs, my voice ringing out in between the crashing sounds.

"You see, you don't know me. I'm standing right in front of your table and you pretend I'm invisible. The problem is that no matter who I am you should behave simply for the sake of decency. But as I said, you don't know me, and I'm not just another face. I am the new English department head and you answer to me until you graduate."

I began to pace back and forth.

"I have a terrible feeling about this crew . . . a premonition. See, I believe that what I've witnessed in this lunchroom might be bleeding into your class work. So, show me right now that I'm wrong. I want a paragraph. Subject: 'what is expected of me in the lunchroom?' I want it properly titled, with brainstorming in the margin and an indented first sentence that restates the question and offers a global remark. I want that backed up by three sentences containing reasons and evidence, and a conclusion that mirrors the intro. Watch your focus, keep the content fresh, organize it intelligently, let in personal, intellectual style, and watch the freakin' grammar. You have three minutes. GO!"

It was slow at first, but within half a minute, they were working furiously. I hadn't given them enough time to finish, and I was glad.

"Time!"

Not one kid threw down his pencil in anger. They all set them down slowly and looked at each other with haunted, defeated glances.

"Good," I said. "Now that I have your attention, I will talk about what is going to go on in this cafeteria from now on."

The students gave me new nickname for that episode: The Terminator. One of the security guards promised me an Air Force One jacket because I flashed him straight back to his old drill sergeant.

But I didn't feel good about it. I felt drained and used and it wasn't over. For a higher good, I had committed a smaller sin by making writing the punishment, and the kids deserved better. If I didn't follow up on the work in hand, the exercise became nothing more than a beating, soon forgotten. I'm not a beater, I'm a builder. And I wasn't about to have my lessons dismissed like the passing conversations of strangers on the subway. That is why I took over the ninth grade for the entire next day.

It began as a display of power to show that I could manipulate their daily routine, but turned into something else. I had the students working hard until the last minute of every period. But by the end of each class, kids were asking my advice, shyly requesting that I look at their poetry. It was a relief and sadly beautiful, but disappointing, because I had achieved it through force.

That thought, that feeling followed me and lingered as I considered my son's question. And right before I answered him, a last image formed in my thoughts: an art gallery, darkened after hours, lit only by the dim security overheads in the hall. Mounted on a huge easel, the Big Picture loomed in the middle of the shadowed lobby. I wasn't cowering before it as my parents had, nor was I contributing to it. I was sweeping beneath it, my blue sleeves rolled to the elbows, maintenance badge clipped to a pocket, headphones over my ears making me oblivious to the silence, my old eyes tired from trying all those years to interpret the small portions illuminated on the canvas by the glowing, half-moon arcs of the miniature display lamps at the bottom of the frame. I was satisfied now to keep my glance where it seemed to belong— down, following the trails of my broom as its bristles caught some renegade ball of tin foil, flicked piece of corn, or snapped bottle cap.

"Come here," I said. Max nestled back in the crook of my arm, and I spoke toward the wall the way people so often do.

"Max, Santa is more like a feeling than a real person." I looked down to him and his eyebrows were up in questioning arches.

"Then you're the one who brings the presents?"

"Yes," I said. "But listen, this is important, Max. You can't go telling all your friends that there's no Santa. I mean, some kids wait all year for him."

He pursed his lips and nodded. Then he reached up, played with my sideburn and stared at my forehead.

"Dad?"

"Yeah."

"Why do they tell us there's a Santa?"

I sighed.

"Because it gives us something to hang onto, Max. It's called faith. It's nice to believe in something. I guess we make stuff up for the people who need it the most. Kind of like the Eagles, you know? We always believe they can win a Super Bowl even though they never do."

He was looking at me with intense concentration.

"I understand," he said.

I believed him. I just wished I didn't feel so empty inside.

I came home late the other day and there was something sitting on the dining room table. It was a green, clay paperweight shaped like a football— uneven laces, misshapen edges, a hairline crack starting to cut its way through the middle. Letters and numbers colored like candy canes were affixed to the top ridge with Elmer's glue. They spelled simply:

"2006 CHAMPS!"

And the card underneath it read clearly in my seven-year-old son's clumsy printing,

"Merry early Christmas. Love Santa."

Serge Shea

Invisible Predators

R ay had reservations about entering Margot and Teddy's house. Legally it might be considered breaking and entering—this was a fuzzy line since he had used the key hidden under the piece of slate to the right of the back door. Although he knew for a fact that Margot and Teddy were away for most of the summer, an irrational fear of getting caught momentarily seized him. He finally convinced himself to enter the house to borrow a pen, because Margot had left a note that required a response:

> *Ray,*
> > *Please work on the roses and maybe put in another bush.*
> > > > *Thanks,*
> > > > > *Margot*

His hands spotted with soil and his arm hair trapping small bugs, he ventured only to the edge of the living room, where someone had spent an immense amount of time and energy matching all the various beiges and angling the couches just so. Going upstairs would be inappropriate, he thought. The air inside was warmer than outside, thick and stuffy like a cotton undershirt caught over your head. The sweat on his forehead started to run down his face. Looking out the kitchen window, he stared at his work. For most of the day he had tenderly wrapped all the rose bushes in cheese-cloth. They looked strange, like rooted packages waiting to be picked up. Light, water, and air still reached them, but their crimson petals were out of sight and the smell, at least to Ray's nose, was less fragrant. Before coming inside, he had doused the cheesecloth with water, and it was possible to make out a red hue where the petals pressed against the cloth. It must be nice in there, he thought, cool and comfortable. He empathized with his flowers; this is what made him a good gardener. Using a ballpoint pen next to the telephone, he jotted on the other side of the note: *Roses are tough this season.*

Ray had spent the whole summer discouraging customers from planting roses in their gardens. Even the most die-hard rose enthusiasts—Mrs. Mulroon and her neighbor Nancy Meyer—had curtailed their desires for the luscious tongue-like petals and settled, for the time being, for something else: daylilies, peonies, dhalias. Margot and Teddy were the only ones who still insisted on roses, despite Ray's friendly suggestions and urgings. It was out of character for Margot, Ray suspected it was Teddy who wanted them. Upon seeing the note, Ray bought another bush, which now gave the garden a total of nine. But roses were the most vulnerable flower. He managed to keep them free of fungus, mold, and infesting insects—spider mites, aphids, thrips, Japanese beetles, and slugs. But like everything else—insects, fungi, people—deer craved roses over all other flowers. Though he had done his best, the normally scarlet-saturated petals were drained, and missing flowers and absent branches revealed green-brown stalks studded with sharp thorns.

The late afternoon light began to turn and Ray got ready to leave. He checked the front lawn and noticed the hedge clippers laying in the grass. He quickly grabbed them and hung them on a nail in the back of the garage. The hedge clippers were technically his, as were the spade, digging shovel, and rusty metal rake. But, somehow, Margot had managed to hold onto them. At the beginning of the summer, when he first started working at Margot and Teddy's, he recognized his tools and was relieved, as if he had found them after years of searching. Lately, though, he hardly noticed them and only sometimes remembered they were once his. Squeezing by Margot's blue Civic on his way out, he wondered if they had two cars at the shore house. Before he could stop, his mind jumped ahead; he imagined the layout of their house and wondered if there was a garden. This was a mistake, the reason he should not have worked at his ex-wife's house. Harder than trying to protect and grow Margot's roses was touching the hems of her new life with Teddy: their home, their cars, their lawn.

For two weeks, Ray tricked the deer into believing a pack of wolves lived in the neighborhood by sprinkling specially ordered wolf urine around the perimeters of his gardens. This and the cheesecloth were the newest in a long line of defenses he employed over the summer, all of which eventually yielded to the deer. Deer are creatures of habit, returning to the same places unless aggressively threatened. After years of residing in the suburbs, they learned that humans were no threat and freely ate from their gardens, roaming from one to the next as if at an all-you-can-eat buffet. For three years, deer had been a growing problem, a problem that saved Ray and his landscaping business, which had tripled since his divorce. Ray didn't hate the deer the way everyone else did. The problem isn't the deer exactly, he would say, the deer have always been here; it's their increasing numbers. Like a tide slowly coming in, they sauntered out of the forest to boldly feast on gardens, making it impossible to keep the red blooms alive. There was no escaping them or their want. They were pests, but Ray felt a certain fondness for them, and not just because they gave him more business. He found their desire admirable. In the same way a chef is delighted to see people devour what he has so painstakingly prepared, the voracity with which they destroyed his gardens was flattering. He wondered how long it would take them to realize there were no wolves.

When he was married, Ray aspired to live in the houses his customers lived in. He would secretly take inventory, estimating the square footage and wondering how many steps it took to get to the second floor. In his head, he replaced his customers. Staring at someone's patio, he would envision himself eating a late Sunday afternoon lunch there with Margot. At these times, he felt more like a prospective buyer searching for his dream home than a gardener. Now he hardly noticed the houses. What he did notice were the people he worked for. Ray looked forward to seeing them. He didn't know them well, but through the years he had come to know their habits. Mrs. Davidson hung her laundry out back because, even though she had a dryer, the fresh air smelled better. Plastic dump trucks and pedal cars littered the Carlton's yard, and underneath some ferns he discovered a whole battle scene set up with small plastic army men. He had once sat with the Hallo-wells and drank a beer while they had dinner. The more he got to know his customers the more he felt like a stranger, as though he didn't belong and gardening was just an excuse to be there. He was sure people felt the same way about him. He even thought he had caught drivers slowing down to stare at him, memorizing his face so they could accurately describe the color of his eyes and his build to a sketch artist.

Ray wasn't alone in his battle against the deer. In the beginning of spring, as he paged to the five-day forecast, he came upon an article about a hunter. It opened with a description of how angry people were with the rising deer population and went on to describe how this hatred had banded community boards together to demand action. By the last month of spring, a bow hunter was hired to spend four weeks in the woods and thin the population. And now, months after the hunting was over, their anger had turned and was directed at how dangerous it was to have had a hunter. The hunter had gained mythical status on par with Big Foot. People's accounts varied and some were exaggerated; eyewitnesses pinned him for vandalism, anonymous bystanders held him responsible for burglaries, and some speculated about his involvement in a rash of stolen cars. Local government and law officials claimed the hunter was no longer around and attributed the sightings to paranoia. Mrs. Robertson, an old lady Ray worked for, said she thought the hunter was eating her cat's food. The beige square vittles she put out at night were gone by morning, yet her cat meowed with hunger. She also blamed him for the unexplainable noises coming from the first floor in the middle of the night.

"If he's hungry, I would be happy to fix him something. Cat food! No one has any business eating that except cats."

Ray nodded at whatever she said and told her to make sure her doors were locked. Her cat did look emaciated.

The one side effect of the wolf urine was that dogs had also been duped. Smell warned them that a pack of wolves was suddenly roaming the neighborhood. Last time Ray was at the Lambertons', their German shepard, Maxie, came out snarling, baring her teeth through quivering lips. When he arrived this time, early enough to see Mr. and Mrs. Lamberton leave for work, he could hear Maxie barking in the house. As the Lambertons were Ray's wealthiest customers, he usually devoted an entire day to working on their enormous house and garden. By the afternoon he had pruned the azalea bushes—Mrs. Lamberton constantly complained they were too unruly—weeded the garden, and started putting in a half-dozen delphiniums. When he heard music suddenly coming from inside their house, Ray remembered that the Lambertons' son Charlie was home from college for the summer. An hour later, while putting in the last delphinium, the choppy guitar cords and call and response lyrics of a reggae song came flooding out as Charlie Lamberton walked out of the front door followed by Maxie, who started to sniff Ray and the garden.

"Hey Ray mon," Charlie said in a mock Jamaican accent. He had something pinched between his fingers, as if he had just caught a small bug. Then Ray smelled the sweet scent of the smoke.

"You want some, mon?" Charlie asked holding his breath.

Ray knew better, but he had no boss to answer to, and knowing the Lambertons, they would probably be more upset that Ray hadn't indulged their only child.

"Very nice, Charlie," was all Ray said. He felt his head immediately start to float.

"Legalize it mon," Charlie said, not giving up on his accent. Charlie moved to the lawn and just sat there bobbing his head to the music with Maxie lying next to him. Ray found it comical, a nice little treat.

The warm, afternoon sun had grown weak and, at some point, Charlie had disappeared into the house. Ray, still a bit foggy, couldn't remember if he had watered the garden or not. He bent down to feel if the dirt was damp and decided that he hadn't. He struggled to untangle the hose. Letting the water arc into the air, he soaked the plants and flowers. When he heard a twig snap behind him, he thought Charlie had come back.

"You come to check out my flowers, mon?" Ray asked.

He turned around and found two deer in the yard nosing at the grass as if occupying their time until he left. Without hesitation Ray dropped the hose and ran after them. He pursued them through two backyards and into the woods. A tangle of branches and bushes slowed him, and he finally gave up. As he caught his breath, he watched the deer dissolve into the forest, only the white underside of their tails visible as they bounced over fallen trees and small shrubs. He hadn't been in the woods for awhile and was surprised how thick and lush everything was. The deer must have a good life in here, he thought. Then he heard a second crashing noise like more deer following the first group. He moved farther into the woods to see them. He caught a glimpse of a man in camouflage pants and a dark green T-shirt swiftly making his way in the same direction as the deer.

Back at the Lambertons', the water from the hose had pooled into a small puddle. Ray finished his work by spreading the wolf urine, and he could hear Maxie starting to bark.

It was while searching the paper for the weather that Ray saw Teddy for the first time. Next to their marriage announcement was a small black and white photo of them. He almost didn't recognize Margot. Her hair was longer and the newspaper reproduction made her look younger. Teddy looked like a salesman, his smile glued to his face. Ray had met him a handful of times since. Teddy's friendliness seemed condescending, as though Margot was squeezing it out of him.

For three years, he had worked nonstop and never had much time to think about the divorce. They talked amiably every four months or so, which is one of the things that made the divorce even harder. Ray was surprised when Margot called and asked him to be their gardener.

"Please Ray, we tried someone else and he wasn't any good," Margot said. "Teddy is fine with it, and we won't even be around for most of the summer."

This was one of her selling points: he wouldn't have to see her or Teddy. Ray stalled but couldn't come up with a good enough reason to decline. He thought it sounded easier not to see them, but he wondered now if, somehow, it made it harder.

The roses at Margot's made great progress. Ray pulled the cloth apart just enough to get a peek. More buds had developed and started to bloom. Everything had become a deeper shade of red, and the cloth was stretched tight from the new growth. Some tears in the side looked like attempted bites that had failed. The lilies were having a second bloom and the deer hadn't touched the dhalias. He had done some good work, maybe his best all summer long. He ate a turkey sandwich on the wrought iron chaise lounge in Margot and Teddy's back patio. After the sandwich, he dozed off for a few minutes. He awoke with a dry mouth and an urgent need to urinate. On the edge of the garden, yanking the right leg hole of his shorts up high, he tracked his urine down the length of the garden. Maybe, he thought, it would deter the deer. He was still thirsty.

This time entering their house felt more comfortable. He took his time and looked around. The cabinets above the sink contained neatly lined rows of matching glasses, which made his collection of free plastic refill cups and stolen bar mugs seem pathetic. When he finished his water, he dried his glass and put it back in its row. On the refrigerator were photos of family and friends—parents proudly holding their kids or posed in front of houses—some doubled as Christmas cards and wished Margot and Teddy a Happy New Year. One picture of Margot and Teddy caught Ray off guard. Margot had a big smile. Teddy had more of a smirk; his straight, dark hair thinner than Ray remembered. A calendar on the wall marked the days they were gone. In red marker, *return from vacation* had been written in the coming Saturday's box. Ray took note. Two months of vacation. He felt a little self-pity and was embarrassed. The front hall closet was full of winter coats and rain jackets. Ray didn't recognize anything of Margot's and found it disconcerting, as though he were looking in a stranger's closet. Teddy's jackets were fashion choices that Ray would never make or think of making. He took one of Teddy's trench coats down and tried it on. Except for the sleeves, which ended before his wrists, it fit. He looked at himself in a full-length mirror and verified how ridiculous he felt. When he took it off, he could smell Teddy's scent: stale sweat and faint aftershave. He wanted to go upstairs. Suddenly, cutting through the silence, the phone rang. Ray jumped. Even the second ring scared him. On the third ring, the machine picked up and Margot's voice announced they were away. It sent a shiver down his spine; he missed Margot. He felt that somehow he had lost her the same way a child's favorite toy suddenly goes missing, never to be found.

In a housing complex off route 101, where Ray had four customers, he saw a golden retriever, a small terrier, a westie, a lab, and a cocker spaniel roaming in a pack from yard to yard. They moved at a trot with a certain determination. They stopped at gardens that Ray had just worked on and spread out with their noses to the ground, searching for the beginning and end of the wolf markings. An invisible predator. It must drive them crazy, Ray thought.

His favorite customers, the Daniels, lived in the same complex. They talked to Ray more like a friend than a gardener. He always worked on their garden last in hope of running into them. Janice was beautiful with an athletic build; she was training for a marathon. Lewis was strange and soft with short dark hair that was graying. Janice and Lewis's cars were in the driveway when Ray arrived, but neither of them came out. As he clipped the rhododendrons, his fingers sore from gripping the plastic handle, he heard raised voices muffled by the white vinyl siding. Janice and Lewis had fought a lot this summer. For some reason, Ray found it comforting to hear them fight; it made him feel as if they trusted him. Instead of trying to mind his own business or leave, Ray lingered. He had come up with things to keep busy with in order to stay longer. Last week, he stacked the hose into perfect neat coils, which he had never done before. Then he swept their front walkway and took his time cleaning up and watering. He never mentioned anything to them. Not that he should, he was their gardener. But he liked to think of them as friends. After about ten minutes they stopped—or at least Ray could no longer hear anything. He found their silence worrisome.

Headless peonies dotted the Daniels' garden, the flowers cleanly sheered off, only bare stalks remaining. The deer were efficient. A bright yellow color caught his eye. What he at first thought was a wild flower that had naturally come up out of the soil was, on closer inspection, the feathered end of an arrow. Ray unsheathed it from the soil. He had weeded the Daniels' garden many times during and since the hunter had been in the woods. He couldn't imagine not seeing the arrow before. Lewis and Janice came out and said hi to Ray. Lewis handed him a glass of cold water and gave a sigh when he saw the arrow. Janice gave a little look at it and then looked at Lewis.

"I've seen him on my runs in the woods," Janice said.

Lewis was silent, and it took Ray a second to figure out who she was talking about.

"I've even talked to him once," she said with a smile.

"You never told me about that," Lewis said.

"I just said hi. He's harmless. There's something sad about him," Janice said.

"Well, what about this?" Lewis asked, taking the arrow from Ray.

Ray didn't want to fuel the argument. He didn't tell them what he'd seen in the woods behind the Lambertons'. They had enough to deal with.

That Saturday was the day Margot and Teddy returned. Ray got up earlier than usual so he would, hopefully, miss them. The roses bulged underneath the strained cheesecloth. With the small blade of his pocketknife, he cut them free. The branches sprang and shook. The deep red petals and full flowers pulsed like beacons. They surprised Ray. He lost himself in the thick fragrance with his eyes closed. He forgot who and where he was. No longer a gardener at his ex-wife's house, he was just happy to be faced with so many flowers. After a summer of telling everyone they couldn't have them, that it was impossible to grow them, he thought the sight of the full red bushes might throw his customers into a rage. When he finished, he wished Margot could have seen the unveiling. Then, like a pebble in his shoe, it occurred to him again that it was probably never Margot who wanted the roses.

He entered their house. Dirt from his boots spotted the carpet, a twig from his hair fell to the floor, and drops of sweat left a small trail as he walked through the first floor. He had lost all caution. He studied everything. He scanned the titles on the bookshelves, went through the CD collection, opened every cabinet door and drawer in the kitchen. Unsatisfied, he climbed the stairs to the second floor. At the top of the stairs his elbow, dark with soil, accidentally brushed the wall and left a smudge mark. He knew he shouldn't be there. He knew it was just plain strange and stupid, but he was looking for something. Their room was surprisingly sparse. Framed wedding pictures and vacation photos decorated the walls and the bedside table. Opening Margot's underwear drawer, he was faced with a tangle of lacy blacks, whites, and reds, none of which were familiar. He smelled the bar of soap in the bathroom. He even sprayed some of her perfume. He was trying to find out what she was like, trying to conjure her from all her objects. None of it seemed like Margot. He didn't recognize anything. He wasn't sure if she had replaced all her old things with new ones or if he had simply forgotten who she was and what she was like. He found something: her brush. A big black brush with a smooth wooden handle and stiff bristles that had entrapped long dark hairs that trailed off like decorative streamers. He studied it and thought maybe one of the hairs was from years ago when they were married. All at once he was struck hard with sadness and jealousy. Then, as quickly as he ran in, he ran out, almost forgetting to lock the door and hide the key. He left, thankful to soon be lost in the long day of work ahead of him.

The deer were slowly coming back. The possibility of wolves no longer threatened them. For the rest of the day, like every Saturday, he visited his customers, fertilizing and watering their gardens, and collecting checks. There were flowers with small bites in almost every garden, as if the deer were testing their boundaries. The Kelleys' narcissuses were beautiful, but some flowers from the front were missing. The Stanleys' wisteria was in need of water and a suspicious bald patch had developed on the side. The

Mckennas thanked Ray for the gorgeous zinnias he had gotten to bloom; they didn't notice the trample spots on the edge near the hostas. With little faith, he spread the wolf urine. He had used up all his defenses and couldn't think of other ways to keep the deer away. The tips of the Lambertons' hibiscus were nibbled. Charlie Lamberton was throwing a Frisbee to Maxie, who sniffed Ray as he got out of the car. Charlie gave Ray a grin and nodded. As the sun was starting to set, he finished his day by planting a row of chrysanthemums at Mrs. Robertson's to replace the row that had been destroyed in the last week.

"Oh thank you, Mr. Ray. It looks great," Mrs. Robertson said. "You know Mr. Ray, I make him sandwiches and the way he eats them, he's got quite an appetite. I don't think he comes into my house anymore."

Ray was only half listening. He finished putting in the last chrysanthemum.

"Who's this?" He asked.

"You know, the hunter," Mrs. Robertson said.

Ray nodded.

"Well, ask him to do something about the deer, would you?"

"I haven't seen him, but I could leave a note."

As Ray left, he hoped fall would come early and the weather would force the deer to stay in the woods. And the hunter, he thought. Ray wondered what the hunter would do all alone in the woods when it got cold, or what he was doing now. Ray understood what Janice meant when she said the hunter was sad. He sympathized.

Ray had intended to drive directly home, but he wanted to see the roses. He slowly rolled by their house. Teddy's car was in the driveway and a couple windows glowed yellow from the lights inside. He couldn't see past the front yard shrubs, so he pulled over. Night was settling and the sky was the blue before black. As he got out of his car, short harsh *ark, ark, arks* from the dog next door startled him. He hid behind the hedges and peered into the yard. He couldn't believe what he saw. Eight deer surrounded the rose bushes. With large mouthfuls, unconcerned by the thorned branches, they took off entire flowers. Three more deer appeared from the woods that bordered the backyard. Ray didn't know what to do. Another nearby dog started up with high-pitched yaps. Teddy came out of the door with a broom in one hand.

"Get out, get the hell out of here," he yelled to the unresponsive deer.

He walked down the steps with the broom cocked as if it were a baseball bat. With a swing that hit a buck square in the hind flank, the deer only responded by slowly moving to another bush. The deer had waited all summer long for the roses; nothing could deter them.Their desire and instinct were too strong . They couldn't help themselves. A third dog from across the street added to the chorus, letting loose thick, deep barks. More deer appeared from the forest to gorge on the bushes. A couple rested on the ground full from eating. Teddy went over to them with his raised broom and they lazily rose and left the yard. A fourth and fifth dog started barking.

"Don't just stand there, do something. They're destroying my yard!" Teddy yelled.

Ray thought he had been caught, but realized Teddy wasn't talking to him.

"Help me," Teddy yelled again into the woods beyond the backyard. Ray strained his eyes in the failing light, and what he thought at first was a short gnarled tree or an odd bush was actually a man standing just inside the cover of the woods. Every dog in the neighborhood was barking; in concert, they reached a crescendo before stopping. Ray couldn't help but smile. There was satisfaction in watching his work appreciated and destroyed by forces outside his control. Frustrated, Teddy swung his broom in huge exaggerated arcs, but hit nothing. Slowly, one by one, the deer left. Ray noticed Margot silhouetted in a window, watching her husband. He wondered if she found the whole scene comical. The roses were gone and only bare branches and trampled flowers were left. The hunter disappeared into the woods. As Ray started to leave, it occurred to him that he would never be in their house again. He didn't want to grow roses for them again. He decided he was no longer their gardener. He was finished fighting for the season.

Christopher Stanton
Terminal Pursuit

The last thing I said to Corinne in the Delta terminal was, "Have a nice trip, you dizzy bitch," and I felt bad about it. I liked that I came up with "dizzy" off the top of my head because it fit the way she mangled facts and jumped to conclusions. In hindsight, though, "bitch" was too easy an insult. I would have preferred hurling a "shrew" or a "harpy" at her. But that's not why I got on the plane.

I'd never followed anyone before. I mean, sure, I'd *followed* people: I'd followed friends to parties and ballgames, and I'd even followed in my father's footsteps at General Electric. But I'd never tailed anyone. I'd never shadowed somebody.

I followed Corinne on the heels of our falling out. I'd actually stopped liking her three weeks earlier, which was unfortunate because we'd only dated for four. I chalk that up to my problem with confrontation, or rather, my former problem. Someone who jumps on a plane to prove a point can no longer be said to shy away from confrontation.

Corinne and I were going away for Labor Day weekend, but not going together. I was heading to Atlanta to see my college roommate, Ned, and his wife, Paula, and Corinne was off to Cincinnati to see someone or other. (She had fed me her itinerary no less than four times, and somewhere around the third helping, not only did I stop taking it in, but I willed myself to purge every detail I had ingested.) In one of those serendipitous events that can only occur when you're no longer interested in someone, our flights, which we'd booked before we met, were ten minutes apart on the same airline. A breakfast date was a no-brainer, and it saddened me that I wasn't looking forward to it. It seemed like such a waste of fate.

Since there is no Philadelphia International Airport House of Pancakes, we found a clean-enough spot close to our terminal. I ordered a couple ham, egg, and cheese sandwiches while Corinne instructed me to make sure the cashier didn't overcharge—because, according to the sign, cheese should be included—then left to find a table. The guy working the grill was too efficient for my liking, so I tried to distract him with a question about where the local hot spots were. He threw me by asking where I was from. "Oh, I'm from here," I said. "I just don't know where any of the hot spots are." He laughed and handed me the sandwiches. Three minutes, from order to plastic orange tray.

At the table, Corinne sat with her hands folded, guarding our coffee. She asked me what took so long. "The guy liked to talk," I told her. Then she asked if I counted my change. I pretended that the chair's squeak drowned out hers and ignored the question.

"Isn't this nice?" she asked. "We're having breakfast together in the airport." Corinne loved commentary. She'd interrupt a conversation to tell you what a good conversation it was, as if she were required to report back to someone on its progress.

"We sure are."

"Did I tell you what happened at work on Wednesday?"

"You killed a man?"

"No. But I could have. My boss gives me no direction, no support. I'm new to the department, but he's never taken the time to really show me how things work. I have to keep asking the people around me for help . . . "

Here's the punch line: She caused a $53,000 error because her boss neglected to tell her to cross-check column seven of the monthly transition report with the last page of the weekly status spreadsheet. I didn't know what it meant, but to be fair, the fault wasn't entirely hers. It was, however, the second time that week that she had been an integral player in a blunder that cost GE tens of thousands of dollars.

I managed to interject the requisite "oh" or "really" at all the right spots as I replayed a scene from three nights before in my head. We'd gone to see the latest Bruce Willis movie and she had complained—twice—about how unusual and distracting it was to see him in a dramatic role. It was exactly the kind of comment you'd let slide if it came from someone you cared for, but pounce on with both feet when said by someone whose every nasally criticism was eating at your patience like acid. You would have no choice but to rattle off a list of every one of Bruno's dramatic roles you could think of, from *12 Monkeys* to *The Sixth Sense*, just to claim some small, meaningless victory. You would do so politely, but in such a manner as to leave no doubt in her mind that Bruce Willis was indeed a goddamn fine dramatic actor and that she had better find more valid things to complain about next time. At least, you would do that the second time she said it. At least I did.

When she was through with the saga of the botched spreadsheet comparison, she stopped talking and picked up her sandwich. With Corinne's stories, there was never any winding down, like: "So, anyway, I'm not sure what I'm gonna do about that." They were always self-contained, and when they were over, you'd better be ready to jump in with one of your own, pronto. More than two seconds of dead air and you'd hear, "You're awfully quiet" or "Are you in a bad mood?" That was one good thing about her repeating stories in exactly the same way—I'd actually be able to see the end coming and prepare for it. I'd heard the one about her breakup with her last boyfriend three times, for instance, and was well aware of my cue: "He didn't even offer me any breadsticks. He thought his hunger was more important than mine just because he was a guy." Bam. End of story. You have a second or two to pick the next category or you forfeit your turn.

Luckily, the coffee had jump-started my synapses and enabled me to prevent any pause that would trigger her taking my emotional temperature. The day before, I had gotten a promotion because the results of a lengthy and difficult project I had overseen had exceeded everyone's expectations, including my own. My boss said some very flattering things, and I was feeling pretty good about myself. Even though I planned to end it with Corinne the following week, it seemed extreme, like a hostile deception, not to share this piece of good news with her. Or maybe I was proud and wanted to brag a little.

"You want to know my opinion?" she jumped right in.

"Sure." (No, no, I don't.)

"I don't think you should take it." Arms folded, lips pursed, head shaking.

"What? Why?"

"To me it's all about the bottom line. They should be making you a manager, not giving you this other position. You're going to have all this new responsibility and basically be doing your boss's job, and they're not compensating you for it. You're letting them take advantage of you."

I should clarify a few points: 1) There are strict qualifications for becoming a manager in my department, and I had not yet met those qualifications. The promotion I got was quite fair; 2) I would not be doing my boss's job and never said I would be; 3) I was seriously considering finding out what Corinne would look like wearing a ham, egg, and cheese hat. I told her points 1 and 2 in a tone that implied point 3.

"Well, I didn't know that, Bill," she said. "I can only give you my opinion based on what you tell me. You should have told me that."

"I *did* tell you what the promotion entailed, you just didn't listen."

"Don't yell at me."

"I'm not yelling at you." I wasn't. I swear.

"You're getting upset. I asked if you wanted my opinion. You shouldn't have said yes if you didn't want to hear it."

I was essentially whispering at this point, partly because we were in public and partly because I didn't want to give her the satisfaction of making me lose my temper. "That's right, Corinne, I did ask to hear it. And you have every right to your opinion, just like I have every right to disagree with you. And that's what I'm doing—disagreeing with you. I'm not yelling at you. This isn't a *fight*. This is a difference of opinion. All right?"

Practically cowering, her voice small, she said, "You're frightening me."

Because her histrionics suggested a strong possibility that a deranged skycap lurked behind me with a machete, I scrutinized her face for a long moment to make sure she was in fact talking to me. Finally, I said, "What are you *talking* about?" I don't know whether it was because of what I heard in my own voice or what I saw in Corinne's eyes, but I immediately realized how ridiculous this—all of it—had become. With the resigned chuckle of the exasperated, I said, "Look, let's just forget about it." I waved off the conversation and lifted my coffee with one fluid motion. "You ready to go?"

We went back to the terminal in silence. I'd been lectured and insulted—and inappropriately *feared*, for crying out loud—and my adrenaline was still rushing. I walked her to her gate, which was four past my own. I had no choice.

Corinne and I had met in a GE diversity-awareness seminar and ended up going out for drinks afterward. She was impressed when I opened the car door for her and when I reached for the check after drinks turned into dinner.

She told me a lot about herself that night. She told me how her mother had no interests outside the walls of their row home in the Northeast, and that her father liked it that way. She told me everyone in her family criticized her for going to college, advising her not to waste the time or money since she'd only wind up getting married and staying at home anyway. She told me about an ex-boyfriend who declared that women "can barely drive and can't parallel park for shit." She told me that, in her family, you could cure cancer and solve world hunger, but if you couldn't pee standing up, you'd better put on an apron and serve somebody who could. She told me she was beginning to think all guys were complete assholes. And then she told me she thought I was a gentleman. So, I knew what I was getting myself into—she *told* me.

Even so, the sting of our final exchange at the gate caught me off guard. "You're just like the rest of them," she said. "I didn't think you were, but you are."

"What do you mean?"

"You can't handle a strong woman. You're threatened because I have my own opinions, and I'm not afraid to express myself."

I was floored. That's what she thought had just gone on here? That's when I shot off that salvo that caused me mixed feelings: "Have a nice trip, you dizzy bitch."

I bolted back to my gate and, trembling, stared at CNN Airport News, unable to focus long enough to make sense of the closed captioning. A middle-aged reporter with obvious career problems was surrounded by a herd of normal-looking cows and one that looked like it had been shaved, if that's even possible. I had no idea if the story was about a prank, an experiment, or an incident of paranormal activity, nor was I sure which description best fit the episode I'd just gone through.

Even though this unexpected turn allowed me to cross "Break up with Corinne" off next week's To Do list, it upset me. I was mad for a lot of reasons, but the reason that trounced all others was that I realized that when Corinne landed in Cincinnati, she'd report to her friend—whom I'd never met and whose opinion should have been meaningless to me—that she had just ended it with "another one." I would join the ranks of Breadstick Guy and Parallel Parking Guy and Lord knows what other guys. And I just couldn't have that. I was not—and my stomach knotted when I thought I would be referred to as—Airport Guy.

Who even knew what the real stories were with those guys anyway? Maybe Breadstick Guy *did* offer her a breadstick, but she was so engrossed in trashing his predecessor that she didn't hear him. Or maybe she was already working on a poppy seed roll and never in a million years would he have guessed she'd even consider chasing it with a fucking breadstick. And maybe Parallel Parking Guy had a legitimate beef with some drunk woman who totaled his car. I had no idea. All I knew for sure was that in her version of *our* little spat, I would be the goat, and her all-men-are-assholes world-view would be further validated. Not on my watch, sister.

I changed my ticket at the counter and headed back down the terminal.

When I got to her—our—gate, I hid. My entire plan consisted of avoiding detection until we got to Cincinnati. I figured I'd work out the rest of it on the plane. I ducked into the men's room, fished a different shirt out of my carry-on bag, threw it on, and topped myself off with a plain black baseball cap and sunglasses. It wasn't much of a disguise, but since she wouldn't exactly be looking for me, it would probably be enough if she happened to glance my way.

Back in the terminal, people had started to board. Corinne was in line, studying her ticket, and I took my place about a dozen people behind her. When I reached the cabin, she and her bag were engaged in an epic battle against the overhead compartment and I sidled past in full-on stealth mode. My seat was three rows behind hers, next to the bathroom. I prayed she hadn't finished that coffee.

I spent most of the flight rehashing this relationship from when it took off to its crash landing. It hit me that one of the reasons I'd kept seeing her well beyond the relationship's expiration date was the criticism my married friends had leveled at me. They felt I was too judgmental with new women, too quick to find that fatal flaw. I felt their assessment was too harsh. Yes, I was picky, but that's a trait more people should cultivate. It was true, though, that I hadn't had a decent relationship in four years, so I wanted to stick this one out as long as I could—if it failed, no one could say it was for lack of trying.

Staring at the back of Corinne's head, I thought about our first date, a week after the seminar. A few days before we went out, I told her what I had in mind—a Branford Marsalis concert at the Mann Music Center and a late dinner at a hot new BYOB downtown. Her response was deflating: it all sounded very nice, but we didn't have to plan every minute; we could "sort of play it by ear."

Throughout the next couple of days, each additional suggestion I offered met with the same curious response. That tactic went against every dating impulse I had and contradicted the only principle about women I knew with absolute certainty to be true. But if she didn't want me to put any thought into our date, if she actually preferred that I had nothing planned, what could I do? Well, what I *did* do was spend nearly an hour on the phone with her that Saturday morning trying to dredge up date-worthy activities.

That evening, I picked her up at her parents' house, where she still lived at the age of thirty-one, for reasons she never explained beyond a murky allusion to a broken engagement some time before. Her mother answered the door, maintained steady eye contact with my shoes, and pointed me inside, where her father sat watching TV, one hand glued to the remote, the other nestled in the sweaty gulch between his ample man-boobs and distended gut. He hacked something resembling hello and waved the remote, and I plopped down in a chair next to the couch and pretended to watch stock car racing until Corinne came downstairs.

We headed into the city to execute phase one of the agenda we'd finally scraped together: seeing an IMAX film about ancient Egypt at the Franklin Institute. On the way, she pointed out her favorite store.

"We have a few minutes to kill. We could just pop in here and look at dresses for a little while." Her tone made it clear that she was joking, and I was happy to play along.

"Or I could just drop you off and circle the block for 20 minutes."

"What are you saying—that if your girlfriend wanted you to help her pick out a dress, you wouldn't do it?" It seemed our little game had been called due to a freak storm.

"No, I'm not saying that at all. But it probably wouldn't make my list of favorite things to do."

"A lot of guys like to pick out clothes for their girlfriends."

"No, actually, they don't." I've never been more sure of anything I've ever said.

"Even for special occasions? So if your girlfriend wanted you to help her pick out a dress for an affair you had to go to, you wouldn't do it? You wouldn't help her?"

I wasn't sure if we were talking about present-day Corinne; future Corinne—who had evolved into my girlfriend for the purposes of this ham-handed attempt at an argument—or some other nameless but equally excitable girlfriend-to-be. But I was pretty sure I knew how to answer the question. Deep breath. Slow, deliberate speech: "If my input were sought and my input were valued, then sure, I would love to help her pick out a dress."

"Oh, OK. Isn't this nice? We're on our first official date." Her brow unfurrowed, her jaw unclenched, and she smiled. And I don't mind telling you, the abrupt transformation was a little unnerving. I'd caught a small glimpse of it the night we met as she discussed the shortcomings of her previous boyfriends. I'd heard it over the phone once when I joked that, despite Pete Sampras's intense strength training, he still wasn't half the man Venus Williams was ("Are you saying women shouldn't lift weights?"). But I have to tell you, seeing the Hulk change back into Bruce Banner before your eyes is something else altogether.

When the pilot welcomed us to Kentucky, I thought I'd accidentally followed the wrong woman onto the wrong plane. I double-checked my flight information and learned that Cincinnati's airport is actually *in* Kentucky. That wrinkle seemed somehow appropriate for this odyssey.

Corinne rose, extracted her bag from the overhead compartment, and stood in the aisle, so I ducked down in my seat. I hate when people make blanket statements that begin, "There are two types of people in the world," then go on to use some half-baked metaphor about dogs and cats or football and baseball or Bert and Ernie. Having said that, there are two types of people in the world: those who leap to get their shit together as soon as the plane lands and stand in the aisle until the flight attendant releases them like the bulls in Pamplona, and those who wait, reading, for the heart-attack cases to leave so they can gather their stuff in peace and disembark.

Corinne is definitely in the former category, and so am I, which probably only added to our fundamental incompatibility. During our first date, after a particularly prickly discussion about gender bias in dry-cleaning costs, she said she could tell we'd be able to have "some really great fights together." At the time I thought it was a flirty, if somewhat odd, thing to say.

But given where I was now and why I was there, I'd have to score that particular point in her favor.

The Cincitucky Airport, or whatever it's called, has a pretty decent food court, with plenty of places to eat and hide. Corinne sat at the lip of the seating area near the McDonald's, checking her watch every few minutes. I was enjoying the success of my cloak-and-dagger mission so much that I rewarded myself with an enormous latte and sat about twenty feet from her, obscured by a dried-out fern.

The problem with following someone, I quickly learned, is that you are at the mercy of that person's timetable. You probably don't see a lot of anal-retentive, control-freak P.I.s about to pop a forehead vein waiting for flight attendants to give them the go-ahead to get off a plane; by the very nature of their jobs, they have to be relaxed and easygoing. (You want to go cheat on your wife for a few hours? OK, I'll just hang out here in the car until you're done. No hurry. Take your time.) I, on the other hand, was so antsy waiting for Corinne's friend to show up that I shredded my coffee's cardboard sleeve and found myself nibbling on my protective fern.

Initially I thought I'd take a cab and follow them but decided against it for two reasons: First, I had no idea where her friend lived, and I wasn't willing to pay a $100 fare—twice—on top of the $812 I had dropped on the last-minute connecting flight to Atlanta. Second, showing up at her friend's house would teeter dangerously close to stalking territory. True, following a woman onto a plane, unbeknownst to her, after you just broke up might also be viewed as stalkerish behavior. But it could just as easily be considered one hell of a romantic gesture. And that's the way I intended to play it.

My plan was to make my presence known shortly after the friend showed up. I would stroll up with a sly grin, introduce myself to the friend, and ask if I might steal Corinne for just a moment. I would gaze into Corinne's shocked eyes and say that I felt miserable about our fight and that I just couldn't leave things that way. I'd say that I didn't have much time before my flight to Atlanta, but suffering through a long holiday weekend without patching things up between us was unthinkable. I'd say that my anger back in Philadelphia wasn't because she was a strong woman—I loved that about her—but because she had touched a nerve about my promotion. I would say whatever bullshit I had to, and I knew that she would buy it because she didn't want me to be Airport Guy any more than I did. About a week later, I'd tell her that things weren't working out.

Through my thinning fern, I saw Corinne pop up from her table, wave her arm, grab her bag, and trot off from the food court. Her friend—Becky, I now remembered—barreled away from her husband, Chip. The two women collided into a tight hug.

78

On my way toward Corinne and her friends, something she had told me about this couple came back to me. She pitied Becky for having to clean up after Chip, who did nothing to help out around the house. His routine, Corinne said, was to come home from work, drink beer, watch sports, and restore old cars in the garage. She told me that when they were in college, she and Becky were adamant that, if and when they ever got married, their relationships would have to be fifty–fifty. And here, just four years after becoming Mrs. Chip, her best friend had gained forty pounds and lost all perspective. She saw Becky as a combination of caretaker, slave, and doormat.

After she and Becky finished hugging and lying about how neither had changed since the last time they saw each other, Corinne moved over to Chip for a perfunctory air-kiss exchange. Chip took her bag and hoisted it over his shoulder, and they walked toward short-term parking while I readied my approach, hovering close enough to hear their conversation.

"So, did you have breakfast with Bill this morning?" Becky asked. "How are things going with you two?"

"Don't ask. He flipped out on me at the airport."

"What? What happened?"

"It's a long story. He's just another jerk, that's all. Another insecure ass-hole. I knew it would come out sooner or later."

I couldn't have asked for a better line to land on, but just as I started my final descent, Becky and Chip held back for a beat and allowed Corinne a very small lead. As she prattled on about how Airport Guy had done her wrong, I saw I wasn't the only one expecting to hear this story. Behind Corinne, Becky and Chip turned to each other, rolled their eyes, and smiled. Chip winked at Becky, and she wrapped her arm around his waist before continuing the conversation.

"That's too bad, sweetie. Don't worry, you'll find somebody great before you know it."

I stopped following them and just stood there for a minute, wondering what I was doing in Kentucky when people were waiting for me in Atlanta.

Jaime Leon Lin-Yu
We Are Pomegranates,
We Are Apples

My best friend Rachel is tired. On Mondays Rachel dines with her boss, the baby diva of the East Asian art world. She is the only assistant he has not fired after ten days. On Tuesdays Rachel gets a shiatsu massage, and if she needs it, goes to see "Frah-ank," who charges one hundred dollars per haircut, but trims Rachel's hair for free. On Wednesdays she works out at 24-Hour Fitness with Winston Chu, a dentist who finds her "intimidating," yet wants to take her to Jamaica. On Thursdays she stops by Rob Syto's happy hour in Center City, which caters to the newest crop of Asian American yuppies. On Fridays she rides the R5 to La Fortune in Ardmore, where celebrated chef Andrew Palacee emerges from the kitchen to greet her. He fills her up on beluga caviar nestled sweetly with sour cream inside an egg half-shell, seared foie gras with quince, and Granny Smith apples baked with lemongrass. Then he gets her drunk on four hundred dollar bottles of pinot noir before driving her home. Last week, he asked, "Would your parents approve of me?" while caressing her cheek and brushing the bangs out of her eyes. He is two years older than her father.

On Saturdays Rachel goes (weather permitting) to the farmers' market in Manayunk with her boyfriend, Knucklehead Neil (my nickname). He is easily irritated, especially when Rachel hunts for antique mirrors, or wants to refurbish old rocking chairs that creak more than rock, or looks for the perfect squat pumpkin for Halloween. Neil typically bitches about how he needs to relax on the weekend, not drive her all over the country looking for princess silver tea sets. Rachel says that Neil doesn't understand "these kinds of things." I find that he doesn't understand anything at all.

Finally, on Sundays Rachel has brunch with me. I usually invite my husband Jake to join us, but he always finds something else to do—play pick-up ball, pay bills, sleep in. Sometimes we get our nails done at one of the Korean places lining the streets of Philly. They treat us extra nice because we're Asian. As we push the door open, a gentle tinkle of bells announces our arrival. They ask us with hope shining in their eyes, "*Ah yung ha say yo?*" I smile, feeling like a child with a hand in the cookie jar, and shake my head.

"Chinese," I say and they nod, as if I just won second place in a beauty pageant. This is when Rachel (never failing) whispers to me, "Maybe we should learn some token Korean phrases—we'd get a discount that way." That's Rachel for you, always trying to bend the rules or manipulate circumstances to her advantage.

I roll my eyes, but I say quickly before Rachel can throw a fit, "Not knowing how to speak Korean is pretty much the same as not being Korean."

On Monday Rachel's cycle starts all over again, sometimes with different men, depending on who has flown in that week. For example, there is Thomas from the London office, who has a live-in girlfriend, but claims it's not serious. He bears exotic soaps and promises of Bora Bora. Rachel keeps the soaps she likes (citrus) and gives me the lavender and sage. At every mention of Bora Bora, we go swimsuit shopping. As we browse the racks, Rachel yammers about the spiritual benefits of vacations, especially ones in the South Pacific. I tell her that unless she's paying for her own airfare and her own room, it's not a good idea.

"We need to think of a name for him," Rachel says, referring to Thomas.

"Other than Thomas?" I ask, knowing that when she says, "We," she means "you." She wants a codeword for Thomas to use when others are around and as something to legitimize his place in her life. "We" decide to call him the "beau."

Neil, the boyfriend, is the conditional giver. He measures everything carefully, tit for tat. For example, if Rachel and Neil eat Cajun barbeque (which Rachel loves), the next night Neil insists on hot dogs, despite Rachel's loathing of processed meat. It never enters Neil's mind to be flexible because to his reasoning, he had just been nice. Now it's Rachel's turn.

When I ask why she's with him, she sighs and says, "He brings me that much closer to the proverbial white picket fence."

"You know that he would never paint it," I say. *Jake would.* But I bite my tongue.

"But he fits in so many other ways," she says, her voice thin. "We have the same interests, same goals . . . "

"So you would have the big beautiful house, but a really shabby fence." As usual, Rachel ignores me. My advice floats in front of her and even over her. It's not until it is almost too late that Rachel remembers what I have to say, so she must store my words somewhere, maybe in her back pocket, like some kind of lucky charm that is only remembered when all else has failed.

*　　*　　*

This Saturday Rachel ditches Neil and Manayunk and accompanies me to the country to pick apples and celebrate the anticipated arrival of fall. The "country" is a two-hour drive into Jersey. I lure Rachel out of her cozy apartment and into hiking boots with promises of an "apple tasting," thinking that sounds relaxed and fun, like "wine tasting."

Autumn is our favorite season. I once joked that I wanted to name my daughter Autumn; to which Rachel replied she would never forgive me. This time of year we get excited about the little things: V-formations of noisy geese; orange, red, and yellow leaves; caramel apple ciders at Starbucks; and for me, jogging through the city to enjoy the cool slap of fall air against my cheek. Rachel prefers to stay inside, planning elaborate feasts using seasonal ingredients.

Rachel's newest fall obsession is the pomegranate. She loves them in salads and is enamored with recipes that call for them. I keep telling her that apples make a better autumnal fruit—easier to find, simpler to eat, and packed to the gills with antioxidants. But Rachel has discovered the joy of picking pomegranate seeds. She curls up on her sofa or in the plaid armchair in my apartment, holding the fruit so close to her face that her cheeks become flushed with splatters of dark juice. To me she is Gollum, whispering, "My Precccccious" as she meticulously carves out the kernel-like seeds, cramming a few at a time into her mouth.

When I say that I just want apple pie, to hell with this pomegranate sauce thing, Rachel says that apples are the plain Jane cousins of pomegranates (after all, *pomme* is French for apple). In my mind, apples trump pomegranates any day; apples are so universal they can be transformed into anything. But I suspect it's the exotic, mysterious quality of pomegranates that excites Rachel.

Today we are apple picking, which I haven't done since childhood. Rachel grumbles as I park the car. She grumbles again when I hand her a basket and an apple picker. She grumbles some more as she follows me out into the fields, sidestepping children and their parents. I duck under low-hanging boughs, brushing her grumblings off me.

"I wish Neil liked this kind of stuff," is the first thing she says that doesn't annoy me.

"Oh, really? You don't even like this. You haven't stopped complaining."

"But this is real," Rachel insists. I refrain from asking what she means by "real." I continue picking wine-sap apples instead. Their tartness is perfect

82

for baking. Jake will love it.

"Why is there such a bad connotation between women and apples?" Rachel asks, angling the long, skinny, metal arms of the apple picker high above her head. "Tell me, oh wise, former English major."

"I don't know. There's a lot of allusions to it. Eve, Snow White . . . hey, there's Johnny Appleseed. There's a guy for you." I carry my nearly full basket and set it between two trees. "In dream-speak, apples represent possibility."

"But I thought they were the forbidden fruit."

I watch Rachel close in on a large, shiny red globe and in one quick motion, pluck it and drop it into the basket at my feet. I lean over and move it to another basket, where I find several yellow apples among red-spotted ones.

"Hey! Watch where you put those! These are golden delicious. You just plucked a macoun."

Rachel rolls her eyes. "God forbid!" She grabs the offending apple and tosses it lightly into another basket. She stretches her arms over her head and yawns.

"I'm tired," Rachel declares, collapsing into the dry grass. "Is it bad that I'm done for the day?"

"Lazy."

She grins. "You know what else is forbidden fruit?"

I go back to apple picking.

"Pomegranates." She laughs. "I bet you didn't think of that. Persephone and Hades, remember? You told me that story."

I shrug. She continues, seeming to speak more to herself than to me. "Persephone was taken by Hades into the Underworld but her mother, Demeter, loved her so much that she convinced Hades to let her go. Hades agreed, as long as Persephone didn't eat anything in the Underworld. But she did—three pomegranate seeds. As a result, Persephone spends half the year with Hades and the other half with her mother, which is why we have seasons." Rachel sighs. "All it took was three little seeds." As usual, Rachel focuses on technicalities. "Do you think," she says, "that Hades has sex with her?"

"What are you talking about?" I finally turn around.

"They're married."

"Against her will."

"So he has sex with her."

"I guess."

"Wouldn't that be considered rape?"

I walk back to the where Rachel sits and hoist the apple basket on my hip. "I guess. Let's drop these off at the weigh station."

Rachel grumbles again, taking her sweet time getting up. She makes a big show of wiping bits of dry grass off her ass and shakes out her ponytail.

"Irhafanewresipeforponegratessas," Rachel mumbles, her hands reaching for her hair, an elastic hair tie in her mouth.

"What?"

Rachel pulls her hair taut. "I have a new recipe for pork chops that calls for pomegranate juice in the sauce. We can make it tonight along with pie." Her face brightens. "Oh, I know! We can make apple ice cream too! I'll bring over my ice cream maker."

The apples are heavy and Rachel is turning entrepreneurial. I don't think I can afford to walk leisurely. "Uh, I can't."

"Jake won't mind. He can have dinner with us."

"It's not that. We're meeting Tom and Ana in Bryn Mawr for dinner." I hurry towards the main barn.

Rachel tries to keep up with me, but starts to lag.

"I told you on Tuesday about this," I say.

"Uh-huh."

When I get to the weigh station, Rachel is some fifty yards behind, a lime green speck topped with black hair wandering around the empty fields between the barn and the orchard.

"Hey!" I drop the basket and wave my arms over my head. Rachel ignores me, pretending to look at scenery.

Fine. Let her be that way. She'll have to talk to me sooner or later. I'm her ride back to the city. I snap at the woman in the brown corduroy overalls to hurry up and weigh my stupid apples.

We're both quiet on the return drive. Finally, I break the silence.

"I *did* tell you about Tom and Ana."

"I'm not mad about that," Rachel says. She removes her boots and curls her feet beneath her.

"So, what is it then?"

"Don't worry about it. It's got nothing to do with you."

If we were on the phone having this conversation, I would ignore her fake-calm voice. But we're stuck in the car for another hour. Her silence makes me want to scream. Instead, I take a deep breath.

"That's crap and you know it. Tell me the truth."

Rachel pinches her lips together. She has chewed off most of her lipstick. "Like I said, don't worry about me, go and have fun with Jake and your other couple-ly friends."

I pound the steering wheel. "God, Rachel, that's bothering you? You know that we're not the kind of people who only have couple friends."

"But you're having dinner in Bryn Mawr."

"It's just dinner."

"It's *Bryn Mawr*. That's like—you know, neat and tidy." I'm having difficulty hearing Rachel because she's mumbling. She holds her neck stiffly, looking out her window.

I pass into the right lane so that I can slow down, think, and still drive at the same time. "What exactly is your problem?"

"You know, we went apple picking," Rachel says. "You made this big deal out of it and kept talking about it all week long, so it seemed natural that we would hang out tonight. I even cancelled my date with Neil."

Oh. I broke a girlfriend rule. I've raised expectations and then crushed them.

"I'm sorry if I gave you the impression that we were going to spend the whole day together," I say.

Rachel sighs. "I guess I have to get used to the fact that you're married now and don't have as much time as you used to, when we could pick up and go whenever we wanted without having to consult anyone."

"But I thought you liked—at least wanted and understood—the whole white picket fence thing," I say, flushed. "But, maybe . . . I mean, do you only like it when it suits you?"

Rachel takes her time answering. Little drops of water splatter onto the windshield. I turn on the wipers. Squishy noises fill the silence.

"I'm getting tired of this jigsaw puzzle of my life," she says with such sad, grand importance and heavy emphasis on the word "tired" that I believe that it really hurts her to say what she is thinking.

I want to shake the drama out of her. Instead, I try for serenity and take the non-offensive route. "I'm sorry if I hurt your feelings. That's why we do brunch on Sundays, to make sure we see each other. Besides, you're the one with the heavy schedule."

"I don't want to get left behind."

"You're *not* getting left behind. Where are you getting that impression? We're just in two different places right now. You just need to find the right guy." I say this a little faster than I intended, possibly giving Rachel the impression that I'm exasperated.

"Not from lack of trying. Maybe I need to find a 'Jake.'"

I ignore the possible sarcasm. "Yes. You need to find someone like Jake, whose middle name is understanding."

"I'm going to die alone," Rachel moans. She leans her cheek against the window.

"Okay, Miss Melodrama." We laugh a little and another mega fight has been avoided. Had this been a few years ago, I would have given into temptation and stopped the car and Rachel would have jumped out to hitchhike and I would have followed her, screaming in the rain.

We drive the rest of the way in companionable silence. As I make the turn into Rachel's neighborhood, she asks, "Are you around tomorrow night?"

"Not really," I say with deliberate vagueness. "I don't know what we're doing, but I'll see you in the morning at Fork."

"Oh, okay. Well, have *fun*." She nearly spits out the last word.

I pull to a stop in front of her brownstone building. Rachel opens the door, unfolds her legs and says almost blithely over her shoulder, "I'm going out with Thomas tomorrow night."

"What?" I don't have the energy to ask specifics, but guilt leads to concern. I hate it when he's in town. Rachel slams the door behind her, closing any opportunities for answers.

*   *   *

Rachel runs on Asian time, which means at least ten minutes if not half an hour late. I stand in line at Fork, counting the parties of people before me in line. One, two, three, four . . . at least a forty-minute wait. I grab my cell phone and think about telling Rachel that we need to switch brunch places, that Fork is too commercial, too touristy, and that people who aren't in the know come here. We're no better than transplants, but that is, of course, what we are. Not recent transplants, but we're still transplants who should know better. But this is the Philly we both know. This is the city that Rachel convinced me to come to, introduced me to, and helped me fall in love with . . . the commercial, touristy, too obvious, City of Brotherly Love, otherwise known as "Killerdelphia."

I moved here a little over two years ago. I didn't know where else to go; divorced at twenty-four, doomed to be part of the "starter marriage" phenomenon. I had been living in Portland, the city of roses, but in my mind the city of wet pine trees. Weepy, sloppy, drippy trees whose needles had turned mushy from my crying.

"Come back to the East Coast," Rachel told me one night. "Come home."

And so I went. To the City of Brotherly Love. To Fork on Sundays, to my armchair-snuggling-Belgium-waffle-eating-rollerblading-on-Kelly-Drive life with Jake—whom I met soon after I moved here—and, of course, to Rachel.

"Hey, daydreamer," Rachel greets me. She wears a pastel blue Burberry coat, unbuttoned so that the classic plaid peeks out with every step she takes. Her long black hair is tied back in a loose low ponytail and she has her chic nerd glasses on. "How much longer?" she asks, gesturing to the line ahead.

I click my cell phone shut and drop it in my shoulder bag. "Where were you?"

Rachel brushes her hair out of her eyes. "Had a fight."

Neil. Of course. The never-ending drama.

Surprisingly, Rachel doesn't want to talk about it. Usually she rehashes every single detail. I am her walking, talking diary.

Still, as we are seated, I ask, "So, what did you and Neil fight about? What did he do this time?"

Rachel buries her nose in the menu despite the fact that she knows it by heart. Suddenly she looks up, resting the tip of the menu against her nose.

"I offered Neil a pomegranate." Rachel taps the menu edge against her nose. "At first he didn't want to try it. He was afraid of ruining his shirt. Said they were too sloppy. I told him it takes time to get to the heart of the fruit, but he got frustrated."

"Really."

Rachel drops the menu, letting it slap against mine, nearly knocking my mug of tea over. My hands scramble to grab the tea and the menus.

Rachel's eyes are sparkly, but not glitzy. I'll order some pumpkin muffins to make her feel better. Pumpkins are a much safer fruit.

"I'm seeing Thomas today," she says.

"I know. You told me yesterday."

"He's leaving on Tuesday."

"Does Neil know?"

"Yes."

"How?"

Rachel slowly and maddeningly says, "I told him."

"No wonder you fought." I sip my tea, resisting the urge to chastise her. After all, she's a grown woman.

"I know what you're thinking," Rachel says, "and I don't want to hear it. I just need to know if you'll be around later, just in case."

"In case of what?"

"Just in case." Rachel plasters a sunny smile on her face as the waiter comes up to take our order. She gets the lox scramble and I, blueberry pancakes. Business as usual.

*   *   *

When I get home, Jake is still asleep. I shed my skirt and blouse and crawl under the covers. Jake opens his eyes and kisses the tip of my nose.

"That was quick. But I'm glad you're back." He snakes his right arm around my chest and squeezes tight.

I pat his hand and think pleasantly of boa constrictors. "Rachel has a date."

"Hmm."

"But not with Neil."

"What do you want to do this afternoon?" Jake buries his face in my hair.

"Rachel's going out with Thomas tonight."

"Uh-huh."

"He's the Hong Kong guy."

"Yeah."

"Remember I told you about him?"

"Nope." He kisses my neck.

I take a deep breath. "Uh, we might have to meet up with them for dinner or after for drinks, depending when Rachel calls."

"What?"

"She probably won't need back-up, but we should probably stay close to home, just in case."

Jake groans. "Another day of Rachel-saving." He rolls away.

I nudge him with my foot and then wrap my arms around his back, kissing a spot between his shoulder blades. "I can go alone if you're too cranky. I thought Rachel was your friend."

"She's *your* friend," Jake sighs. "I guess I missed the part of our marriage that states that you have to save Rachel from strange men because she lacks the common sense to save herself." He unwraps my arms, his back still facing me.

I lean over. "That's not fair."

Jake opens his eyes. They are flat, like obsidian. "I don't want to help Rachel cheat on Neil."

"But she's not really with him. Dating Neil isn't really dating him. He's such a non-entity, you know that. You met the guy."

"Yeah, he's a tool. I don't get why she can't break up with him." Jake pushes me away—gently, but it's a push nonetheless. "She has plenty of other options."

"Because technically, she never said she was exclusive with Neil. He just assumed, like he assumes everything."

"When are you going to get that you're not her savior?" When I don't answer, he sits up. "So, what are you going to do? Stay here all day?"

When I nod, Jake snorts. He putters over to the bathroom. I stare out the window, surveying the sunshine, trying to figure out a way to salvage our day. I can hear him pee.

"Want me to make coffee?" I call out as he flushes the toilet.

"Don't bother."

The floorboards creak under Jake's weight. He appears in the bedroom doorway, his hair standing up and to the side. "I'm going out." He throws the paper onto the duvet and treads not-so-lightly to the kitchen before I can think of a reply.

I stay in bed until Jake leaves, the front door slamming behind him. I pull on some wool socks and one of Jake's mangled yet incredibly soft T-shirts from his adolescent burger-flipping days and pad into the kitchen looking for a clean mug. There's a half a grocery bag of pomegranates from Rachel on the counter. I open it and a sickeningly sweet smell threatens to overpower me. The pomegranates are tender, some with squishy spots. I choose the firmest one, and peel back the skin using a paring knife and my fingernails. My mother taught me how to eat pomegranates because pome-granates are guaranteed to be complicated. I pick my way through the firm yellow flesh not meant for eating, staining my fingers, careful not to burst any of the kernel-shaped seeds in order to get to the heart of the fruit. I tuck the seeds in the pocket of my cheek, savoring them until I unearth the rest of them, eating those seeds as you cannot do with other fruit.

Sucking the juices with one hand cupped under my chin, I walk over to my closet in the bedroom. Pomegranate juice drips through my fingers as I survey my clothes, deciding what to wear should Rachel need me tonight. My teeth hurt; the seeds are too sweet. But as I swallow, I notice an odd kick, the last departing taste of the fruit, not sweet or sour, but sharp, a reminder not to forget. At first I think it's a bug, but all I see in my hand is tough orange-red skin and spongy pulp. And perfect round little seeds, small with a hard layer of shiny, dark sweet juice.

*　　*　　*

It is past midnight when the phone rings. I shake myself awake and jump off the couch, glancing at the clock near the television. The phone seems too loud, the rings reverberating off the walls and the windows.

On my way to the kitchen, I pass the bedroom. Jake sleeps the deep sleep of the dead, after a day of soccer in the park with his friends. His brown hair is spiky from sleeping on it. I resist the urge to smooth it down.

The phone is in the kitchen, hidden beneath newspapers on the counter. I fumble with the receiver. "Hello?"

"It's me."

"It's about time." I lean my back against the counter's edge. The uneven tiles dig in my lower back. "Where have you been?

"Out."

"Did you have a good time?"

A pause. Then, "Yeah, I guess."

"I take that as 'no.'"

"It was fine. Really. Thomas picked me up and we went to dinner. I wanted lobster, so we went to this place near Rittenhouse Square . . . and then went back to my place for drinks, you know, had some wine . . . "

"Maybe you should get some sleep," I say, thinking how much more clearheaded both of us would be in the morning.

"I don't think I am going to see Thomas again." Rachel's voice cracks a bit, like she is either about to cry or has just finished.

"Why?" Concern causes my voice to rise a little. "What happened?"

"Nothing. It's just that he wanted to stay over and I refused. I tried to call him a cab and he got mad, saying he flew all the way from London, called me a tease, but I told him that I had a boyfriend, well, actually I said I was seeing someone, so Thomas knew, but he got so mad and called me a bitch."

"Rachel." I fight to keep my voice calm. "What exactly happened tonight?"

"He . . . he . . . " Rachel starts crying so softly that I can barely hear her. "He raised his hand and I ran out of my apartment. I ran down the stairs, screaming. You know Mr. and Mrs. Henderson?"

"On the first floor, yeah, I know them. Did they hear you?"

"Yeah, Mr. Henderson. He . . . " Rachel hiccups. "He came out and yelled at me for making such a fuss. A 'fuss' he said. I love old people language." Rachel pauses. "Some other neighbors opened their doors, too. I didn't know what to do so I barged into the Hendersons' place to hide."

"Where was Thomas?"

"He had followed me down the stairs and when he saw Mr. Henderson, he left." Rachel gives a small laugh. "Little ole Mr. Henderson scared off Thomas."

"Oh, god, Rachel. This could have been serious."

"You think?" Rachel blows her nose. "It's pretty bad, huh?"

"I don't think you should be alone right now."

"It's okay. Mrs. Henderson walked me upstairs."

"Is she there now?"

"No. I asked her to go away."

"Okay, then. I'm coming over." In a few quick steps I'm in the bedroom, covering Jake with a blanket and scribbling a note, the phone still clenched between my left shoulder and cheek. He's going to hate this, but that can wait until tomorrow morning.

When I arrive, Rachel is sitting on her sofa wearing flannel pajamas, her knees pulled up. Her eyes are puffy and her hair is wrapped in a towel, wet from a shower.

I sit beside her, tentatively touching her knee. "Hey."

"Hi." She smiles weakly. "You didn't have to come over. What is Jake doing?"

"Sleeping. And of course I had to come." I start to get up. "I'll make some tea."

Rachel grabs my wrist and pulls me back down on the couch beside her. "I don't want tea."

I see a basket of pomegranates and feel inspired. I hand her one. She pokes a small hole using the edge of her thumbnail, and carefully peels enough skin back to expose three little seeds. "Such a minor technicality," she muses.

"Like the boyfriend factor."

Rachel bobs her head slowly. She looks at me with no particular look. "Maybe I am better off as an apple."

Despite the childish sound of it, I hug her knee and feel a rise of tears. "Why do you say that?"

Rachel shakes her head. "Because. Because you polish it and bite it and then it's over. Pomegranates . . . are so messy. Takes skill to eat them. You have to appreciate them, not everyone likes them." She pauses. I am startled by her long sentences. "I did tell him I had a boyfriend. I tell all of them that. They don't seem to listen."

I don't know what to say. I think about Eve and her outstretched hand, the apple balanced on the flat of her palm. I think about Persephone and three little pomegranate seeds, hard at first in her mouth, then with one bite, an explosion of flavor sealing her fate. I realize that I could explain technicalities to Rachel until the sun rises . . . if I wanted to.

Pomegranate juice is dripping down her chin. I hand her a napkin to wipe it off.

"I think, that maybe you were always a pomegranate," I say, choosing my words carefully. "Sometimes, though, it's not so bad to be an apple."

"Yeah, but right now, pomegranates are in season." Rachel holds out her fruit smeared palms and sticky fingers. "Hand me another one." I do and we eat the entire basket of fruit. We are absorbed in our meticulous picking and peeling, completely immersed in joyful stickiness, forgetting everything else but the orange-red hearts in our hands.

Xavier Richardson
The Good Pretender

W hen did I stop paying attention to my wife?

Ten years ago we were strangers coming out of the same movie—back when Center City still had theaters—moving in the same direction. I remember the crisp night air against my face, the click, click, click of a traffic signal green/yellow/red, the scent of fresh baked pastry.

"Do you smell that?" Lillian's voice was made for FM radio.

"Yes."

"Where do you think it's coming from?"

We followed our noses to a bakery a couple of blocks away. The windows were dark. She misstepped over a join in the sidewalk. I caught her.

"Closed." Our lips were close enough to feel each other breathe.

"I should have known better." Her eyes stayed in mine. Time had stopped and wouldn't move again until we did.

Tonight my wife got into bed, turned toward her nightstand, curled up into herself and pulled the covers up to her neck, as though she had lost interest in me. I don't know how much time went by before I shut off the lamp, only that she didn't ask, and I didn't volunteer, what was on my mind. Out of habit I pulled her to me and wrapped around her. Out of habit she relaxed her cold feet against my shins. The soft fragrance of lavender bath oil was the last thing I remembered.

* * *

I came into the mirror behind Lillian. She tugged at the hem of a navy blue blazer, spun toward me and asked if I thought she was getting fat. I shook my head. She sighed at her reflection and said that since her last promotion she no longer had time to work out.

We no longer had time for a lot of things, but I wasn't about to bring that up. I offered dinner at O'Hara's, her favorite restaurant from our West Philadelphia days. It had been a long time since we had enjoyed each other's company over a good meal. She reminded me that we had to attend a dinner tonight for one of her firm's senior partners, kissed me, whirled out of my arms, was down the hallway, the stairs, and out the front door. I heard her car leave before I moved again.

Lillian liked being a trial attorney for a mid-sized law firm with a reputation for taking on large corporations like the insurance company I worked for. I hadn't been excited about my career for a very long time. I didn't know how, but this had to have something to do with the distance between us.

*   *   *

Low passionate swearing came from Miriam's corner office on the twenty-second floor of the 1818 Market Street building. She was on her hands and knees gathering papers into manila folders. I walked in and took the folders from her and helped her up. She thanked me, pushing a lock of dark reddish brown hair out of her face, then asked if I was strong enough to move the file cabinet behind her or if she would need to call maintenance.

I set the folders on top of the cabinet, grabbed one end and swung it out. More folders, leaning on the baseboard, flopped down. I picked them up and handed them to Miriam. She kept hold of my hand.

"Thank you, and thank you for coming. True to the end. I set the challenge, you meet it without an interruption of your casual aloofness that with a little refinement might even pass for style. How many times a week do you work out?" Miriam was the one woman in the office tall enough to look me in the eye without tilting her head awkwardly. She only had to raise her eyes slightly.

"Four."

"Does Lillian work out with you?"

"No."

"You must wear gloves. You don't have calluses."

"I wear gloves."

"Grey Flannel." She finally let me go. "Such a subtle scent. You almost have to be in a man's arms before you know he's wearing it. Most of the boys here prefer something a little more arrogant. But if you can smell it across the room, there really isn't a need to get closer. Grey Flannel draws you in. To fully appreciate it, you have to get close. It was Richard's scent when we were starting out. I work out or run every morning. Not Richard though. We're the same age, but people think he married a younger woman. How much do you bench press?"

"I only lift to stay in shape." I pushed the file cabinet back against the wall.

"Ted seriously underestimated you. He thought your success consisted of two parts luck, one part charm and personality, and one part trickery. He was convinced you were pretending to be someone you are not. You were just so slick he couldn't figure out how to expose you. His heart really wasn't into exposing you anyway. Your success was his success."

"Ted told you that?" I tried not to give her the benefit of my surprise.

"He didn't see any other explanation for an untrusted black male being able to structure landmark deals where his trusted great white warriors couldn't get past their charts and graphs." Miriam was enjoying the sound of her own voice more than usual. "But you must forgive Ted. He can trace his values back to Plymouth Rock. Anything above the understanding of the village elders is pretty much witchcraft to him. He feels the same way about my being a woman and improving on his numbers—well, technically getting you to improve upon what you already did for him."

"I see." I looked out the window at a construction site across the street. Some part of Center City was always being renovated, expanded, razed or rebuilt.

"You know." A dash of tongue left dark red lips wet. "I was a lot like you at your age. If you weren't so cold toward the hand that feeds you . . . "

"My hand feeds me."

She raised a finger, using it to measure her words. "You need to loosen up sometimes. Stop being so sensitive. Pretend to be friendly if you're not interested in being a friend. Take it from me—around here, no one knows the difference."

"I'm not a good pretender."

"You don't have to be. At this level people see what they want to see as long as you don't make it too hard for them. Nobody can afford new enemies. They have mortgages, timeshares, vacations, children's tuition, wives, mistresses, car payments. . . . They go along to get along. You should try it sometime." She sat on her desk and crossed her legs. "You might even find yourself liking it."

"If my best isn't good enough, nothing I have ever will be. There's no point faking it."

"As much as we like to think we mean to this organization, if we both dropped dead tomorrow, there'd be a moment of silence and then life would go on."

"I have a meeting in less than an hour."

Miriam laughed. "You really think I dislike you, don't you?"

"I think you like me about as much as I like you."

"Any woman in her right mind would have to be afraid of a man with such tight control over his emotions." She straightened the hem of her skirt. "Unless you're the biggest pretender of all."

"My meeting." I tapped my watch.

"I know you're not this way with Lillian. You can't be. How could she deal with it?"

"I don't doubt that had you tried to have this conversation at the beginning of your tenure, we'd have the kind of relationship where we share things about our spouses. For whatever reason, we went in a different direction."

"I like the fact you chose 'We' instead of 'You.' You accept your part of the blame. However, has it ever occurred to you, if you were better liked by your peers I wouldn't have been able to do what I did to you?"

"Nobody in this office has had more success than my staff."

"That keeps you in a job. It doesn't get your budget approved. It doesn't get you assignments or resources. I'm the only one who can do that."

"I used to wonder if I couldn't meet one of your little challenges, would you have lost an important client over it?"

"You needed a war just as much as I did. While everybody else was trying to figure out who I slept with to get this job, you were the only one who would fight me."

"Just as I thought. You have a timeshare too."

"You enjoyed your role as much as I enjoyed mine. You can't stand here and tell me none of our clients offered you a job. You could've gone to a competitor."

"You're speaking in the past tense."

"I'm telling you that you had any number of options. And what did you do? You chose to stay in an unfavorable working environment, fighting for supplies and resources for projects nobody else wanted, for a boss you didn't like." Miriam slid off the desk. We were eye to eye again. "Tell me you didn't love it."

"I love the people who work for me, but I wouldn't expect you to understand that."

"If not for me or somebody just like me you wouldn't have excelled the way you have. And you served as my example. Everybody saw how hard I was on my top VP. You have no idea how that kept the other execs in line." Miriam sat back on her desk. Her skirt shortened from above her knee a considerable way up her thigh. "I've been asked to take a position with Headquarters."

"Congratulations."

"I'm strongly considering recommending you to replace me."

"What would I have to do in return?"

She checked her watch. "I don't want you to be late for your meeting."

"Very well then." I started to leave.

"And Adam."

"Yes."

"By helping me get my promotion you've already done what you have to do."

*　　*　　*

I met my best friend for lunch at Le Castagne. As Cassius got older, his women got younger, the relationships shorter. Today's date exuded a self-assuredness and grace that bespoke class and intelligence. She was not the kind of woman who usually interested him.

"This is my sister, Dr. Lucinda Dupree." Cassius put his arm around his guest. "She's in town to visit her favorite brother."

There was no family resemblance. Cassius and I had been friends since college. I had met his brother and another sister. Like Cassius, they had long angled faces, slashing eyes, and mouths that gave their smiles a dark cunning. Lucinda's face was small and round with high cheekbones. Her eyes gentle. Her smile honest.

"Doctor?" I didn't know what else to say.

"Religion and History." The sleeve of her jacket hit her glass.

Hours later, sitting in my weekly staff meeting, instead of an analyst giving a projected cost report I heard the ring of a gold button on Lucinda's sleeve knock against the side of a glass, the tiny scrape of the glass moving a few inches across the table, a splash of wine. Lines and numbers on an analyst's flip chart were replaced by the rich red hue that washed over Lucinda's hand, the baby blue of a napkin that made the red disappear, her eyes wide with apology.

"Ellison." Cassius had called me back to reality when my eyes stayed in hers.

"Adam." At the staff meeting it was my top assistant's voice.

This hadn't happened since I met Lillian.

"Are you two okay?" Cassius offered his sister more napkins.

"Yes." Lucinda seemed to emerge from the same daze I was in.

"If you and Lillian weren't the happiest couple I know, I'd swear you were flirting with my sister . . . making her nervous."

"Now you know how I feel when you and Lillian flirt."

"But that's harmless. I never make Lillian nervous."

"He wasn't flirting with me . . . were you?"

96

"No. It's more like I was caught off guard."

"How?"

"Talk as though I wasn't even here." Cassius threw his hands up.

"It's just that I've met Von and Drucilla. You aren't what I would have expected."

"And how is that?"

"I'm calling Lillian. Did I mention Ellison's wife is a lawyer, a good one too?"

"How long have you been married?"

"Nine, going on ten years."

"How many children?"

"We don't have children."

"Let me guess. Her career?"

"She wanted to. Blame me."

"What do you do?"

"He's a vice president at Susquehanna Commonwealth Insurance. The information, marketing, and operations directors answer to him."

"It sounds more impressive than it feels."

"Why is that?" Lucinda asked.

"Because of the president, Miriam Parish," Cassius said.

"According to her it was tough love."

"I know you're not buying into that."

"She got herself kicked up to HQ and she's recommending me to replace her."

"You don't believe her."

"Even if she doesn't mean it, all I got from Ted Simmons was a handgun in a fancy leather case. What could I do with that?"

"Maybe he knew what it would be like to work for Miriam."

This lapse was out of character. I had known most of the people around this conference table, in this stolid room, since before I met my wife. There wasn't a better New Accounts Manager than Sean Milligan. All he needed was a department head to take his ideas seriously. Donna Culver kept Large Group running. She was also the first person I turned to in a crisis. Charlie Layton had forgotten more than most of us would ever know about Local Group, but prior department heads wouldn't look past his lack of a degree. John DeLessio ran Brokered Accounts with an unorthodoxed ingenuity that only he understood, but got results. Sam Glassier, Jill Greenberg, and Matt Pfizer came to me as employees no one else wanted. Now they were unit managers everyone on the floor wanted to work for. If I were offered Miriam's position I would have to pick between Sean and Donna to replace me.

"Forgive me, I was a little distracted. I've got an announcement to make."

"What's up Skip?" Sean asked.

"HQ snatched up our president."

"The witch is dead, the witch is dead, hi-ho the witch is—"

"Nathan, let's keep our mourning civilized," I interrupted my personal assistant.

"Yeah right, mourning. Anything you say Skip." He was smiling from ear to ear, as was everyone else.

"May I propose a respectful gathering to commiserate our mutual sorrow, a wake so to speak?" Charlie Layton proposed. Charlie never had an unkind word to say about anyone.

"A wake?" I was trying to maintain the proper respect, but Miriam had brought this on herself, and Charlie's proposal deserved at least a smile.

*   *   *

My wife's car was in the garage when I got home. She was in the bedroom, in front of a mirror, in her underwear, holding up dinner dresses to herself. "I am getting fat." She poked a clothes hanger into a slight looseness around her middle.

I dropped my jacket over the rocking chair she'd given me for one of my birthdays and told her she wasn't.

"You're just saying that. I didn't used to need a bra to keep these up. And look at you, soon they'll be saying I married a younger man."

"You're not getting fat, we're getting older." I tossed my shirt over my jacket and went to my wife. Her chin found its familiar nook in my shoulder. "I asked you to grow old with me, remember?"

"Yes, but I didn't think you meant so soon."

"Believe it or not, you're far more attractive to me then you've ever been."

"Maybe it's because I'm feeling vulnerable and really need you to make me feel attractive, but thank you." She kissed me.

"You were always vulnerable, you just didn't realize it."

"To you and you alone. You're the same way. Not even Cassius would believe how you can be with me." She unloosed my belt and unbuttoned my pants.

"I met him and his sister for lunch."

"Do you think he'll ever settle down?" she asked.

"Why do people say 'settle down'? That's what silt does on the bottom of the Schuylkill."

"I thought you were tired of me. I know I'm not the easiest person in the world to put up with." She rolled down her stockings. I unhooked her bra.

98

"I guess we're alike in that too." I stepped out of my shorts.

"We're doing this like we're too used to it." Lillian wiggled out of her panties.

"And we're really not that old either." I sat down to take off my socks.

"If we're like this now, how will we be in our fifties and sixties?" My wife's hands seemed weighted to her lap.

"I can still see us standing at that red light, ten years ago. Remember the scent of those pastries? The way you laughed when the bakery was closed. I love to see you laugh, Lillian."

"You used to make me laugh. But do we owe each other the rest of our lives as a thank you? Shouldn't we still be doing something for each other?" My wife hugged herself as though the room had grown cold.

I held out my arm, she tucked herself under it. "Just you being there when I turn out the light, cold feet and all. . . . You don't know how much that means to me. I love you Lillian."

"I will always love you too, Adam Ellison. Just knowing that when all is said and done I'll have your arms around me and you'll let me warm my feet on you, has helped me make it through more days than I care to admit. Lately you haven't touched me otherwise."

"I've wanted to."

"I'm right here."

*   *   *

I began to suspect Lillian might be having an affair. Maybe someone caught her eye the way Lucinda caught mine. I ran from the feeling. It hung on through every kiss, caress, every motion. While she was in the bathroom getting ready for dinner, I thought about going through her purse. Instead, I got up and went down the hall to one of our spare rooms.

I'd wanted this house out in Chestnut Hill because I saw a deer grazing on the land when the realtor brought us to look at it. The raccoons are a menace, more so than the squirrels were in West Philadelphia. Looking out the window I could see I would have to get out the riding mower this weekend or call a landscaper. I was leaning toward making the call. When we first got the house, taking care of the yard connected me with it. I sweated, grunted, groaned, panted, and broke my back, albeit in the tamest sense of the word, maintaining well-kept grounds that squished underfoot after other traces of a rain had evaporated.

What was wrong with me? Maybe I only wanted to convince myself Lillian was having an affair so I could see Lucinda with a clear conscience, and just because I pursued didn't mean she would acquiesce. Either way she'd probably tell Cassius. Maybe nothing was wrong. Maybe things were the same as they had always been and I had changed. There were too many maybes, except Lillian couldn't be having an affair. I would have known the same way she would if I started seeing Lucinda.

*   *   *

On the way home from dinner the highway was wet from an earlier downpour. Scattered raindrops moved down the windshield. Lillian asked what was wrong?

"I was thinking how Miriam's leaving is affecting people."

"Where is she going?"

"She took a position with Headquarters."

"Why didn't you tell me?"

"I meant to when I got home."

After what happened before we left the house Lillian did not ask how I forgot. For a while the only sound was the slush of tires over wet road. I slowed to let another car merge into our lane and the slush lessened. Before it picked up again, Lillian said, "Hal Schwartz is having an affair. That's what Sheila and I were talking about in the kitchen."

"What's she going to do?"

"You knew?"

"What was I going to say?" We were passing the gates of a huge cemetery, set far back, up on a hill, concrete pillars backlit against the night.

"Why didn't you tell me?"

"I gave my word."

"I can't believe you didn't tell me. It makes me wonder what else you're keeping from me."

"It shouldn't."

"Give me one good reason."

"Miriam told me she's recommending me to replace her."

"Don't change the subject."

"She's an Independence Hall tour guide. Don't ask me her name. . . . Hal's a neurologist. I can't see what they could have in common." An eighteen-wheeler passed us, Betty Boop silhouetted on mud flaps waving in a wet tire spray.

"What does she look like?"

"You think he'd introduce us? I told him we couldn't discuss her if he wanted me to be comfortable around his wife."

"You and I are about the same age as Hal and Sheila."

"Has she cheated on him?"

100

"That's not the sort of thing she would tell me. She's too good of a lawyer. . . . Adam, have you ever thought about being with someone else?"

"Whatever our problems, you're the only woman I want to be with."

"I count on that. The way we've been lately . . . maybe I'm taking too much for granted."

"We both do."

"When we get home I want you to love me like you mean it."

*   *   *

In the morning Lillian rose as radiant as she had been that first night under a streetlight.

"Well at least one of us is happy." I wanted to feel like I felt helping her track down the pastry aroma.

"Something's still bothering you."

"Why didn't we have children?"

"We agreed. Neither of us wanted the responsibility." She got up.

"We had a lot of work to do on the house. We were sharing a piece of car that broke down once a month."

"Well, there you go." She began taking out clothes for work.

"I wanted to establish myself first. I didn't want to bring a child into the world I couldn't take care of. We could barely take care of ourselves."

"If we had wanted a child we could've found a way. People who had a lot less than us have been finding a way since time began." She swung a skirt and jacket toward me, shook her head, hung it back up, took out another and slung it across the rocking chair.

"Money isn't an issue now."

"Money hasn't been an issue for a long time."

"Stay home with me today."

"It's Memorial Day this weekend. We'll go down to the timeshare, just the two of us."

"It always comes back to the timeshare."

"You feel better after we spend a few days sailing, hiking your volcano trails, and touring those old Jamaican ruins. How does that sound?"

My wife was pretending things were back to the way they were supposed to be and she wanted me to pretend with her. As she walked down the hallway toward the bathroom, I went to the dresser. Lillian sang Phyllis Hyman's version of "Betcha By Golly Wow." I sorted through faded receipts and dog-eared photocopies of tax returns. The shower came on. I thumbed past pictures of us on our honeymoon, birthday, anniversary cards, a hairbrush that belonged to my father.

Lillian sang. I moved on to the deed to our house and insurance policies. The revolver Ted Simmons gave me lay in its leather case on top of a neatly folded towel. The chrome-plated handle fit well inside my grip. Lillian's voice continued to fill the house. I closed my eyes. The first thing I'd noticed about Lillian was her voice:

> . . . *Write your name across the sky*
> *Anything you have to try . . .*

I was supposed to be too proud, too strong, have too much going for myself to be thinking like this. I wasn't angry or scared. In the back of mind I knew I was overreacting. This didn't make sense. It gave me goose pimples. So this is what it felt like to make my own rules.

"Adam?" The shower had stopped. Lillian's footsteps were in the hallway.

All those years of playing by other people's rules.

"Adam?"

The phone rang electric needles through me. I dropped the revolver.

"Adam?" Lillian was almost outside the door. She didn't deserve this. I used my foot to slide the gun under our bed. The phone was on her nightstand. I reached for it with fingers still stinging from that first ring.

"What was that sound?" She was looking at the mess of papers and pictures on the dresser.

"It's Ted Simmons." I covered the receiver. Headquarters was acting quickly if they were going to offer me Miriam's position before her promotion was officially announced.

"Adam?"

"I was talking to Lillian." I was getting ahead of myself. Ted wouldn't offer me the position over the phone. First he would want to gauge my interest, then set up an interview with the board of directors.

"I hate to be the bearer of bad news," he said, and I knew Miriam's position was going to someone else.

"Who did you name?"

"Name for what?" Ted asked.

"Miriam told me she accepted a job at HQ. She also told me she was recommending me to succeed her here." I felt Lillian's arm around me.

"I wish I could have brought you into the loop sooner. Maybe this could've been avoided. We could've gotten your help."

"What happened?" I was looking at my wife, touching her cheek. She squeezed my hand and mouthed *I love you* with such sincerity I wondered how I ever doubted her.

"You're the only executive who didn't complain about her. From what I understand that's more a testament to your resolve than her behavior."

"Someone filed a lawsuit?" In spite of our differences Miriam was a woman of her word. I didn't like her methods, but she got things done that I doubted I could have, things Ted didn't when he ran the office.

"All of that was resolved before she resigned." Ted sighed. In my mind, I could see his trademark, wide, gold-framed lenses, deep lines creasing his ruddy complexion, his free hand mopping through his snow-white hair, like I'd watched him do in other crises. But I'd never heard his voice this heavy. "Adam, Miriam was in an automobile accident. She didn't survive."

"Miriam was in an accident," I told Lillian. "She didn't make it."

"Oh my god. Was anyone else hurt?"

I asked Ted, but I already knew. Miriam had been alone, the road scenic, the crash spectacular.

Rafael Reyna
Ecrasez l'infame

Waldman sat beside the podium. She looked at me, a smiling diamond or hummingbird turned-on. But she soon looked to forget me (the face in the crowd), the nail in a porch board. And it wasn't easy sitting straight.

At the Political Action conference Waldman was a pro-life bitch. Center City in Philly, Monday.

Brunette—a sixty-year-old Naropa baby. Worn and battle-ripped, rubbings of a thousand years, she was a namesake of a renamed twin. She wore a red shoe divorced from heel, danced it up and down on folded leg. Nail polish green, silken-balloon shirt, she was kitten restless, tigress in heat, ready to spring beneath a literary fog light. I considered shouting her name.

"Waldman, you're beautiful!"

Naturally, I didn't. With Rip Van Winkle dead, you can only hold your elbows and be quiet and wait in the hole. This be the new age of robotic jock-straps, this be the age of electronic Abu Ghraibs—Had I yelled that to Waldman? One can only imagine somebody coughing and the world in a Jersey storm of stultification.

Around me sat the orchard lawn scholars, some college furies and, of course, the gift: Waldman, cringing and disheartened . . .

When she finally got up to talk politics at the podium it was 4 p.m. in Conference Hall. As she stood, she swung a bell ringing. "Dick Cheney has not served! John Ashcroft has not served!" And she spat things like, *ecrasez l'infame!* and *hasta la victoria siempre!* And the Che washouts stamped their flags, cheering. She balled her fists and rumbled sink water, her throat milky as clam chowder skins—she was dead! and dying! for all those Tenderloin Marxists and dirt-mound Indians.

And then she gave a slide show named after an Italian quack-show artist named Gustavo Bandini. She recited a poem while chiaroscuro colors changed on the walls and that hotshot director flapped his wings. The idea was that Philly was to vote, that we were to oust the Tyrant and turn the city green again.

That night I scoffed over my last cup of coffee and thought about Waldman getting us hot to vote and how she believed the WOOOO WOOOO really meant something. I looked at Waldman's army of pins with tanks upside down. They were so happy to be doing what they were doing, but somehow pitiable, sad actors, sad elephants in the circus game, so sad in fact that even the bums looked at them funny, as if to say, "Where's the picnic?" The crackies rolled their heads in the penumbra, blanketed with felonies and recalling that in the Third World, when soup goes bad, the men throw stones at the Gods.

That following day of November 7th I never made it to the polls. Pissed and full of American muscle, I swore never to go—I was debilitated and inept. Mornings like those I was more apt to shit bricks and lay against stonewalls with the shades down—the sun shone and it was a day like any other. It was not in my character to vote for lesser Tyrants, to pick the lesser evil, my own draft, my own patriot act of arrest. So I did not vote, and as I said before, I was inept.

There was a flyer around town about Waldman speaking again in Center City. This was Election Day and she wanted all the blacks to vote. She wanted all the white suburban ticketeers chanting the Om litanies in the hood. I could only imagine her, door to door with lollipops, gritting her teeth . . .

That night she stood in Love Park shouting with a megaphone. She said the Bowery in the sixties was only the beginning. And she said surely that the Evil Empire would end, and that her mission here had been accomplished. The bush was in flames and the flames said to us, *ecrasez l'infame* and Philly would turn green again.

And we all awaited the Verdict on that very regular evening. A bearded college boy stooped by a television in his white van. The whole crowd bent on toes, asses squeezed shut, silently cheering but not quite yet. Waldman was to give the victory signal. But as soon as that college boy whispered the Verdict in her ear, she dropped the megaphone and held her face.

I laughed mightily and damnably.

A French expatriate lady next to me squawked. "How can you laugh? How can you laugh at a time like this?" And I felt guilty. She told me she was an artist. She specialized in going across the Midwest putting up rainbow propaganda and studying which rednecks tore her signs down. "This is the end. He will not fund the program. I am done for." She wept like we were all gone-bad Chinese hamsters and she, in particular, was dying.

I walked to SEPTA in the dark with Penn's statue above me, a reaching stone god in a city of ill-begotten stones. I had the ANSWER pamphlets in my hand, pieces of paper that would end up glass mats on old furniture. As I walked around lit-up City Hall, I recognized Waldman. She sat on the curb alone with chin in hand, around her the wind blowing up misused propaganda. I mustered the courage to say hello. She looked up at me, pissed, a tired crazy creature in the corner. She was still gorgeous, one of the most attractive women I had ever seen, sixty with lizard lips that belong on the edge of boxed wines.

"Can I help you?"

That grey voice—she wanted alone with her dust and stones, and I was an intruder, suddenly feeling sulfurous as a tick rooting in her veins. But I saw the Howl in her eyes. Look at Waldman—a yellowed creature on the edge of the dark and curbed with winos and tapeworms, a broken heel beneath the king of kings—the poet's poet. *She* was *dying*! I had to say it— I knew if I didn't, I too would have shot myself in the bathtub.

"Waldman, you're beautiful."

She looked at me like I was crazy. I expected it. She switched crossed legs and shook her head—stared me down like I the dogshit and she the heavenly mothball beneath the mattress.

"Meet me tomorrow at 5:30, Sixteenth and Fairmount. We'll need a chickenshit like you."

She spoke and grimaced with that deep caramel rumbling. I smiled, fool that I was, and thanked her. She nodded and must have squinted holes in my back. That was the beginning of the Revolution and it couldn't come too fast for me.

C. Natale Peditto
The Veterans

On the television above the bar, World War II was remembered with comic relief: a clownish company of G. I. Joes and Janes hoarding cigarettes in foxholes, blowing the faceless enemy to kingdom come. All the while the jukebox played loudly over the sound of the TV in the Russian-American social club. It was a late August Sunday in Philadelphia, and the dwarfed ailanthus tree beyond the back window by the pool table, where the sun's glow settled against the barrier of iron bars, reminded one of a jungle tree. Nothing but brick wall and rubble outside. You could have fantasized tropical Pacific jungles, or the sweltering devastation of Midway Island or Guadalcanal.

Kaminski sat half drunk behind the pool players. When it was his turn to shoot, he lifted his stick like a lance as he kicked back the shaky wooden chair and stepped to the table. He wasn't looking at anyone. Kaminski had once fought in the ring. He still retained a sense of the theatrical. The young men looked at him with amusement while the older men sipped their beers at scattered tables along the empty dance floor, emitting long spiraling cigarette smoke signals in the heated vacuum of the hall. A shaft of sunlight suddenly breached the shade and solitude of the bar, illuminating the long room. Kaminski shot sloppily and his eight ball dribbled into the corner pocket followed by the cue ball.

"Aaah, you fuckup," Kaminski's road buddy, O'Hara, cried from behind.

Kaminski walked the long way around the pool table, to the table where O'Hara sat next to his nickels and dimes and the short full glass of port wine that Kaminski had bought for him.

"Shut up and drink your wine," Kaminski ordered.

O'Hara was quiet and hesitant, like a little brother. A small wiry man in his early sixties who coughed and wheezed, O'Hara worked the freighters as a seaman when he was fit and able. Lately someone had promised him a job, and he was always sad when there was a prospect of shipping out.

"Whatsa matter?" Kaminski said, hovering like a bear over O'Hara, "Don't you like your wine? It's good wine. Hey, bartender, ain't this the best wine in the house?" The bartender, a recent immigrant from Ukraine who spoke six languages but was often ignorant of the inbred subtleties of most of them, was usually anxious to please. This time he shrugged his shoulders and looked for an ashtray to empty. O'Hara sipped the wine to please Kaminski.

Kaminski enjoyed intimidating people, though no one really took him seriously. His fluid eyes revealed a gentler soul. Years ago, he had chosen to camouflage his broken fighter's face with a full length of dirty gray whiskers, a Santa Claus beard that cascaded along his downy-haired barrel chest.

The banter around the pool table would rise to shouting and recede to subdued, bibulous invective following each rotation. The TV was audible now, but no one paid much attention to the movie. There was normally an air of surrendered expectation about the place. All this aside, today was different. For some reason, the juices of life were flowing through Kaminski, engendering desire with hope.

"Hey, O'Hara," Kaminski nudged his companion. O'Hara smiled sanguinely. "Whadya say we go back to my place and give the old wifeski a pop? She needs at least three or four jumps a day. Or do you want my sister? She gives good head."

O'Hara played Kaminski's game. "Your wife gives better head."

"I'll let you for fifteen dollars," Kaminski offered.

"Fuck you," O'Hara countered. "She'll do me for free. She told me you can't get it up anymore."

"Oh yeah," Kaminski continued. "You should've heard her this morning screaming for me to stop."

"You mean she was screaming for you to get it up!" O'Hara scored.

"Oh shit," Kaminski bluffed. He had neither a wife nor a sister. One of the younger men thought that Kaminski was disgusting and told him so. Kaminski ignored the kid. Kids were heartless. Kaminski chuckled and pulled closer to O'Hara's ear, breathing a wino's whisper. "Hey, I have something I want to show you in the men's room."

"Whaddya talking about, dirty pictures?"

"No. No." Kaminski looked self-satisfied and complacent as though his secret gave him the day's edge. O'Hara just wanted to sip his wine quietly, mesmerized by the movement of the billiard balls.

"Alright, you don't have to go into the john with me."

Kaminski confidently slipped a small aerosol can from his pocket. It resembled a can of cologne spray. He held it in front of O'Hara's face and waited for his friend's response.

O'Hara was puzzled by the label. It read INSTANT STUD.

"It's for your joint, stupid," Kaminski declared. "Spray this stuff on your prick and you can screw for hours at a time."

O'Hara was unconvinced. "How much did it cost you?"

"Nineteen ninety-five," Kaminski responded.

"Nineteen ninety-five! Did you get a guarantee with it?"

"What guarantee?" Kaminski studied the can with the seriousness and concern of a mother eagle.

"Never mind," O'Hara allowed.

"It's worth a try, ain't it? You tell me the last time you had some vigor in your trigger."

"Leave me alone, Kaminski."

"Come on. Are you coming with me or not?"

"Where?"

"To the American Legion hall. They got broads over there."

"Nah."

"Come on," Kaminski implored. O'Hara finally agreed to go along, only after Kaminski had bought a few more rounds. They had to help each other out the door of the club.

Kaminski owned an old Cadillac Sedan de Ville, which he drove no faster than thirty-five miles per hour, laughing all the way to the Legion post about his intentions. Just as Kaminski had promised, there were women hanging out at the bar. Most of them were in their late sixties and older, with hardened faces and adipose arms, shameless drinkers who were not to be messed with. All the men in the place were working stiffs who had come to watch the Phillies game and tie one on. Now that the game had ended, those who remained sat stone faced and apathetic over their beers. The women sat in a boisterous clique at one corner of the bar. There was Rosie, a large, heavy-breasted woman; the Hagstrom twins, a former women's pro-wrestling tag team; as well as a few other tough-looking females. Kaminski and O'Hara walked over to the corner, pulling stools by the women.

Kaminski tugged on his beard, his eyes scanning the women. They knew Kaminski well and enjoyed mocking him. "If it ain't Kaminski," one of them called. "Hey, girls, Father Christmas is here. And he brought one of his little elves with him, too. Did you bring us any toys, Father Christmas?"

"We got something for you alright," Kaminski snickered. He elbowed O'Hara, who hung at the bar with a half-conscious smile faintly lighting his besotted face, trying to accommodate his companion.

"What'd you bring us?" Rosie asked.

"I could use a new husband," one of the Hagstrom twins joined in. "Mine doesn't work anymore."

Kaminski said, "Forget your old man. Which one of you wants a date with a fabulous lover?"

"Me," one of them answered. "Who you got in mind?"

"You're looking at him. I've come to give you the thrill of a lifetime."

The group of women exploded into a simultaneous chorus of *whoooa!* followed by an earthquake of laughter. Kaminski had lost one round. He sat next to his silent friend, trying to summon a new strategy while the women continued their harassment. It was no holds barred. As far as they were concerned, Kaminski had invited their abuse.

"Takes more than a bowl of Wheaties, Kaminski. What were you reading today?—one of those magazines? He probably seen too much. Opened up all those old possibilities for him." More laughter and more insults. "Maybe your friend there can hold it up for you while you're doing it." They all laughed again while Kaminski remained silent. He bore it all with a leaden smile. Finally the women cooled and went back to their own conversation.

"A lotta help you are," Kaminski said, jabbing at O'Hara.

O'Hara was silent. Then he told Kaminski that he had to leave. "I'm supposed to be on the ship tonight. It's sailing. Can you drive me down to the Tioga pier?"

"Just hold on. I'll get you there. Just give me a few more minutes. Old Rosie's alright. I'll catch her when she comes back from the toilet."

"You ain't got a chance, Kaminski. You must be crazy tonight."

"It's a hot night, and I want to try this stuff out. All I have to do is show it to her. These dames ain't had anything hard between their legs since the Japs bombed Pearl Harbor." Kaminski laughed. "They dream of torpedoes every night and wake up sweatin'."

Kaminski waited for Rosie to return from the restroom and stopped her on her way back to the bar. Kaminski reached for her wrist, but she avoided his hand. "What do you want, killer?"

Kaminski poured it on. "Just a little of your time. You know I'm always thinking of you."

"Sweet talk," Rosie smiled. "I like you too, Kaminski. Now can I go back and join my friends?"

"I thought you'd like to take a ride. I have to take my buddy down to his ship in Port Richmond. Why don't you come along?"

"I don't think so. Some other time." Rosie was already walking.

"Aw, come on. It's a nice night for a drive."

By this time, Rosie had returned to the bar and her friends. Kaminski realized these women were unconquerable as a cadre; but Rosie hesitated a moment and said she'd join him.

"You're not going with that bum!" the older of the Hagstrom twins interrupted.

"Mind your own damn business," Kaminski told her. The Hagstrom twin got off her stool to fight. Rosie placated everybody. Kaminski knew he had scored when Rosie told the girls that she needed some fresh air and that Kaminski had promised to bring all of them a bucket of fried chicken from Colonel Sanders. Kaminski didn't mind about the chicken—everything had its price, even Rosie and the Hagstrom twins; besides, if things worked out as he hoped, he wouldn't bring Rosie back to the Legion hall. The twins warned them not to eat all the chicken before they returned.

The threesome picked up O'Hara's gear at his rooming house, then headed down to the waterfront in Kaminski's Cadillac. Kaminski unstashed a bottle of wine from beneath the front seat, and they passed it amongst themselves, toasting O'Hara's bon voyage. Rosie sang, and O'Hara drifted off in half sleep.

"Like a little baby, ain't he?" Rosie commented.

"Yep," Kaminski agreed.

O'Hara dozed, his head resting on his sea bag clutched in his lap. He gave the impression of someone who might be going on his last voyage.

"Now why can't you be more like him?" Rosie asked. "He's really a gentle soul. And you go dragging this poor fella around, acting like a fool, and he has to put up with all your crap."

Kaminski cast a meaningful eye at Rosie who sang on dreamily. Either she was lost in her own reverie, or she was ignoring his intentions completely. Kaminski handed her the bottle of wine again. They finally delivered O'Hara to the gate of the pier. They watched him stumble up the gangplank and waited for him to give them the high sign that he was aboard. When O'Hara waved for them to leave, Rosie let go a slobbering outpouring of grief.

"It makes me so sad. Just like the old days. Like seeing the boys off. Ah, we used to sing 'I'll be Seeing You,' as the bombs burst overhead."

What a cornball old hag, Kaminski thought. "Whata y'know about bombs? We burst our eardrums," Kaminski declared. "Migraines. O'Hara wears a steel plate."

Rosie was weeping. "Oh, Kaminski, I'm really sorry. But you don't know. I lost a boyfriend in that war."

"Life is for the livers," Kaminski admonished her with a cavalier gesture. "We're bound for my place. We can bury old memories."

Rosie didn't give Kaminski an argument. At least, not until they were in Kaminski's room and seated on the bed with the wine between them. Kaminski put his arm around Rosie's shoulder, and Rosie sighed, "It's no good."

"Whatsa matter, Rosie? Don't you want a little lovin'?"

"You're something, Kaminski. Carrying on, like you're some kind of stud, the way you did at the Legion hall. What makes you think you're the answer to every woman's dreams, huh?"

"Well, you left with me, didn't you? I thought you wanted to be with me tonight."

"You mean you thought I wanted to get laid? Maybe I just wanted to spend a little time with you. You ever think of that, like being friends or pals?"

"Yeah, well, I'm a lover, too."

"I don't doubt it, Kaminski. But going to bed with a man ain't something I do at the drop of a hat."

"Well, when was the last time?"

"I don't remember."

"Come on, *cheri*," Kaminski whispered, rubbing Rosie's shoulder.

"We're too old anymore. That's just it—we're too old." Rosie reached for the bottle they were sharing, and took a sip of wine.

"Aw, come on. I got something to show you." Kaminski pulled out the can of Instant Stud. He placed it on the rug in front of them. It stood sentinel.

"What's that supposed to do?"

"Exactly what it says."

Rosie fell backwards. Her laughter shook the bed. "You must be sick, Kaminski. That's what they call a novelty item. You've been rooked."

Now she was laughing and crying at the same time.

"Novelty item, huh?" Kaminski murmured disappointedly. "Did you ever try it?"

"Nope. You know you amaze me, Kaminski. The older you get the harder you try. You'll probably kill yourself trying."

"Well, it would have been a novelty any way you looked at it." They were both laughing now, Kaminski rolling over onto Rosie.

"For old time's sake?" Kaminski pleaded.

Rosie shook her head and groaned in near exasperation. "Well, okay, for old time's sake," she agreed. "But promise me one thing."

"What's that?" Kaminski asked. He could already feel an old urge gradually repeating its connections inside him.

"Promise me we don't take off our clothes."

Kaminski was baffled. "Well, how the hell are we supposed to do it?"

Rosie continued to laugh, lying on her back, Kaminski atop her, bathing him tenderly through her dress in mounds of blushing flesh. "Carefully, my love." Speaking softly, in short fluttering breaths, she told Kaminski, "Carefully. . . . "

B.J. Burton
Alexandra in the Middle of the Night

It was late Friday night, or early Saturday morning. Alexandra shut the door of the bathroom, locking herself in. Through the small frosted window at her right she could see the hazy glow of the streetlight at the corner of Sixteenth and Pine. She flipped the light on. The neon bulb flickered unexpectedly, making eerie flashes in the mirror. Her hands gripped the edge of the sink as if it were falling from its foundation. But it wasn't. Alexandra was holding on.

She'd had chocolate and caffeine after four p.m. that day. It was amazing, she thought, after spending most of her twenties and her early thirties drinking up to twelve cups of black coffee a day, now at forty-two, half a cup of green tea from Wawa and three half-melted Hershey's Kisses from her pocket at 4:15 in the afternoon were keeping her awake.

Except that wasn't true. Alexandra knew exactly why she couldn't sleep. It was what he said, *what he said* (was it minutes ago?), that made her bolt out of her soft bed as if stung by a yellow jacket.

Alexandra puffed her warm breath onto the mirror over the sink, making a little cloud of vapor, then drew a little heart with her finger into it, then a big "X" through it, then finally smudged it out altogether. Reflected in the mirror was a face she didn't recognize. Half asleep, she felt wounded from the jagged edges of an interrupted dream.

A blue silk nightgown hung inside out on the back of the bathroom door. One small rip on the right side underneath the arm was a reminder of a first night's passion with a new man. The nightgown was three years old. The man was sleeping in her bed.

Alexandra unloosened her grip on the sink, took off his overly starched white shirt that she had quickly thrown over her shoulders, let it fall into a rumpled pile on the floor, and opened the medicine cabinet.

"Let's see. Cotton balls, Tylenol, Advil—Why am I keeping Advil when it gave me a forty-five minute nosebleed the first time I used it?—Bactine, Neosporin, toothpicks, razors, Band-Aids, old Ativan, big scissors, little scissors."

She brought the big scissors up to her shoulder-length auburn hair.

"Maybe I'll give myself a little trim . . . "

The big scissors with the orange handles had been in her possession since a college roommate from Lancaster County gave them to her when she was learning how to sew. "Sewing?" she reminisced. "What was I thinking?" She remembered actually making some sort of peasant dress, an apron (*an apron?*), and some curtains out of pink paisley bed sheets one summer. "Hmm . . . " she thought, "bed sheets . . . "

Alexandra imagined strolling calmly across the hardwood floor in the hallway and onto the multicolored braided rug in her bedroom to where the man was sleeping. She imagined trimming just a little section off his brown bristly mustache, taking a quarter-inch or more off the back of his wavy, almost-curly hair.

Alexandra once read in a self-help book that if a man hurts you more than three times it's time to move on. She remembered that the author (a woman, of course) was recently divorced and remarried, and was relating her experiences to other women so they wouldn't hurl themselves headfirst and unknowingly into similarly unpleasant circumstances. Alexandra feared— believed—that she had done exactly that.

Alexandra had just finished a year-long round of therapy with Dr. Dolores. Many of their sessions had focused on Alexandra's turbulent childhood, no matter how often Dr. D. gently suggested to her that it would be more beneficial to focus on the present.

An episode she remembered in fierce detail involved a Crosby, Stills, Nash and Young album, given to her on her sixteenth birthday by her best friend, Lee Ann. As Alexandra was stepping out of her father's Ford Country Squire station wagon one day after school, the album slipped out of her book bag and fell onto the concrete garage floor, just as the electric garage door was closing. Alexandra started screaming, which for some reason caused her father to start pushing the buttons on the remote. The garage door went up and down, up and down several times on top of the album, leaving it shattered. When she first described this event to Dr. D., Alexandra was inclined to agree with her therapist that her own perceptions were wrong, and this was indeed an accident—the result of a malfunctioning garage door. However, in succeeding sessions, and after considering alternative angles and possibilities, Alexandra came to the conclusion that her perceptions were right in the first place, that this was indeed a deliberate, malicious act. She came to that conclusion because of one thing—her father's reaction afterwards. She remembered her father casually glancing at the black pieces of vinyl shining in the sunlight. "Oops," he said. "Sorry." And with a broad smile, not even looking back at the chards of broken plastic, or at Alexandra, he strolled happily into the house carrying his briefcase. Alexandra imagined herself flicking a lighted match into his Ford Country Squire station wagon, setting it on fire. "Oops," she thought to herself. "Sorry."

An interior designer by profession, Max—the man in her bed—was adept at deception. He had achieved success turning ordinary office spaces into dazzling displays of opulence that disguised the true nature of their occupants: an insurance company looked like a restaurant, a clothing store looked like a movie theater, a doctor's office looked like a hotel. Max said he had learned to use his imagination to the fullest. But to Alexandra, this seemed more like just plain lying.

Whenever Alexandra described the end of her short-lived marriage, Dr. D. told her, "A man like that is not going to make you happy." Nathan—the "man like that"—pursued other women throughout his engagement and marriage to Alexandra, but she didn't see it at the time. It was only after Nathan had too many late nights at work and too many dental conventions in Las Vegas that she began to suspect something. When he finally confessed to her that there had been many, many, many women, Alexandra fell deep into the abyss. Her therapist was right. Nathan had not made her happy.

Alexandra thought she had learned something from all that—that now, if a similar situation presented itself, she would see some warning signal, a red flag of recognition that would propel her to, as the author of the self-help book said, "Run, girl, in the opposite direction, as fast as you can!"

So it happened that Alexandra found herself holding the bathroom sink in the middle of the night. This man, Max, the one sleeping in her bed, had now hurt her four times.

After her divorce, Alexandra made a promise to herself to focus on her life and finish her architecture degree at Temple. She wanted to know how to create things that would be real, functional, and lasting. She planned to do this while working full-time as a receptionist in the architectural department at Day and Zimmermann.

One early spring evening three years ago, Alexandra was studying some exterior Corinthian columns at the Art Museum when Max showed up at a Young Friends of the Endangered Azaleas fundraiser held at the museum on the same night. Alexandra, in T-shirt and jeans, was sketching the details of the capital when a man with a mustache and wavy, almost-curly hair, wearing a tux and carrying an empty wine glass and a crumpled paper cocktail napkin approached her and complimented her drawing.

115

His presence startled her. She pressed her black Conté crayon hard into the paper. The end cracked off, popping like a pebble into his empty glass.

As he handed her the piece of black crayon, his steel blue-gray eyes beamed into her. "You're an artist?" he asked. "We're related! I'm an interior designer."

Soon they were walking along the slate trail, discussing their likes, loves, and passions under a canopy of shedding spruces and pollinating pines. Max weaved it into their first conversation how miserable and alone he felt in grade school, being the only one in the class with an "x" in his name. Alexandra had felt the same way.

"I hated being called Maxfield."

"Oh, me, too! I mean, I hated being called Alexandra."

"Kids used to tease me. 'Hey, Max, how's your field?' I hated it."

"Me, too! Kids used to call me Alexandra Graham Bell."

On subsequent evenings, they spoke intensely—about feelings of isolation after the breakup of their marriages, about the benefits of the no- versus low-carb diet, and about the plight of endangered plants and animals everywhere. Max was saving the temperate rainforest of British Columbia; he was saving the endangered orange-bellied parakeet of Australia; he was saving the rare plumleaf azalea of the southern United States. And Alexandra thought he was saving her.

And so, with their shared experiences, especially of being picked on because of the distinction of having an "x" in their names, Maxfield and Alexandra forged a friendship.

Alexandra told Max all about Nathan and about not wanting to be involved because she was still reeling from the divorce. But Max pushed in the gentlest of ways. He spoke to her in whispers, in a kind and sympathetic voice that made her believe him and believe in him.

Gazing into the bathroom mirror, Alexandra focused on her mouth. It was still red from kissing him, before he told her his latest bit of news.

Yes, she acknowledged it. He had now hurt her for the fourth time.

She unlocked the bathroom door and peeked out. She heard his rhythmic breathing in the next room. She remembered how she left him. He was rolled up in the covers, taking up more space in her bed than he deserved.

"He has the kindest eyes," Alexandra told Lee Ann.

But, Lee Ann warned her, "I'd tread cautiously if I were you."

Marie said, "He's gorgeous. You go with it, girl!"

And Sally, always the pessimist, said something like, "Get out of this as soon as possible. I can't even tell you why."

Sally had exceptional sixth-sense abilities. She once called Alexandra at two a.m. to tell her to check the toaster oven after she had a dream about burning cinnamon toast. Alexandra had, it turned out, left the toaster oven on. It wasn't cinnamon toast, but a blueberry bagel that burned to a crisp and almost set the apartment on fire. The smoke alarm, with battery intact, never went off.

Alarms in Alexandra's head should've been going off, but they weren't.

"A man like that is not going to make you happy." But that was a man like Nathan and this was Max. He seemed so different.

Wads of wet, crumpled Kleenex lay on the floor, having missed their intended goal of the trash can. It looked like a small snowfall had fallen in Alexandra's bathroom, but it was more like a storm—a January blizzard raging with all its intensity inside her heart and inside her head.

Four times.

The first time was when she and Max had taken a trip to Atlantic City. Hot, sticky city summer days were replaced by a luxurious weekend at the Borgata, complete with complimentary champagne and a concert featuring Patti LaBelle. On the way home, they stopped at the Thirty-Forth Street 7-Eleven in Ocean City. Alexandra bought a 32-ounce Big Gulp and finished it before getting back into Max's black Lexus sedan.

When they arrived at the Egg Harbor Toll Plaza, Alexandra politely requested that they stop at the next gas station. As they approached the only decent rest stop on the Atlantic City Expressway, Max floored it, saying he wanted to beat the weekend traffic back to the city. It was when they were halfway through the Pine Barrens that Alexandra, now in agony, threatened to relieve herself on Max's climate-controlled, reclining leather seat with the built-in massager if he didn't pull over. Max finally stopped. In an effort to gain some degree of privacy, Alexandra fled deep into the woods, lest any glimpse of her be seen by westbound traffic. When she tried to return to the car, she found herself surrounded on all sides by dagger-like thickets and deep brush. She started yelling for Max, who, after about fifteen minutes, came to her rescue. In the meantime, she had trudged through the worst kind of poison ivy imaginable. Her throat started closing up, and she and Max soon found themselves in the emergency room at Jefferson. Max turned into a raging stranger. He yelled angrily at Alexandra for causing him to lose his good drive-time record, causing her throat to close up even more. He became so exasperated that, after spending the night in the hospital, Alexandra felt safer taking a cab home the next day. She missed a week and a half of work, and still Max was angry at her. And although he was knee-deep in the same woods, Max never got a drop of poison ivy.

The second time was when Alexandra came down with a strange stomach ache the weekend she and Max had planned a trip to the Arizona desert to see the blooming spring flowers. It was Alexandra—too sick to travel—

who insisted that Max ask his old college roommate, Joe, to accompany him. Alexandra's stomach ache soon revealed itself to be smoldering appendicitis. She was alone and upset during her emergency surgery and during the next two weeks while Max and Joe were "lost" in the desert.

The third time was when Alexandra found out that Joe was not Joseph but JoAnne.

But Alexandra decided to go against the advice of her latest self-help book and, as she would call it, "give him the benefit of the doubt."

"It's just like camping with your cousin or your sister," Max explained. "We're friends, that's all."

Except he had never mentioned that Joe was a woman. Alexandra found out herself when a receipt from the Walgreens in Flagstaff fell out of Max's windbreaker, listing not only a pack of Energizer batteries and Coppertone 30 sunblock, but Ph-balanced Secret deodorant and a box of Tampax.

Three times should tell you something. Four times is your heaviest iron frying pan whacking you on the backside of your head. Four times, and all your best girlfriends should have an intervention with you if you don't fix things.

The fourth time was tonight—just after Max had kissed Alexandra goodnight as they were fading with unfinished sentences toward dreamland. Max started telling her not about how great she looked, not about the fabulous beef stroganoff that she had cooked for dinner, not about the wonderful book on endangered azaleas she had given him for his birthday, but all about a new woman who had joined his interior design firm—that they had been spending long lunches together, and that he thought they'd end up being very close, because she—like Joe—enjoyed spring desert flowers blooming in Arizona, and she wasn't prone—like some people—to getting things like poison ivy and appendicitis. And, he thought, he should probably tell Alexandra that he and Elizabeth (oh, yes, Elizabeth had a "z" in her name and always felt self-conscious about that, too), having just traveled all day back from a design conference in Montreal, had to spend the night together in one room at the Sheraton because all the hotels in Albany were booked solid.

At the end of his very long monologue, Max turned suddenly, accidentally knocking Alexandra solidly in the temple. She shrieked with surprise more than pain, jumped up, and ran into the bathroom, locking the door behind her. It was as she was closing the bathroom door that she heard Max yell to her, "Oops! Sorry."

Alexandra realized she had been in the bathroom for quite some time now. This was her place, and what had just happened had no business happening to her in her own apartment. She slipped her old, torn nightgown over her head and leaned toward the mirror. Alexandra gazed into her eyes and noticed the tiny flecks of gold in her brown pupils. She studied the blond highlights in the auburn hair that swept boldly across her forehead. She observed her high cheekbones, recently revealed after she shed eight pounds on the South Beach Diet. She saw a person who was strong enough to leave a cheating husband without money and without a job, a person who was strong enough to put herself through college even when her father kept telling her she wasn't smart enough, a person who was strong enough to express to the man sleeping in her bed exactly how she felt.

Alexandra splashed water on her face, removing all evidence of tears. She grabbed a fistful of hair with one hand and the scissors with the orange handles in the other. Taking a deep breath, she closed her eyes, then stopped.

Alexandra imagined this: unlocking the bathroom door, the neon light flickering then going out altogether, feeling her way along in the darkness, stepping across the hardwood floor toward the bedroom, tripping on the braided rug, the scissors flying directly at Max sleeping soundly in the middle of the bed. She heard herself say, as the silver blades flashed in the air, "Oops. Sorry."

It was probably close to five a.m. now. Alexandra opened the medicine cabinet again. She grabbed the old bottle of Ativan, popped the little white pill in her mouth, and turned on the faucet. Making a cup with her hands for the water, she swallowed the pill. The edges of her hair were wet now. She tucked the damp strands behind her ear.

She unlocked the bathroom door. Keeping the neon light on, she closed the door slightly behind her, leaving a sliver of light to guide her way back to the bedroom. She stepped into the dark hallway. Walking slowly in bare feet across the hardwood floor, she reached the bedroom doorway. A dark gray predawn haze filtered through the shade. Max shifted in the sheets; his rough, unshaven chin was facing her, his breathing was heavy and deep. She leaned over him, her long auburn hair lightly stroking his neck. A bead of water cascaded from the corner of her eye down over the side of her face and landed on his shoulder. She kissed his cheek and gripped his tanned forearm; polished nails pressed into his skin. Morning traffic was just beginning to build as she held the scissors behind her back.

Josh McIlvain
Health Insurance and the Girl

O ne day, on my way to the train station, a pretty girl in light blue scrubs popped out of Jefferson Hospital and I thought, I need her for a girlfriend.

Her blond hair was in a bun and her neck was suntanned, her face was healthy and bright. She had a faint smile as if amusing herself with a private joke. Her blue eyes glanced at me as I walked by. They were friendly and inviting, matching the color of her scrubs. Girls in scrubs have always turned me on. Scrubs have the cozy accessibility of pajamas mixed with the fetish of professionalism. And despite being designed for uniformity and drabness, scrubs accentuate a woman's body, clinging to her with the slightest movement. Even small breasts lift scrub shirts off bellies, forming a tent for your head.

Walking down 10th Street toward the train station, I was careful not to go too fast and lose track of her. With the help of large reflective first-floor windows, I kept an eye on her trailing behind me. I slowed at intersections so that we waited together for the lights to change. By the time we were a block from the station, I was sure she was destined for it too. I opened the large glass door just as she was coming up and held it for her. She smiled, mouthed "Thank you," and trotted down the steps. I followed her to my train platform.

The R3 to West Trenton train pulled up. "No, no," I whispered as she leaned toward it. "Yes, yes," I continued as she stepped away when the doors opened, knowing I could never afford dating someone in Bucks County. Three minutes later, my train pulled up and she stepped aboard the car down from me. She's an R7 girl! I took a seat, forcing down thoughts of my hands on her naked body. I was too excited to make an approach, especially if it required stumbling to the back of the train. I had to plan the seduction rationally. Should I quit my job or ask her out first?

For the past two years, I had been dreaming of spending a year making a record of my songs before I turned gray. If I picked up a part-time coffee shop job and used all my savings, I'd have about fifteen grand for the year—enough to squeak by. The majority of my time would be spent writing songs, playing guitar and recording a CD on my low-tech equipment.

Standing in the way of my dream, however, was the sentinel of health insurance. I could not afford not having it and I could not afford paying for it on my own. Though I had used it only three times in five years, health insurance was a security blanket my thirty-five year old body dared not live without. And health insurance plus rent equaled a thousand dollars a month, which would leave me with three thousand for the whole year for all other expenses. $8.22 a day would not cover phone, electric, student loan (yes, still), credit card, and food bills.

But the sentinel had just been waved aside. The one hundred thousand pound boulder had proved a dry leaf, picked up by the slightest breeze and blown away. This girl was the perfect solution to my health insurance dilemma. She would fulfill my medical needs and a sexual fantasy to boot.

The solution seemed so obvious that I was surprised I hadn't thought of it before. My ex-girlfriend's sister had been an intern. Whenever my ex left the room she would stare longingly at me, slip a finger in her mouth and refuse conversation, shaking her head naughtily whenever I spoke, especially if I spoke about the weather. She was good at computers and was always quick to help, help that included putting her perfumed breasts two inches from my nose while she leaned over and commandeered the keyboard as my less technologically advanced girlfriend stood behind her.

Also, the intern who was the roommate of a girl I sang with. I'd go over with my guitar and chit-chat with my singer friend and her roommate—short, skinny, flat chested, with dark hair and a tight little ass—would come in dressed in loose fitting scrubs, plop in her chair, spread her legs wide and talk about how her ovaries were making her bounce off the wall she needed it so bad. Having a live-in girlfriend at the time, I didn't pursue the roommate, but her sexual frankness turned me on. She had a little moustache, which increased my attraction because I imagined the details of her face and what it would look like next to mine, my fingers touching her lips, and the little beads of sweat stuck to the small black hairs by the corners of her panting mouth.

In fact every girl intern I have ever met has been afflicted with extreme horniness. It's fearsome how man-crazy she is. She comes home, she wants a love slave to leap on her, tear off her scrubs and fuck her against the front door before she can put down her keys, toss her on the couch and fuck her over the arm, roll her on the floor and fuck her till her back is tattooed with

121

the carpet pattern, pick her up and fuck her down the hall till every framed museum print smashes on the floor, fuck her on the cluttered kitchen counter with her overdue bills stuck to the sweat on her ass, fuck her in the shower while her hand yanks the shower curtain off its hooks, fuck her against the wall till her feet come off the floor and fuck her so violently in bed that the sheets became one big dripping wet stain. Then, the fucking done, she relaxes for an hour or two before putting her scrubs back on, getting a twenty-four ounce coffee from Wawa and returning to the hospital for another fourteen hour shift of bloody vomit, morbid jokes, and catnaps.

What the girl in scrubs would need from me was to be a sex object. Few men qualify for this job. Being a male sex object is not easy, especially when called upon at odd hours and intermittent days to perform in a non-stop frenzy. She doesn't have time to flatter you, adore you, make herself vulnerable because she worries what you think of her. She doesn't give two shits what you're thinking as long as you're getting her off—she's got lives to save! But becoming a male sex object appealed to me.

For an annual salary of thirty-one thousand six hundred fifty dollars, I had been working as a publishing coordinator at the University Press for three years after an even worse paying two years writing brochures for an historical society. In my twenties, when I should have been focusing on a profitable career or at least a viable music career, I had stumbled drunkenly from waiting tables to selling records to hammering dry wall. By the time I turned thirty my old friends owned houses and were making babies and my new friends had gotten younger and younger. That's what spurred me into the publishing world—a desperate attempt to seek the comforts of a career before I had become too old for entry level. But after five years, doomed to continuous lateral movement, I dreaded the prospect of another year lost in a windowless room, a year of emails and phone calls to authors and editors, photo researching and light copyediting for books I couldn't understand, and long pauses of inactivity under the deadly glow of fluorescent lights.

*   *   *

The day after I discovered her I went to the train station prepared to wait till she appeared. I knew hospital hours were unpredictable but I had no other option and at the station I could read. I never read enough anyway.

I sat on a platform bench for three hours and glanced at the steps so many times that I read less than thirty pages. Finally, I decided to go home on the 9:45. If she didn't appear, I'd wait again tomorrow. If she did appear, I'd . . . well, I hadn't really thought that through.

At 9:40, she came down the steps, in scrubs, a green backpack over her right shoulder. I stood up, arms hanging down, thumb in book, and checked the information monitor. She walked by, stopped several feet later, and looked down the tunnel for our train.

"Train is always late," I mumbled.

She turned her head, her mouth open, teeth just visible.

"Huh?"

"This train is always late," I repeated, my words echoing harshly.

She rubbed her nose before answering, "Yeah, I was afraid I might miss it."

"I missed the last one."

Her sharp blue eyes stayed on mine.

"You must have been waiting a long time."

"Yes," I said, stretching out the word as my mind struggled for a way to open up the conversation. Then I raised my book high in the air. "But it's not so bad. Gave me a chance to do some reading."

"What are you reading?" she asked and stepped toward me.

"*Lord Jim*. Conrad."

"Oh. Is it good?"

"Can't put it down," I said and brought the book down. I stepped in her direction. "Do you read? I mean, I assume you read, but—"

She read. She liked Borges, Marquez and a lot of Latin American writers I'd never heard of. I said I liked Vonnegut and Martin Amis and some other writers she knew. The train came. We both got on. We sat together in a three person seat, she by the window and me by the aisle and we leaned toward each other like horses. I asked if she worked at Jefferson and she said yes and I asked her her stop and she told me and I said, "Oh, the one before mine," while I calculated when to ask her out so I could get her number without creating the awkward situation of her running off the train and me trying to find pen and paper because I still hadn't gotten a cell phone. I told her I was a publishing coordinator at University Press but I was soon quitting and devoting myself to music. She told me how she loved music and admired musicians, though she wasn't musical herself.

Suddenly we were two stops away from hers.

"Would you like to get a coffee or a beer sometime?"

"Sure," she said, "when were you thinking?"

"I only just thought of it," I blurted out and we both laughed. "What's your schedule like this week? I'm your basic nine to fiver."

"I'm free right now," she offered.

We got off at her stop and walked to a nearby bar. She told me her name was Celia.

The bar was full of locals, including a couple I had once waited tables with. They still worked at the restaurant, having complained bitterly about it every day for seven years. I waved hello and ushered Celia to a table by the front window.

"Who are they?"

"They're the black hole of depression."

We drank our beer and talked music, more books, sports. She was from Chicago and liked the White Sox, the Bulls and the Bears in that order. I said I liked the Phillies, the Eagles, the Sixers, and the Flyers in that order. (She never mentioned the Blackhawks.) We agreed that there wasn't much of a rivalry between the two cities and that made it easy for us to get along. Then we fell silent and smiled at each other.

A little after one, I walked Celia to her place, the first floor of a small brick duplex. We stopped at her walkway. She looked up at me and stood on her toes for a second. She did it a second time and I kissed her. She grasped my neck and held me to her lips. My hands went to her side and my fingers felt the warmth of her body through the thin poly-cotton fabric.

"I noticed you on the street yesterday," she said, loosening her grip on my neck and pulling her lips back.

"I know. I noticed you too."

We kissed again, exchanged information, and kissed some more. I watched her go in and then I left. The mile home went by in a happy blur. I cleaned my kitchen, took out my garbage and fell asleep content.

*   *   *

"How about Thursday?"

"Thursday works."

"Hold on," I said and put my hand over the phone.

My co-worker Abbey idled by my desk holding book proofs, swaying, waiting for my attention. She was pale and thin with a sporty mop of hair and a smile that seemed to belie stomach pain.

"Look, the proofs! Two years of aggravation right here!" she announced. "American Methodism as Exemplified by Political Expression in Rural Midwestern Communities, circa 1835 - 1860. I think it'll be a bestseller."

"Let's hope."

"My son is in the questioning stage. He always asks what I do. Then he asks why."

I nodded. Abbey sighed. She turned around and disappeared down the hall. I uncovered the phone.

"Great, so Thursday."

Thursday night King Sunny Ade and his band spread the Juju rhythm while we danced close and fast and grabbed and rubbed each other, shouted and drank. On the last train home, we made out the entire ride, her hands twisting my shirt and my hands squeezing her neck and thighs, and neither of us caring if our loud smacking noises disturbed the other riders.

"I want you to come over and I want to do things to you," she whispered in my ear before sticking her tongue in it.

We hurried off the train and to her home. She pulled me inside. The apartment had low ceilings and hard modern angles but she had a very comfortable couch that we fell upon, our arms around each other, our mouths open and together. We stripped to our waists and then to our underwear and later to nothing at all. Soon after that she excused herself. She came back with a twelve pack of condoms and I realized I was in for a very long night.

After several hours and many orgasms we fell asleep clasped together on the couch. A little throw-over barely covered us while her air conditioner hummed loudly and her naked body kept me warm. She woke me up two hours later offering a cup of coffee. She bit her lower lip and I noticed how the indent reflected the slight unevenness of her front teeth. I thought what a beautiful thing and I laughed.

"Why are you laughing?" she asked, laughing too.

"Because it's so fucking early," I said.

"I know. I'm sorry. Here, have this."

I took the coffee. She was dressed in her scrubs. I was naked with a hard on. I sipped the coffee, which had little effect. I struggled into my clothes while she watched. By the door we held each other. The smell of her clean hair was comforting and I could have slept standing up, my face nestled in the arch of her neck. But off we went—she to the train station and me home to wash, put on clean clothes and go to the office.

The quiet at the University Press, which I usually equated with death, was comforting this morning. I sat in my swivel chair, gazing at the charcoal gray carpet, creating exotic patterns with my sleep deprived eyes. When my co-workers arrived saying, "Good morning!" I smiled and responded with a soft "Hi," genuinely pleased to see them. The world looks so much better after a night of unrestrained passion. For a while, anyway.

*   *   *

Celia, having worked the late shift, came to my place Saturday morning wearing her scrubs. I grinned in expectation of taking them off. She kept asking me why I was grinning and I kept saying I was happy to see her. I made strawberry pancakes and thick bacon and served fresh orange juice.

125

She ate seconds and said she'd never had the luxury of dating a guy who cooked. I knelt by her chair and slid her scrub pants to her knees and kissed her warm meaty thighs. She dropped her fork and started panting. She kicked off her pants and drew me up on the chair. I hoisted her up, her back arching over the back of the chair. She brought her shirt over my head, and I admired the blue light on her white skin before putting my mouth over a tit.

"Fuck me. Fuck me," she ordered and punched me in the back.

We came to a conclusion on the chair, moved to the bed, made love a couple more times, fell asleep and woke up at five. Celia stretched, popping her breasts out from under the sheets, and said, "I haven't slept that well in ages." Then she rolled on top of me and had me again. Then she returned to work.

After seeing her to the train, I stood in my living room for several minutes, unsure what to do with the rest of my evening. It dawned on me that I needed exercise to survive as a love machine. So I went for a long bike ride in the park. I rode fast. I sped through puddles and over roots and down a gravel path and almost spun out into a stone wall. I stopped next to the wall to calm down. That was exactly the type of injury I had to avoid, even with a medical girlfriend.

That night I sat in my living room playing guitar, going through a catalogue of songs I was considering for my recording. Halfway through a song about subterranean lovers running through caves and frolicking in reflective pools, I stopped abruptly. Technically, the morning's sex-a-thon had been our third date. I had to quit the University Press soon so that she would take my artistic lifestyle for granted; if I waited for the relationship to stabilize, she might suspect my projected medical dependency on her. Plus, my immediate freedom from employment would allow me to accommodate her shifting schedule. I believed this relationship had legs, enough for three months at least—and if three, then probably six. If six . . . well, six is a big hurdle.

But what about that part-time coffee shop job for the extra cash? Where was I hoping to do that? Coffee had been my friend throughout my tenure at University Press. I had first seen Celia because I had stopped by a new coffee shop after work to reactivate my brain—otherwise I would have never been walking down Tenth Street at that time. Maybe I only wanted to work at a coffee shop because it was one of my few positive associations with the last several years. I enjoyed sitting at a little café table, sipping coffee and reading the paper. But working at a coffee shop would be an entirely different experience, perhaps a really bad experience, and had I ever even met a barista I liked?

"Fuck it," I said and hit my guitar. I was too delirious from the sex for serious thinking. I sang again about the subterranean lovers, who after skipping about the underworld decide they want to see the sun and end up as toast.

The next night I met my friend Tim in town for a beer. Tim, a librarian, had been living off unemployment for three months. He hadn't worked at all during that time because he'd brought a wrongful termination suit against his employer and he couldn't weaken his grievances with a new job. But Tim hated not having a job and couldn't sit still. He spent his days pacing around his girlfriend's apartment reading comic books, the TV tuned to the Sci-Fi Channel, the stereo blaring and the computer on for email and news.

"You seem happy," he said gulping down his first beer. His girlfriend didn't drink so Tim took advantage of any opportunity to put several down. He belched loudly. I waved my hand in front of my face.

I told Tim about meeting Celia, excluding the health insurance angle.

"You fuck her yet?"

"Um, well . . . "

"Yeah you fucked her. Yeah, that sounds great," he said. "Me, I've got this crotch rot I can't get rid of."

Drunk, walking back to the train station in the humid late summer air, a heaviness crept over me. It was something I experienced frequently. My muscles went slack and my body weighed me down. My brain dulled without recourse to thought, except thoughts like, "I have transformed into a slug" or "I'm so tired. If I saw a mushroom cloud right now would I even be concerned?" The heaviness increased on the train. I looked out the window through my tired, half-wasted reflection into blackness, knowing that seven hours later I would be riding this train in the opposite direction to the University Press.

I got off the train, walked down to the street and leaned against the post office box under the trestle. For a long time, I looked down the street. Light from the street lamps emerged in scattered beams through the leafy darkness of overgrown trees. Their branches arched over telephone and power lines and intertwined above the street. Night bugs buzzed, chirped, rattled, clicked. A car drove by.

The payphone by the station steps rang and a man emerged from the darkness of the parking lot and answered it.

"Well that's creepy," I said to myself and went home.

I figured I would be fast asleep after dropping my exhausted body on my bed but money matters crept into my thoughts and my brain began to swim with anxiety. The pragmatic aspect of my relationship with Celia, with her as my private health insurance, would only succeed by keeping Celia seduced. The last thing she needed was a difficult personal life. If our relationship stopped being free and easy, if every time she suggested we do this or that and I paused the I-don't-think-I-can-afford-it pause accompanied by an impotent shrug, I'd be in jeopardy of losing the benefits of her medical training. Besides, I wanted to treat Celia to things. I wanted to take her to a nice restaurant and slide my hand across the tablecloth and between lighted candlesticks and squeeze her hand, bring it to my mouth and kiss her between her knuckles. I wanted a weekend together in the woods in a log cabin with no electricity but a big fireplace and plenty of firewood, a thick rug to roll around on and big fluffy cushions to make love against, and several bottles of decent wine.

When I woke up, however, my doubts about quitting seemed inconsequential compared to my hatred of having to crawl out of bed and go to work. I would find ways of keeping Celia happy because I would be so happy not to have to go to work in the morning.

*　　*　　*

"Roy, you have any time this morning I could meet with you?"

"Sure, 11:30 okay?" Roy was the manager of my department. He was a kind, intelligent, tweed coat-wearing, white-haired widower, who knew a lot about Eighteenth-century Philadelphia printing technology.

"Yes, thanks," I said and hung up. I'd give four weeks. With four weeks I could squirrel away more money including an extra vacation day's pay. I could organize my future and find the ideal coffee shop where the pay was decent, the work undemanding and my coworkers congenial.

Roy would ask about my plans. If I told him the truth, he'd try to change my mind out of concern for my well being. I had to convince him I was taken care of. I had to come up with a story to satisfy his concerns.

"I'm going to California."

"Wonderful, I love California. Where in California?"

"San . . . Francisco," I said, thinking, however, that if I were going to California, I'd go to L.A. for sunshine and women, but San Francisco sounded more responsible considering my so-called publishing background. Then I had a premonition of Roy, who liked good coffee and, because he lived alone, liked reading dusty books in coffee shops, entering my coffee shop, ordering a cappuccino, his kindly face lighting up upon seeing me, then turning sad with the realization that I had never made it to California, something had gone wrong, and I had been too embarrassed to ask for my job back and now I was down on my luck, a thirty-five year old barista boy working short days at $8.50 an hour plus whatever meager tips were collected in the college fund tip jar that was really for paying down an overdue phone bill.

"Do you have a job lined up?"

"No," I said. Roy's face swamped with worry. "I have a temporary one

128

for money. For more permanent stuff I have . . . leads. I have friends there who work in publishing."

"That's good. Where?"

"Where they work? Can't really remember, I always get it mixed up with Harper Collins but it's not. Something like Harper Collins."

"I hope you'll use me as a reference."

"Thanks, I was going to ask you about that," I lied.

I left Roy's office and let out a deep breathe. My heart started thumping with joy. I had a serious urge to sprint down the hallways and jump up and slap on office windows, shouting, "I'm a free man, you hear? FREE MAN!" I speed walked out instead, barely containing myself, and went for lunch.

I bought an Italian hoagie with the works from my favorite truck stand and sat outside on a brick wall. The sun beat down on the campus and a few students straggled around with backpacks. I unwrapped my hoagie and ate with gusto. Everything was great now—food was nourishment for the soul, the sun triggered photosynthesis making living things grow, earnest young people would learn about the world and I was going to make music for the next year. The hoagie tasted so good, I regretted that I would no longer be in close proximity to my favorite hoagie makers. So I bit off smaller and smaller bites of my hoagie and chewed them for longer and longer periods of time, staring absently at a brick wall with reflective windows, savoring each morsel. Then it was over. I wiped the oil from my hands and went back to the office.

I called Celia's cell. "Not interrupting an operation, am I?"

"Nothing major."

"You sure? Because I know hospitals . . ."

"Baby, you know hospital workers. What's up?"

"I quit. I gave four weeks."

"No shit? Good for you! That's so inspiring."

"Thanks." I closed my eyes, happy to hear her approval.

"I wish I could be so bold."

"But you've got a real job."

"I guess. I always wanted to go into acting or something like that."

"For real?"

"Maybe when I get my loans paid off."

"When will that be?"

"Years."

"You can always act for me."

"We can role play."

"I want to celebrate," I said. "When can I see you next? How's Wednesday?"

"I can't Wednesday, I'm going to Chicago for interviews. I'll be back Thursday."

"Interviews? What are you interviewing for?"

"Residency programs. It's really between Chicago and Boston. Boston for the reputation, Chicago because it's home. But it's really whoever chooses me."

"Philly's not in the picture?"

"No, I . . . no."

"When would it start?"

"Like three months or at least that's when I'd be moving."

I lost my ability to speak. My skin went hot and I broke into a sweat.

"I'm sorry, I probably should have told you before we, uh, before we started fucking," she said with a quiet laugh. "Things have been happening fast and I've been caught up in the moment, you know."

I had to say something to keep from collapsing. "Yes, yeah, um. No, I mean, it's logical."

"You still want to hang out with me, right?"

"Of course, of course. Hey, I think it's great you're doing your thing."

"You're really the one doing your thing. You're pursuing your dream. You quit your job to go for it, man, that takes guts."

"Right."

"So listen, what about Friday?"

"Friday?"

"I'm free Friday night."

"Oh, yeah, let's do Friday. I'll get tickets somewhere."

"Great, and I'll buy dinner." She paused. "I like you, you know."

"I like you too, Celia."

"We'll have some fun while I'm still here."

I hung up and lowered my head to my desk and knocked my forehead against the edge twice. I put my finger in my mouth like a bit to keep from screaming. I stared at my keyboard. I could call Roy and say I had a change of heart. But what would I say to Celia? Would I have to dump her to avoid explaining why I suddenly had to continue working at the University Press?

I noticed two paperclips that had fallen below the space bar. For some reason, it became imperative for me to get the paperclips out. I got another paperclip from my desk drawer, unfolded it into a hook and on perhaps the tenth and fourteenth tries, managed to extract the paperclips.

"What 'cha doing?" Abbey asked, holding a coffee mug that said "World's Hardest Working Mom."

"I dropped some paperclips," I said.

"It's always important to retrieve those. God forbid we lose a paperclip around here."

With great effort, I smiled. Abbey raised her eyebrows and then shuffled down the hall. She seemed to disappear into the gray.

With four hospitals in Center City, there would never be a shortage of pretty interns to cover my medical needs. I called my doctor for a final check-up.

Jon Petruschke
Bragging about Annie

I watched the Culture Club's crowded dance floor from the bar, unable to spot my brother Dan. As I scanned the dancing mass, a young woman stood out to me. I noticed her large, pretty eyes, carefree smile, and short haircut. She looked European—high cheekbones, olive skin, dressed very nicely in linen. I wanted to dance, particularly with her, but was stiff with the inertia of inhibition. I tried to talk myself into *carpe diem* and other motivators. Then I spotted Dan dancing with a girl. Neither of us had gone on a date in months. I had worried how he'd feel if I met a girl tonight and he didn't. The DJ mixed in the next song . . . *Sometimes I feel I've got to . . . Run away I've got to . . . Get away* . . . I was ready for more than just foot tapping. I slipped through the crowd, finding a niche on the dance floor.

The young woman I'd noticed danced with another young woman and was gleaming with sweat. Her smile made me think she was on drugs. I figured x; her dancing was too precise for alcohol. I'd heard ecstasy elevates body temperature and can lead to dehydration—perhaps this was why she was so sweaty.

Dancing in flip-flops is limiting, so I pulled them off and shoved them into my back pockets. Freedom was worth the risk of squashed toes. Soon the heat penetrated like the music, and I was wiping sweat from my brow and shaved head. I glanced at the girl, achieving brief eye contact. She smiled her indiscriminate, general smile. I debated dancing closer to her. I had to do it before fear and logic intervened. So I danced by her side, in front of her, behind her. The DJ mixed in a new song . . . *You spin me right round, baby . . . Right round like a record, baby . . . Right round round round* . . . We exchanged glances as we moved—she still smiling, me too intimidated to. I thought of my "cold, stoic appearance" and other complaints I'd heard from people. It was my shyness, but shy or not, I was eager to appear happy to this girl.

"I have that watch!" she said, grabbing my arm.

I'd bought the watch, a *Jurassic Park* watch, in a Burger King.

She let go of my arm, looking surprised. As we resumed dancing, my foot hit a wet spot on the floor. Losing my balance, I careened towards her. She flinched, but I caught myself before toppling onto her. Carefully, I began dancing again.

"Didn't mean to go lunge at you," I said, grinning over my embarrassment.

"Oh?" she said, looking confused.

Had she misheard me? *Didn't mean to blow lunch at you. Didn't mean to goat love at you. Didn't mean to throw lozenges at you.*

A new song came on. We looked at each other, not recognizing it.

"Would you like a drink?" I quickly offered.

"Sure. A water."

"Two waters," I told the tall, attractive, blond bartender.

"What?" the bartender yelled. She looked irritated, like she knew I was wasting my time and hers with a girl I had no shot with.

"Two waters!" I shouted.

The bartender plunged two cups into her bin of ice. I asked my dance partner her name.

"Cass."

"Cat?"

"Cass."

"Kath?"

"No. Cass, as in Cassandra." The music was loud, getting louder it seemed.

"Sorry," I said, worried she might just walk away. "I'm Jon."

"Nice to meet you Jon."

"You too. For a second I thought you'd misheard my question and you were telling me you owned a cat."

"What?" she said, straining to hear.

"I thought you were saying you had a cat."

"Oh."

"Cause I have a cat," I said.

"Yeah?"

"Yeah."

"I don't own a cat," she said.

I again worried that she might walk away, tell the bartender what I had said, and then they'd laugh at me.

"Hey!" the bartender yelled, startling me.

She handed me two cups of water. I left a dollar from my sweaty hand.

"So what do you do?" I asked.

"I work for an historical home society."

"Really," I said, battling to conceive of a better follow-up than, "Then . . . what do you do?" or "I like it that you used 'an' rather than 'a' before 'historical.'"

"What do you do?" she asked.

"I'm a social worker at a psychiatric hospital."

"Really?"

"Yeah. And, well, I write too."

"I guess you'd have to. What do you do at the hospital?"

"I'm a counselor. I meet with patients, run groups, plan treatment, that sort of thing."

"Really?"

I couldn't tell if she was interested because it seemed interesting, or interested because it seemed dubious.

The music ended and the lights came on. I was glad to see that no expression of horror crossed Cass's face when she looked at me. Cass's dance partner joined us. She was Cass's former college roommate, Shana.

"You know what? That's my brother, Dan," I said, touching Cass's shoulder and pointing. My fingertips on her shoulder weren't necessary, but she didn't seem to mind.

Dan and the girl he'd befriended waved from across the emptying room. As the three of us waved back, Cass and Shana smiled at each other. I hoped it was because they thought it was cute my brother and I were out together, not strange that I pointed him out.

The three of us looked at each other, then looked away.

"I'll be right back," Cass said, and went to the bar.

"So where'd you two go to school?" I asked Shana.

"Swarthmore."

"Oh, okay."

"You've heard of it?"

"Yeah."

Cass returned and handed me a napkin with her name and phone number written on it. I thought, *It's not her real number.*

"I'll call you and maybe you can come see my cat. She's a special cat, I ought to keep pictures of her in my wallet. To show people."

My humor floundered; I had advanced from weird to creepy.

I waited two days to call Cass. I hated adhering to the rule about not calling a girl too soon. I left a message for this girl in college the day after we'd met. She never called back and told one of my friends I was a "clingy freak." I hoped Cass would reveal herself as the type who wished I hadn't waited two days to call, but I'd met that kind of girl before—her neediness became unreasonable, then volatile. Maybe I wasn't sure what I was hoping.

I planned what I'd say and called. I got an answering machine. I slowly enunciated my name, a reminder of who I was, and both my home and work numbers. I hung up, relieved. Now it was up to Cass to call back. But was leaving my work number too much?

Cass called me at work the next day.

"I can't talk right now," she said. "I just wanted to let you know I got your message. I didn't call back last night cause I got in late."

"Thanks." I was surprised by her courtesy.

"Can I call you tonight at, how's . . . nine o'clock?"

That night my phone rang at nine.

"Wow, nine on the dot. You're pretty reliable, huh?" I said.

"I said nine, right?" she asked, not sarcastically, but verifying.

"Yeah, you did. I guess I'm not used to people doing what they say."

"Oh?"

"People sometimes don't do what they say, especially in the dating world."

"Oh."

"Anyway, it's good to finally get to talk without having to yell past loud music and my tinnitus," I joked.

"I'm actually surprised you didn't call sooner," she said.

"I waited two days."

"I just thought I'd hear from you the next day."

I suspected I was out of compliance with another rule.

"To see if you got home okay?"

"I wasn't thinking that exactly, but that would have been nice," she said, not bothered, but I knew this could be a first strike.

"This might sound ridiculous, but I was following the two-day calling rule."

"The what?"

"You're supposed to wait two days after you meet someone before you call them. People sometimes get annoyed if you call too soon, like you're needy or overbearing."

"You must've had some trouble with people you've dated," she said.

"I suppose."

"Where do you live?" Cass asked.

"Ambler. With my friend Megan."

"Megan?"

"Don't worry, Megan's not really a girl. She is, but we're like siblings, mutually repulsed by each other, but close according to a sometimes inexplicable bond. Where do you live?"

135

"South Philly, Rocky's neighborhood," she said. "But, I'm originally from Maine."

"Interesting, I dated a girl in college who was from Maine. That actually explains a lot."

"What's that?"

"Well, she was a really genuine and honest person, and you seem to be too. When you were dancing, at first I thought you were on ecstasy or something because of how much you were smiling, but I realized you were really just enjoying yourself."

"Did I hear a meow?" Cass asked.

"Yeah, it was my little cat. She's quite interactive, if you talk to her she meows back."

"Is she a Siamese?"

"Nope, she's a barn kitty, aren't ya Annie?" I said, a couple octaves higher than my normal speaking voice and realized I could be treading from cute and humorous to odd.

"So, you said you write, didn't you?" Cass asked. "What do you write?"

"Poetry, stories. What are your passions?"

"My passions are traveling and food. Are they important to you?"

"Definitely," I lied, wondering how I would explain myself.

"I'm going to Italy this fall and I'm so excited. It'll be my third time. Where all've you been?"

"I've actually never been out of the country or on a plane."

"Wow!" I could tell she was smiling.

"It's something I want to do. I like traveling, seeing new places."

She asked what my family was like.

"Pretty standard," I said, proud of the stability. "I have three older brothers, my parents have been married for a long time, and my grandmother lives with them."

"Are you the black sheep?" she quickly asked with a snicker.

"My brothers and I, we're all pretty different. I feel like a black sheep. I'm not all into being a man's man and whatnot." I was suddenly concerned she'd think I was gay. "I'm not gay though."

"Oh? Okay."

"I don't have a problem with gay people or anything, girls just sometimes think I'm gay, and I'm not. I'm just not your typical guy. I had a friend in college who'd intervene with every pretty girl I approached and ask them if they thought I was gay."

"Really?"

"Yeah, and they usually said yes. So I'm a bit touchy with that."

"Actually, I did wonder if you were gay when I first saw you . . . "

"Damn."

I managed to laugh with her.

"You know, the whole stereotype about gay guys dressing well. Sorry about that. Anyway, I should probably go."

"Do you want to see my cat sometime?"

"What's the deal with your cat?" she asked.

"I have the best cat," I said with exaggerated enthusiasm.

"Why don't we just have dinner sometime?"

"That sounds good. But, um, I'm not too experimental when it comes to food," I warned, feeling sheepish.

"What does that mean?"

"Well, what'd you have in mind?"

"How about . . . pizza, or Chinese?"

"Better go with pizza."

There was a pause.

"Okay, let's see here. I could do dinner in . . . next Thursday," she said.

"Next Thursday?"

"Yeah, next Thursday."

"So not this Thursday, but like in two Thursdays?" I asked. I was available for dinner any night between now and the end of time.

I was to meet Cass at the 12th Street Gym at six o'clock. But I arrived early, so I decided to have an iced coffee at a nearby café. The caffeine exacerbated my nervousness and my paranoia about why the café's all male clientele were staring at me. When I met up with Cass, she informed me that we were in the gayborhood. She preferred this gym because she didn't have to worry about guys looking at her.

We headed to South Street for dinner, shared a pizza, and went for a walk. It was a mild July evening. Cass showed me a couple historic homes that her agency maintained, and recounted history that was charming and, surprisingly, not boring. Cass asked me why I thought there was so much mental illness in America. I tensely muddled my answers with, "and whatnot," "this and that," and "you know." I anxiously cracked poorly timed jokes, intelligent questions evaded me, and interesting thoughts were out of reach. The evening ended much earlier than I thought it would; after a couple hours together, she said she had to go home and prepare for her very full tomorrow.

"This is probably a long shot given the bookedness of your schedule, but do you want to go dancing tomorrow night?" I asked.

"I'm busy the first part of the evening, but I could meet you later on."

"Wow, great! My brother gave me some passes to Egypt for my birthday.

It's not my favorite club, but admission's free and it might be fun. Here, I brought some passes, in case you were interested, and if you want to invite anyone along."

"Alright, I'll see you tomorrow night."

I attempted to kiss her, but received a cheek.

Cass met me in line outside Egypt.

"Is your car nearby? I'd like to put my bag in it."

As the two of us walked the three blocks to my car, Cass told me that she had started getting serious with a fellow.

"I almost didn't come tonight," she confessed. "But you seem really nice, and we had fun dancing before, and I think you'd be a fun person to have as a friend. I really mean it when I say I want us to be friends."

My nervousness emptied, leaving only disappointment. I felt stupid and lonely.

"I appreciate you coming. If you hadn't, then I would have been wondering what went wrong," I said, trying to ease her discomfort. It was the first time she seemed nervous to me.

"That's what I figured," she said. "So, anyway, happy birthday. Now let's go dance."

I had too much to drink. But in the early a.m., Cass was willing to accompany me for a snack at Silk City, where I had arranged to meet my roommate. Stylish, artsy-looking twenty- and thirty-something-year-olds filled the diner. I considered my singlehood and inability to mingle with strangers like these; it was disheartening. I ordered fries and withdrew into a quiet and forlorn inebriation.

"So how long have you guys been friends?" Cass asked.

"Since high school."

"What'd you do tonight?" I asked Megan.

"Peddled my ass on the street."

"Figures."

I watched Cass eat a hotdog with mustard and onions.

"How can you eat that?" I finally asked.

"I was craving it."

"I thought you were into eating exotic stuff?"

She smiled and said, "That's true, you remembered. I don't know, I guess this is exotic to me right now."

She looked over at Megan and said, "I told Jon that my two big passions were food and travel, and he said pizza was the safer choice between pizza and Chinese when we went out."

They laughed.

"Yeah, that's Jon, not too adventurous. I've known him for a long time, so I can give you all the dirt," Megan said, chuckling. I wanted to clobber her.

"I've definitely been intrigued by him . . . "

"And his lack of smiling, right?"

"Yeah!"

"Yeah, he looks like a Nazi, but when you get to know him, you find he's really just a pink sprinkle."

They were only teasing, but I silently damned my drunken state—too drunk to effectively return banter, not drunk enough to cause a scene.

"I've been trying new things to eat . . . and I want to travel more," I said.

Two weeks later, an employee at a local psych hospital went berserk, arriving for work with a loaded rifle. Then a recently fired employee from my hospital called with threats to shoot all of us. So my boss sent me home and gave me the next day off. Having had no luck coaxing my friends out for a drink or a movie, I called Cass. I reached her answering machine and hung up. Then my phone rang.

"Hi, who is this? I just hit *69."

"Oh . . . um, it's Jon."

"Jon? Oh, hi Jon, how are you?"

"Good, I was calling to see if you were free tonight. I don't have to work tomorrow so I was calling around to see if anyone wanted to do something."

I explained why I had the day off and she said she was busy, but we talked for a while. I asked about her family.

"I was adopted," she said, "and raised by my family in Maine. My birth-family lives in Louisiana. I found them a few years ago, they're Cajun."

"That's pretty wild," I said, uncertain what Cajun was.

"Cajun's a mix of French and Native American," she said.

"That's funny, I thought you looked European, but I wasn't sure about your dark skin."

"Yeah, apparently I have the Cajun look."

"I don't mean to offend you or anything, I guess with my job it's the way I think, but do you think you've had any problems or difficulties from being adopted and whatnot?"

"Quite the opposite. I feel I've been blessed with two families."

"Well that's good." I tried not to sound disappointed.

"But I do have an issue," she said in a playful tone.

"Really?" I said.

"Yeah, it's hard to say though."

"Take your time, I could tell you about all of my issues and whatnot," I

139

said and laughed.

"You like to say that a lot, don't you?"

"What?"

"Whatnot."

"Hmm, maybe, I didn't really notice. Let's get back to this alleged issue."

"Let's talk about something else."

"Okay." I said, but felt terrible now.

"So I'm not available to do anything tonight, but this Thursday I'm free."

"Really? *This* Thursday? Not next Thursday?"

She giggled.

Wednesday night she called, asking if we could move things to Friday night, and rather than dinner, she wondered if I could . . .

" . . . read to you?"

"Yeah, you see," she explained. "My birth-father is coming to visit from Louisiana, and I need to clean my apartment on Friday. I was wondering if you'd be interested in reading something aloud to me while I clean, maybe one of your favorite authors?"

"Sure, that sounds fine," I said, bracing for the onslaught of hell I was certain my friends would give me.

"Maybe she's just into casual sex," one friend suggested.

"Anyway," I said. "I was thinking I'd bring over a bottle of wine and read something really good to her, then maybe read some of my own stuff."

"No, no, no," another said.

"I don't know if you should read any of your own stuff, man. You never know how that could go," a third said.

"And not wine, something harder," the first said.

"Tequila!" they shouted in unison.

"Tequila? I don't think she's a big drinker, and this isn't really a date. I mean, there's this other guy," I explained.

"Don't worry about him," they emphasized.

"Yeah man, I brought tequila over to a girl's one time and we ended up naked on her kitchen floor."

"Yeah dude—tequila. You'll be gettin' it on before any apartment cleaning gets done!"

They assured me tequila and some decent erotica was the way to go.

I arrived at her apartment with a bottle of red wine and a book of Hemingway short stories.

"Wine!" she said with surprise when she opened the door.

140

"Yeah, I wasn't sure if you drank though."

"Sometimes. I don't know how much cleaning I'll get done, but that's fine. Are you hungry?"

As we walked back to her place, carrying a pizza, we turned onto her street. I stopped and raised my arm to stop Cass. There was a man on a bicycle, circling around in front of her apartment, and then pedaling away from us. After he was a block away, I lowered my arm.

"Did you know that guy?" she asked.

"Yeah, unfortunately. He's an ex-patient of mine."

"Really?"

"Yeah, and he's a sexual predator."

"God!"

"So I didn't want him to see us, or where you live."

"Yeah. Thanks."

I was excited by the opportunity to be the expert.

"Come on, let's go inside and eat," I suggested.

We ate the pizza and drank the wine and soon Cass decided that the apartment didn't need any straightening up for her birth-father's visit.

"I'd still like it if you read to me though . . . the wine's making me tired, do you think we could lay in my bed while you read?"

"That's fine."

We lay side by side and I read to her. At times she leaned her head on my shoulder, and put her hand on my chest. I pretended not to notice, but wondered if she was leading me on. I planned on making no advances.

After hearing two stories, she said, "It was good meeting Megan. When you told me that you worked in a psychiatric hospital, I remembered how flat your expression was on the dance floor, not smiling much, I thought, he doesn't *work* there, he *escaped* from there." She laughed, then continued, "But Megan said you were on the up and up."

"Yeah. I have a hard time smiling, especially when I'm nervous."

"You were nervous?"

"It wasn't easy getting myself to dance with you."

"Well, I'm glad you did."

There was a pause; then I told her that I had a surprise.

"What is it?"

I pulled some folded pages from my pocket. "I brought along some of my poetry. Would you like to hear it?"

"Um . . . sure."

"Alright, well then, here goes." I cleared my throat. "The first one's called 'Another American Night.'

The TV screen turns
from pixels to Paxils
and I'm stuffed, yet starved,
chewing on the remote.
I defeated consumerism
by buying everything advertised."

She didn't say anything, but she smiled.
"Okay, here are some more, these are haiku I wrote.

Your neck bruises fade—
my deep Valentine's kisses
a few days ago."

I glanced up at her, then read several more.
"I was worried your poetry would be really awful."
"Yeah?"
"And I was going to have to sit through it, pretend to like it and feel really embarrassed for you. But, I'm impressed."
"Unless you're pretending now," I said, smiling.
"I'm not. But when we talked on the phone and when we had dinner on South Street, and you kept saying 'whatnot' and 'you know,' I was thinking, if this guy's a writer, why can't he elaborate beyond 'whatnot'?"
"I get nervous."
"Now I got a glimpse of the whatnot in your poetry, the little details in life you catch. I like it very much."
There was silence and we looked at each other and I figured this was the opportune moment to kiss.
"I'm getting tired," she said.
"Maybe I should get going," I suggested, thinking this was my best opportunity to leave with the audience wanting more.
"Probably, I have a long day tomorrow."
At the door to her apartment, she hugged me and kissed my neck.
"Can I meet your family?" she asked.
"Yeah . . . sure . . . I guess." I didn't know what to say.

Four days later, we had dinner at my parents—with them, my grandmother, Dan, and Rachel, the girl he'd met at the Culture Club.
Cass asked me why her spot at the table was the only one set with plastic utensils.
"Ugh, don't ask. Mom, can you please pass over some regular utensils

for Cass?" I asked, blushing with irritation and embarrassment.

"Oh, you eat with regular silverware dear?" my mom asked.

"Er, yes."

"Jon used to date a girl who would only eat with plastic utensils. Alice, she was a bit strange," my dad remarked.

I grew redder.

"Why was it that Alice wouldn't eat with regular silverware Jon?" my mom asked.

"Because she didn't like the feel of metal in her mouth," I mumbled.

"Yeah, she was odd," Dan said.

"Alright, alright. Let's move on," I snapped.

"What are you two going to do tonight?" my mom asked Cass and I.

Why am I drawing all the fire? Dan's also in range and with a date!

"I don't know, Jon's been adamant about showing me his cat," Cass said.

"Good luck," my dad said.

"Why?" Cass asked.

"We never see her when we go to Jon's," my mom said.

"I'm not so sure he even has a cat," my dad added, his eyes steady on his plate.

"I've shown you pictures!" I argued. "She's really shy around strangers, and you guys get too loud for her. You've got to be calm around her and wait for her to get comfortable and come to you."

"Like playing dead?" Dan asked, smirking.

I resisted stabbing him in the face with my fork.

"So the four of you met that night?" my mom said, trying to cleanly mother away the sibling tension.

"Yeah," I said, knowing she already knew this, but hoping Dan might be the bull's-eye for a while.

"That's so nice," my grandmother said, looking at Cass. "You know, the boys' other two brothers are married. And their mother and I, we've been praying that Danny and Jonny would meet two nice girls."

I coughed out a potato.

After dinner Cass and I sat in my car.

"They're a bit of a handful. And my grandmom's comments . . . " I said, smirking.

"She's sweet."

"Yeah, she is. Gram's eighty-nine. She likes to say 'shit for brains' a lot."

"What?"

"My parents are always getting after her about it. She used to be a really busy person; she still is. But years ago she was even busier—painting and cooking a lot. She'd always complain that the only time she can stop and think is when she's on the pot. When I was a little kid, I thought about this, and one day it clicked. Since we all have shit for brains, when you go to the bathroom, that's the only way to free up more space to think. And that was why she could think so well on the pot."

Cass laughed.

"Yeah, Gram laughed too when I told her that."

We were quiet for a moment.

"You live nearby?" Cass asked. "Maybe I could meet your exceptional cat now."

"Oh yeah! Right!"

At my apartment, we sat together on the large, lime-green IKEA couch. Cass sat Indian-style facing me, with her back against the arm of the couch.

"Are those roads . . . and a town, on your carpet?" Cass asked.

"Yeah," I said, scratching my head. "Megan and I figured the busyness of it might distract from the state of the apartment."

"It looks pretty neat to me."

"I picked up a bit earlier."

"Is Megan out?"

"Yeah," I said. "Can I ask you a question?"

"Sure."

"Why'd you want to meet my family?"

"To see what kind of people you come from," she said.

"You don't think that's strange?" I asked.

"How so?"

"I don't know. I told my mom 'There's this girl who wants to come have dinner with us. I'm not dating her or anything, but I met her recently, and now she wants to have dinner with us, and meet you guys.'"

"I stopped seeing that guy," she said. "After the first couple times you and I talked, I wasn't sure how right we were for each other. You didn't seem interested in life like I am, with food and seeing new places . . . "

"I want to explain that."

"You don't have to, I already like you," she said, smiling.

"Look," I whispered and pointed.

"Is that Annie?"

"Yeah, I'm surprised she's coming out already, I was worried you might not even get to see her tonight. You must seem safe to her."

Annie cautiously approached us.

"Annnnieeeeee," I sang in a high-pitched voice that made Cass giggle. Annie hurried toward us. She stopped at the edge of the couch and looked up.

"Come on girl," I said.

She let out an abbreviated meow and jumped up onto Cass's lap. She looked at Cass, then me.

"She knows her name, huh?"

"Yeah, she's a small cat and rather skittish, but quite smart," I said.

"Wow, she's beautiful. Look at all the colors: orange, tan, brown, black."

"The closer you get to her, the more you appreciate her. Her individual hairs, some of them are all four colors."

I slid to the center of the couch and petted Annie.

"She's really sweet," Cass said, and looked at me.

I held her gaze; it was another opportune moment to kiss. "Maybe you could read some more poetry to me?" she asked.

"Maybe," I said, and ran my fingertips from Annie's back to Cass's hand, and up her arm to her cheek. "Maybe," I said again, and kissed her instead.

Phyllis Carol Agins
Black and White

E dward stands on the corner of Fourth and Chestnut, selling postcards of Philly's glory days, for that's how he thinks of them. He's created the cards himself, taking his father's old negatives and embossing— that's what the young boy in the copy store called it—the old images onto new cards. The tourists love them. The kids swarm around his stand and jam their fingers into the bins. Thank God, he's wrapped plastic around everything. *Look at this*, one lady sighs, *the horses, the trolleys, and the men who sold everything on the street. These are treasures just waiting to be found.* She buys five cards.

He's an entrepreneur, he laughs, just like his father, Jacob, who ran from the pogroms and the Czar like millions of other turn-of-the-century Jews. But Jacob ignored his own history and named his son Edward, trying to capture the gentility of the neutralized American. Edward Burnblatt—quite the WASP, that name.

Edward is eighty-four now, and hits the corner only on the good days. No rain. Forget the snow. No temperatures below fifty degrees. On the bad days and late at night, he stays in his apartment where he weeps sometimes for his dead wife and for his children who have abandoned Philadelphia— one for the Vermont countryside, and the other for that oppressive cesspool to the north that Edward won't name. Some nights, he weeps for his city.

He tells the tourists how he once traveled the streets of Philly with his father—two adventurers who needed to map their territory. He'll add, if they ask, that Jacob was the premier photographer in the city. The man who was the best at focusing its mood: the smells drifting from the port, the smoky breath of booming factories, the translucence of early morning air draped across buildings. Best at capturing the dreams of its citizens, of women bound in corsets and of small boys in short pants who had to wait until their thirteenth birthdays to wear their first manly trousers. Capturing, too, the dreams of men with canes and bowlers and handlebar mustaches, who hung by their hooked elbows on the straps of trolleys that carried them from south to north.

For a long time, Edward wouldn't say—because he had almost forgotten it himself—that Jacob took pictures of tourists, too, for a living, following people, even cajoling them, like a street peddler hawking his wares, and finally cornering them, so they took pity on the photographer who had hidden his *kippa* under an American hat, and who pleaded in guttural English, *Please lady, please.* Exhausted, they would pay him ten cents and write their names in the small pad that he kept in his breast pocket, tucked next to a watch that was missing its chain, because gold was more than he could afford with a wife and five children to feed.

Those tourists were always surprised when the photo appeared in five days—exactly. Always amazed that the man had portrayed them as they hoped to be: handsome, well dressed, without a doubt, prosperous. Absolutely American. They'd sacrifice the photos right then and there, packaging them into hard envelops for the transatlantic voyage to families back home, to prove that America was, indeed, as the rumors promised—the new Eden, full of milk and honey. And weren't they, in black and white, the living proof, fixed carefully by Jacob's chemicals onto durable cardboard?

Lately, Edward will tell anyone, like he does that young reporter for the *Inquirer* one day when he's about to pack up because KYW News has been promising rain, that Jacob kept all the negatives in yellow envelops, neatly labeled with the where and when of the people and places. Maybe Jacob hoped that the tourists would write again, demanding five or even more copies for their family albums scattered about the world.

Edward was fifty-five when he finally decided to open the boxes, searching, he tells the reporter, for a piece of his father in the handwriting, in the photos' composition, in the way Jacob always included a bit of Philadelphia as if to root the tourists in the here and now. He needed to visit his father again, having decided that oblivion was just around the corner, so he'd better hurry up and explore his own history. He never expected to see eighty because Jacob was only fifty when he died, his fingers stained with developing chemicals and tobacco tar.

No, he tells the attentive young reporter, the old days were gone and the new ones are empty. All he wants to do is feed himself because everyone knows Social Security can't take care of a hamster in a cage. He doesn't mind that his friends are dead and his children have rejected his city. There is peace, isn't there, in revisiting the old places through the pictures that his father left him, like an insurance policy taken out one hundred years ago.

147

Edward laughs when the reporter's eyes fill with tears. *That's just how time is*, he tells the young man, as if he's sharing a secret.

The evening the reporter shows up again at Fourth and Chestnut, proudly holding the front page of the City Section in the fading light, Edward is a little surprised. Most people visit the stand just once. Only the man who sells coffee on the corner and brings him lunch comes every day, like a religion.

The reporter is carrying a smile too big for his face. He's got two friends with him—a girl who's clinging to him like he's the next messiah, and a photographer who's marking the moment with his own fast-flashing photos—*click, click, click*. Nothing like the laborious, scene setting of Jacob's photos, with the flash that blinded for thirty seconds and the boom that filled your head. The reporter is pointing to the headline—*Edward Burnblatt, Philadelphia's Living History*—and to photos of the stand and close-ups of Edward that the photographer obviously took on the sly, unlike Jacob, who always got the customer's permission scratched on his pad. Edward is in color because black and white doesn't count anymore.

The camera flashes, the tourists gather to see what the fuss is about, and the reporter congratulates himself at having discovered Edward on his corner. Someone says the mayor is coming—any minute, that is. The tourists pull out their cameras because, surely, something important is going on here, and they must record the event for their personal histories, thinking: *We were there when . . .* They'd figure out that part later. They start flashing, too.

Finally, there are only bright lights before him, and the noise of cameras whirring towards the next frame, the next image. Edward can't see anything except for the utter clarity of Jacob, adorned in sepia, standing in the same spot where the *Inquirer* photographer stands, camera in hand, grinning, absolutely beaming, at his son.

David Sanders
Nothing Matters

Now I know what happens when dwarfs collide. Before? I was dark and invisible. But now I shine again. It's nuclear fusion. *You're a shining star, no matter who you are. . . . Shining star for you to see, what your life can truly be.*

You wouldn't think me stellar to look at me. Gray-skinned, skinny-assed guy lying here naked looking a lot more weathered than thirty-seven. But believe me, I'm afire. White hot. Right there on the ceiling, a new glow against the black velour.

I'm in my room at my mom's. The décor is not to her taste, but she doesn't complain. Mattress on the floor. Brick-and-board bookshelf against the wall. Wooden crate in the corner filled with T-shirts and underwear. Wicker basket in the other corner with dirty laundry. My old turntable on a crate by the window. But overhead? Wide open space. My map of the heavens, spread across the ceiling, each tiny glow-in-the-dark star glued, one by one, onto the black fabric I stapled there.

Perseus, Cassiopeia—the constellations are amazing. Hydra, Phoenix, Monoceros, scattered across the blackness. Like Jackson Pollock with breathing room. My Uncle Warren was afraid of the night sky, said it was too much of nothing for him. But that's what pulls me in. The nothingness. The breathing room. It comforts me. Because I know it's not really nothing, that secret between the stars. Not empty at all. No, no, no. It's full of wonder.

It was Molly who opened my eyes, starting this morning at work with the *Scientific American* scooped off my shelving cart. "You gotta read this article, Danny!" she whispered. "It'll change your whole take on space!"

I didn't really know I *had* a take on space. I just liked looking up and picking out the superhero constellations—Hercules, Pegasus, Orion, the Dippers.

But space itself was pretty much a void. A vacuum. Defined by what it wasn't.

The article was short and I read it all in one standing, hiding myself in the stacks at Bohemia Books with my cart of magazines and books and tapes and CDs, poised to pretend I was shelving if anyone passed by. After all, I've had the job less than a year and I don't want to lose it. Not that I care terribly about stocking shelves and sweeping floors. Not exactly the stuff of dreams. But this being the first job I've had since crawling back home to Philly, and the test that's supposed to prove I've got my feet back on earth, getting fired can't be good, you know? *You've got to change your evil ways.*

So I read this article on the sly, trying to stay out of Karen's radar. Half my age and Karen's already manager. That hurts, especially given I used to own a record store in L.A. Now I'm taking orders from a kid with green hair, a dozen rings and posts pierced through her head, and a neck tattoo of a snake. Of course, I probably look as strange to her—sunken cheeks, speed-demon eyes, flaming red goatee, and waves of hair hanging down my back.

Anyway, this article was pretty good. All that black emptiness of space? According to cosmologists (I love that word), it's not empty at all. No, it's *full*. Jam-packed with stuff we can't see. One cosmologist called it "the invisible cosmic majority," the dark matter that makes up most of what we look at in the night sky. Black holes. Dead stars. Subatomic neutrinos so small they pass right through us. Dark matter. I like that.

Now here's the thing. Once upon a time when I was a lad and life was sweet, back in the olden days before it all got screwed up, I was onto this whole dark matter business. No shit. Long before the scientists figured it out, my dad was there. Me and my dad. Standing in the backyard with Mom and Uncle Warren, and they were pointing at the scads of stars and naming the constellations. Only, I was staring into the space between them and wondering aloud what held the whole thing together. "*Nothing, Danny,*" Uncle Warren said after a bit. "*You can see that for yourself. Too much of nothing.*" My mom repeated the phrase, like she was trying it on for size: "*Too much nothing.*" But it didn't sit right with me. "*How can something be nothing?*" I asked my dad. And he laughed his big, warming laugh and put his arm around me. "*That's the spirit, Danny. You remember that: even nothing's got to be something.*"

And here I am, thirty years later, grown up, burnt out, and Molly comes spinning into my life all jazzed up about nothing.

"Where you been, you don't know about dark matter?" she teased me at work during lunch, sipping ginger ale between bites of pizza in the back office.

"I know a little, but I like hearing you talk about it," I said, shoving another slice into my mouth.

"It just blows me away. Probably ninety-nine percent of the entire universe is something that looks like nothing. Which leaves only one percent for all the stars and galaxies and things we can actually see."

Before I could swallow my cheese and sausage and add some wisdom of my own, she was off and running about galaxy halos and gravitational light distortions.

I'm convinced that Molly has been sent from another galaxy to rescue me. She's a miracle, buzzing all excited like a kid, even though she's a couple years older than me. She landed here at Bohemia as a cashier a few months ago, and contact was immediate. Somehow she's been calibrated to my exact wavelength, and is beaming me these digital brain signals to kick me out of deep sleep and into action. You know, like that space probe that went dormant all those years? And when conditions were just right, scientists beamed special codes to fire up its onboard computers and get it in gear? Well, that's me. I was in free-float so long I lost track of which way was up or down, but damn if she doesn't come along and change all that. Power's back. Navigational systems reestablished. Mission control, we are a go.

Molly was leaning over the table, arranging pieces of napkins and red pepper flakes around the pizza box. It was her model of the galaxy, and she was using it to describe the nature of dark matter.

Leave it to the science geeks to ruin the names," she complained, sprinkling salt over the model. "'Wimps' and 'machos'? Is that Disneyfied or what?"

Actually, I find it funny—WIMPs standing for "weakly interacting massive particles," incredibly tiny subatomic particles, and MACHOs standing for "massive compact halo objects," huge planet-like objects, even bigger than planets.

"MACHOs," Molly said, "have such super-strong gravities that they can actually change the spin of a galaxy, or at least the outer part of a galaxy." She pointed to the far side of the table, her body forming an arc. "Way out here in the halo, which is how they get their name."

She looked great with her body stretched out across the galaxy. She's so small she had to stand on the chair rung to reach. Her outstretched arm was thin and tough like a cord, and I could see the ghosts of needle marks up the inside. I'd noticed them the first day she started working at the store. She didn't try to hide them, and when she noticed me noticing them, she said, simply, "*That's history.*" And I told her, "*I can relate.*"

"But you can't see MACHOs either," she went on. "They give off zero light. In fact, sometimes their gravities are so strong they actually suck light back in. Those are the black holes."

"Black holes are cool."

"Way cool. And there's the neutrinos. Subatomic too, and they trip around the universe, zipping right through any matter in their way. They're passing through us right now."

She looked down at herself as though she might catch one in the act, then glanced up at me, grinned, and faked a glamour-girl pose with a hand behind her head.

"What do you think, a heavenly body?"

"Music of the spheres."

She laughed. "You're a stitch. So you see, these scientists are dividing into two camps. Some are total pioneers, spinning out wild theories without worrying what people might say. Others are the careful experimenters, staying inside the lines, but digging deeper for the details. Totally different approaches, but put 'em together and they're recreating our whole concept about nothingness and the universe."

She sat back and took a breath, then suddenly looked down as though she'd been scolded. "Sorry about that," she said to her hands. "I'm talking too much."

"No, no. Not at all."

"I'm probably not making any sense."

"No, it's beautiful. You're describing the great divide between the romantics and the classicists."

She looked up. "I am?"

"Absolutely. Think Wagner. Think Bach. You're saying that some scientists come up with these bold, soaring chords of new ideas, and others focus on the patterns and the details. And we need them both."

"So that's what I said?" She grinned at me sideways. Her dark eyes glowed behind thick plastic glasses. Black hair, dusted with a few strands of gray, ringed her face.

I brushed a hair from her cheek. "Yeah. It's brilliant. So which are you? Bach or Wagner?"

At that moment, Molly's ex-squeeze appeared in the doorway. He leaned against the jamb, his arms folded like pistons across his chest.

"Pretty fucking cozy in here," he said.

I've known a lot of scary guys over the years, and Chuck is a definite on the list. He's got a good fifty pounds over me, all muscle, and he entered the room like he wanted to be sure I knew it. He loads trucks at the moving company where Molly used to run the front counter, but she dumped him just before she changed jobs. *"He's got a nice bod, but a big fist,"* she told me, explaining both the beginning and the end of the relationship. Trouble is, she didn't get far enough away, and he keeps hanging on, dropping by, taking her places on his bike.

Chuck circled the table slowly, prowling, looking down on us and the mess we'd made. He picked up a torn napkin. He turned it over a few times, trying to figure out what it meant.

"What were you two talking about?" he asked.

"Nothing," Molly said.

I wanted to grin, but caught myself.

Chuck turned on me. "What's so fucking funny?"

"Nothing," I told him. "We were talking about nothing."

Now Molly tried not to smile and Chuck saw that too. His eyes narrowed. His face hardened. I'd seen that look before, seconds before a blade went into my side. Some people just can't take a joke.

Molly was gutsy. "What did you come by for anyway?"

"Party tonight. See if you was going or what, and need a ride."

"Maybe I am, maybe not. What do you care?"

Karen was throwing a bash at her daddy's house while he was in Europe. Chuck's been hanging around the bookstore so I guess he got invited. I don't know why Karen's into him, maybe it's the tattoos.

Molly stood up. "I have to get back to work."

Chuck grabbed her by the wrist.

"Listen . . . " he started to say, but she interrupted.

"No, Chuck. Let go. You got to go, 'cause I have to get back to work."

"I'm just taking you to a fucking party." His voice was a growl. Molly winced. I stood up and reached out toward Chuck.

"Easy there . . . " I began to say, but he swatted my arm away.

"Keep your hands to yourself!" He let go of Molly. "I'll pick you up at eight." Then he was gone.

I stared at the empty doorway for a moment, my arm stinging. "Jesus, that was something." I looked over at Molly, who was rubbing her wrist. "You okay?"

"Sorry about that," she said. She started packing up the leftover pizza and straightening the table like she could clean the whole episode away. Bach or Wagner? Easy call: she's a definite Bach—simple and tidy on the surface but lots happening underneath. And I guess I'm the opposite, a Wagner kind of guy. All that soaring chords stuff. A romantic.

"Can I do anything to help?"

She stopped cleaning but kept her head down. "You already did." She looked up and touched my hand. "Really, thanks."

I took a gamble and started bobbing my head like Chuck. "No fuckin' problem," I said. "But hey! Dat party tonight? Is you going or what?"

It paid off: she grinned. "Maybe, maybe not. Who's asking?"

*   *   *

153

"This dark matter . . . " my mom started to say at dinner, then her voice trailed off. I'd been telling her about my talk with Molly and she was passing the pork chops. Her hands trembled from the effort and she had to give the plate her full concentration until I'd taken hold. "I've been hearing about that."

That's my mom. A hairdresser who knows about dark matter. A cosmologist cosmetologist. Maybe she gets a bit spacey these days, but who can blame her? And maybe we still have our fights. But overall we get along okay. It's no picnic living with your mom but she had no one else to care for her and I had nowhere else to go.

"These scientists think it makes up most of the universe," I told her. "All those black holes, burned-out stars, lost planets, brown dwarfs."

"Brown dwarfs?"

"Yeah, they're the most common thing in the cosmos, only you can't see them. They're stars that don't have enough mass to generate fusion. Stars too small to shine."

"Ahhh," Mom sighed and sat back. "Like your Uncle Warren."

Mom's right. Her brother did his best, I guess, but he never shined. Uncle Warren was night to my dad's day. Dad was bright and full of fire, burning with goodwill, generous with his friends and students and family. Uncle Warren frowned on the world in some private misery. Sometimes he got those serious-funk, cloud-over-the-sun, fear-the-world, depression blues. Mom gets them too. But my dad was like a cure for both of them, a guiding light.

Dad and Warren were close despite their differences. Uncle Warren never married and he was always around when I was growing up, making himself a part of the family. When I moved to L.A. to start my own life—or screw it up, depending on your perspective—it was like he took it personally. And when he came up with his Poconos vacation scheme, I think he was trying to recreate some fantasy happy days of old. Family camping? We should have axed the fucking idea from the start. Hard to believe it was just two years ago. We were driving down the mountain, maneuvering around dark switchbacks looking for a campsite. Dad was up ahead with Uncle Warren, who drove the pickup pulling a trailer. Mom and I followed right behind in our little Chevy Nova. *Drove my Chevy to the levee but the levee was dry.* We came to this one turn and Dad and Warren went right off the side of the mountain. No traffic. No skid marks. Just a flying, heavy leap into the dark.

It's amazing how fast everything can get knocked out of orbit. I scrambled down the mountainside to where the pickup had landed. The impact must have been horrible. Truck and trailer were accordioned into a stand of pines.

154

Dad was thrown clear through the windshield. Warren went through the glass too, but the trailer must have roared up from behind so fast that it caught his legs on the steering wheel. He was stretched out across the remains of the hood like he was reaching for my dad.

Nearly killed Mom to lose both of 'em at once. Hospitalized twice—first for the shock, then for swallowing every bottle of pills in the house. I used to think killing yourself was for cowards and losers, but I'm not so sure anymore. Two things my mom is not is a coward or a loser, but there she was, in my dad's favorite chair, passed out and nearly gone when a neighbor found her. After coming home the second time, she couldn't stand living alone in our big, old West Philly house so she sold everything and moved into this Chestnut Hill apartment.

And me? I went back to California thinking I could pick things up right where I'd left them. Selling vinyl, doing drugs, partying as though nothing had changed. I didn't see the night falling down around me until one evening, late, when I found myself standing on a wall on the top deck of a parking garage looking down five flights of darkness to the concrete below. I couldn't get the image of that crash out of my head. I'd tried. I went on such a coke and speed binge that I had to rip off my own store to finance it. Then I ripped off my friends. Pushed people away. Shut down. Shot out the lights. Piece by piece, I broke apart. Dad and Warren gone. My turn was next, I could feel it. Next in line. Next to nothing. I looked down and my toes were hanging out over the ledge, dipping into the blackness, testing the waters.

And then I was saved. I'm serious. Amazing grace. But there was no heavenly choir of angels. No flash of light. No voice booming down from above. It was very simple, really. A hand reached out and lifted my face. A shift in perspective is all: instead of looking down, I looked up. That's it. Same darkness, just a different point of view. The sky above was as black as the street below. No stars, no moon. Nothing. *"But even nothing's got to be something."*

Okay, maybe I did hear a voice. It was my dad's.

So I took a step back and put myself in detox. The Parallax Center. Zombieville. Where they pin cheerful affirmations and happy faces on your straitjacket. But it beat the alternative, and nine months later I was released to my mom's custody. A new start. The lame helping the lame.

*   *   *

All through dinner, I knew Mom was nervous about me driving at night, but she didn't say anything. And I knew she knew I was nervous about the party, but I didn't say anything either. Classic. So with dinner over, I excused

155

myself to get ready. I put on a bit of the Brandenburg and stripped off my shirt. I wanted to look sharp for a change. Usually I wear jeans and Grateful Dead T-shirts. I'm not even a Dead Head, but I once swapped some dope for a whole case of these shirts, and years later I'm still stuck with them.

I found something in the crate with buttons—a dark-brown dress shirt they gave me at Parallax—put it on, killed the stereo, and grabbed the car keys from the bookshelf. I stash the keys behind my folks' twentieth anniversary photo—a shot of the two of them standing in front of our old house. Their arms are linked, both are flashing huge smiles, and Warren's in the background on the porch holding a happy anniversary banner. I guess I must have taken the photo.

Mom was in the kitchen fussing when I left, putting things away in the wrong places. I gave her a quick kiss and headed out back where she parks her car. I don't drive it much, mostly just to get around, *get around, I get around.* But Karen's father lives out past the Blue Route, so I fired it up and took it 'round the corner for some gas. While I was there I checked the oil and tires. I know, I was balking. Parties can be tough.

But once I was finally on the road and merging with the flow of cars heading out of the city, I felt better. Little Feat was coming out the speakers. The wind was blowing in all four windows, whipping my hair around my head. And my mind was wandering the way I let it go at work sometimes. Pieces of ideas jumped around inside my brain, and before I knew it, this little theory had started taking shape.

See, I figured that if ninety-nine percent of the universe is dark matter and only one percent is visible, the same could hold true for people. Out of a crowd of a hundred, say, only one will be noticeably special and the ninety-nine others will fill in space and make the special one stand out. So in a city of a couple million, only twenty thousand will really shine. That's probably generous. Not that there's anything wrong with the rest of us. Far from it. We might even be better people than those who shine—they just put out more light than we do. We make up the background fabric of the world, the dark matter, the underlying WIMPs and MACHOs and neutrinos who hold it all together. We're like the giant black cape, and a few sequins are stitched on to catch the light.

And I figure that people, all the time, are going in and out of being visible and invisible. Stars burn out. Then they collide with another star, gain mass, and start to glow again. Of course, some people are stars forever, like Hercules or Orion or Jesus or Buddha. Gandhi maybe. Roy Orbison definitely. *Cry-yi-yi-yi-ing.* But for most of us, we stay dark except for special moments of shining—like when we get hitched, or have a kid, or win a prize, or do a good deed, or maybe just make it intact through a tough night. The rest of the time we're the dark stuff of the cosmos, expanding forever until one day we disappear. Or there might be so much of us that eventually we'll suck the whole universe back in on itself in a big crunch of humanity, and something new and unimaginable will appear on the other side. Or nothing will appear. Or maybe that nothing is the something that will appear—who can say?

All I know is that, sitting behind the wheel tonight, cruising along the highway joined by hundreds, thousands, millions of cars all around the world, passing unnoticed through towns and neighborhoods on my way to a party of strangers who were mostly dark matter like me, somehow my little life seemed okay. Somehow I felt like I belonged.

And when I finally arrived and stood in front of a big suburban house ablaze with the energy of the music and dancing and people inside, I was ready for a party.

*   *   *

And what a party! The house was alive with bodies in motion, pulsing to the beat of something techno I'd never heard before. Two big guys in turtlenecks and sports coats stood inside the front door. One with short, black hair was laughing loudly and punching the one with a pony tail. I had them pegged: massive compact halo objects. MACHOs, big and dim at the outer gates of the galaxy. I flew on by with a nod of recognition.

Every room of the house was packed. Dark matter abounded. Dead stars. Lost planets. Brown dwarfs. Black holes. All were there, circling the cheese cubes and pretzel bowls, sucking up booze from the bar, clustering around the computer games, zipping through narrow doorways.

Most everybody was younger than me, but still, I felt like one of them. I joined the flow, a brown dwarf in a brown button shirt, roaming, watching, listening, searching. All around me, turning corners, barreling down hallways, slinking up and down stairs and in and out of rooms, a dense swarm of dark matter wearing slacks and skirts and high heels and sneakers moved through the house, clustering and regrouping, passing from nowhere to nowhere.

Eventually, I made my way to the living room where my hostess stood at the center of attention, radiating her grunge charm and refracting light from fake diamonds pinned through her ears and nose and lip and eyebrows. Her snake tattoo looked positively festive. She held a joint in one hand and a plate of carrots in the other. Decisions, decisions. She took a hit. I took a carrot.

"Great party, Karen."

She turned. "Danny! You did come!" She offered a kiss, pressing her lip post against my cheek. "I'm so glad! Molly's here somewhere. Try the deck, there's a keg out there."

I went out into the backyard, looked up, and spotted Molly immediately. She was on the deck, leaning out over the rail and gazing at the sky. Her arms were bare and her long skirt, a light blue that shimmered in the porch light, clung to her legs. She glanced down, noticed me, and beamed.

"Hey, Danny boy, you made it!" She gestured skyward. "Ain't it glorious?" Then waved me up. "Thank god you're here, I need some decent company."

I took the narrow steps two at a time and landed with a flourish.

Molly laughed and gave me a bear hug. "Glad you came." Then, in my ear, with a kiss, she whispered: "Really glad."

I returned the kiss. On her lips. And that's when things started cooking. First, I felt the hand, heavy, gripping my shoulder. Then Chuck's voice right behind me.

"Whathefuck?" He must have drunk a lot of beer to fit all those syllables into one.

I let go of Molly and turned around. Stupid me, I was still in afterglow.

"Chuckles!" I said. "How's it hangin'?"

"Didn't I say keep your hands off?"

Molly got up in his face. "Would you just butt the hell out of my business, Chuck? Just go. Get out. Get lost. Go away!"

For a few seconds, Chuck didn't know where to look. Which of us was the greater enemy? His eyes, three quarters dim from the booze, swung ominously between us. Then he made his decision. In one swift motion, he let go of me and grabbed Molly by the back of the neck. His fingers practically met at her throat.

"What d'you say?" His jaw had gone tight again.

"Whoa there, big guy," I jumped in, but he ignored me. It looked like one squeeze and he'd snap her neck. I tried again. "C'mon, Chuck, there's no problem here. Okay? It's all my fault, okay? Let go, man. *Really*, let go."

He didn't move, but his eyes kept doing that pendulum thing—back and forth, me and Molly, Molly and me. Molly didn't move either, and I could see pain and panic creeping into her eyes. I was aware of other people on the deck starting to watch us; someone slipped inside through the sliding door.

"Listen, Chuck!" I didn't know what was going to come out of my mouth next. "*Listen*, okay? I figured out who you are. You want to know?"

That slowly got his attention.

"Wha' d'you mean?"

"I figured it out. You're one of those weakly interacting massive particles. You know what I'm saying? At first I thought you were a MACHO, but now I can see you're a WIMP."

Whether brilliant or insane, it worked. He let go of Molly, turned to me, and landed a blow, hard, square in my face. The pain was immediate and immense. Both my hands covered my face as I crumpled to the deck. I heard Molly say, "You are so stupid!" and at first I thought she was talking to me but then I heard her give Chuck a nasty sounding slap. I was still blind, but I knew this could get uglier. There was a deadly second of silence. Then Karen's voice cut through from the direction of the house.

"Hey Chuck! What the hell are you doing out here? Ruining my party for god's sake? You are such an animal. I love it, but lighten up already! C'mon, get your ass inside. I'll get you a beer. And the rest of you, show's over. As you were. Give him room."

I felt a presence descend beside me on the deck.

"Danny, Danny, Danny. God, I am so sorry." Soft hands covered my hands, covering my face. "But *you*! I can *not* believe you called King Kong a wimp! You are certifiable, that's for sure. Let me see."

Molly lifted my hands. She whistled softly.

"Oh man, you are going to have one big shiner."

"As I suspected," I said, wincing up at her. "Dark matter *can* shine."

From somewhere deep inside her came an explosion of laughter. It was like a blown tire, so wrenching it could have been a cry instead. Maybe it was, because her cheeks were wet when she kissed my eye. Then her body was shaking and she was rocking and kissing me, her lips salty against mine.

Molly helped me inside, and I offered to drive her home. She hadn't come with Chuck so we found her ride and told her we were leaving. We made our way through the party and in the living room we found Karen on the couch with Chuck passed out beside her. Karen lifted her diamond-pierced face to us, and a shard of light skipped off the walls. She grinned.

"Sorry about all the excitement, Danny. You okay?"

"Oh yeah," I told her. "Perfect. It was a most memorable party."

She looked at Molly and giggled. "Good golly, Miss Molly. What a scene! What a fucking riot! What are we going to do with him?"

"No 'we' about it sweetie," Molly told her. "He's all yours."

On the way out we said goodnight to the turtleneck boys, then Molly linked her arm in mine all the way to the car. She held my hand the drive home, and kept holding on when I pulled up in front of her apartment building. We sat there, silent, for a long time. Enclosed by the night, part of the darkness, part of that cosmic nothing that holds it all together.

And now I'm back in my room at my mom's. Pain is blazing through my head, reminding me I'm alive. I'll tell you something, getting hit by Chuck was like having a supernova go off inside my head. They say you see stars? It's more like mean, gigantic flares, exploding and expanding until you think your skull's gonna split.

But I'll tell you something else. Chuck's right hook was nothing compared to Molly's kiss. That was the celestial impact right there, the brown dwarf collision. Molly and me, two stars too small to shine on our own, doubling our mass in one grand crash. I'm *still* glowing, lying here on my mattress, a warm breeze blowing over my naked body. Molly's next to me, asleep and curled against my side. And my eyes are wide open, staring at the ceiling. *Shining star for you to see, what my life can truly be. Shining star for you to see, what my life can truly be.*

"Nothing Matters" was first published in the *Laurel Review*.

Edward P. Clapp
The Shanghai Ship to Love

ONE

Imet Elise at a party at the Shore. Two bottles of wine and a number of
body shots later, Elise, a grad student from Philadelphia, and I, a
development associate for a not-for-profit organization in New York,
decided that the Garden State wasn't large enough to keep us apart.

Soon I was spending every weekend with Elise. She was researching
practical applications of third-wave feminist theory in post–*wardrobe
malfunction* society. On Saturday morning walks to the dog park near her
apartment she'd explain her theories on the death of irony and the socio-
political nuances that separated feminists who wore lipstick from feminists
who didn't. The dog park wasn't so much a dog park as a huge sink hole
that'd grown moss over itself, almost self consciously, as if to cover up some
gruesome scar. No fence surrounded it. There was no sign. No convenient
miracle of industrial design doggy-baggy-dispenser/shit-compactor to chuck
turds in. Nothing. Nothing at all indicated that hole was a dog park. You
could ask anyone: "Hey pal, where's the dog park?" and the guy'd point you
right to it. "Right there. Just over that road, pass the tracks, keep going, there
you are. Can't miss it."

The guy was right. You couldn't miss it. No doubt about it—when you
came upon that pestilential chasm, it was certain. Even when a bunch of four-
legged spuds there wasn't yipping and snipping around, sniffing. Even at
midnight, at three in the morning, at 11 a.m. on a school day, whenever you
chanced upon finding the place empty, you still knew it: dog park.

"The neo-cons thought the world would change overnight the day
Britney and Madonna made out on national television," Elise would say as
she sparked a smoke and crossed Baltimore Avenue. "It was a ploy—an

egregious conspiratorial act of propaganda developed by the religious right, thinly veiled as a media stunt facilitated by the left, conceived to drive Middle America further up the ass of father figure fear—"

Elise and I loved going to the dog park. Neither she nor I had a dog but it was where we went to get away from our separate worlds and be together; two strangers from grossly different urban environs convening with nature. Dogs yipping all around us. The robust aroma of dark roasted coffee held close to our noses, doing its best to dilute the equally full-bodied stench of countless canine fecal patties steaming away like mini-heaps of freshly over-turned compost.

" . . . and those two dumb bitches bought into it!"

TWO

For someone pulling in biweekly toilet paper–thin paychecks, spending every other weekend in Philadelphia was about as practical as drinking the days away under a palm-frond umbrella on a resort beach in Puerto Vallarta.

To make these dream weekends happen I had to be wily and inventive. I needed an economical means of conveyance, cheap transport from point *a* to point *b*. A poor man's chariot. Though dire was the dilemma, the solution was obvious as soon as I took the first test drive: the Chinatown Express bus between New York and Philadelphia.

Before it was merely the butt of bad jokes and a known source of carcinogens. Now the New Jersey Turnpike became my highway to love—and the Chinatown bus was my ticket to ride. I had favorite drivers, favorite ticket saleswomen, and favorite kung fu moves I'd subtly exercise at home, in the office, or in the conference rooms of unassuming wealthy corporate marauders masquerading as philanthropists.

The more I rode the Chinatown Express, the more the experience became a part of me.

The hawkers on each side of the line knew me by name . . . or something that sounded like my name. It might have translated to *fuck-wit* in Mandarin but it didn't matter to me. It was recognition and that's gotta mean something.

In Philly, the Chinatown Express picked up in front of a basement-level Asian video store on the corner of Tenth and Arch. No sign indicated that this was a major transportation hub. Like so many bargains, the Chinatown bus was an esoteric thing—you either knew about it or you didn't. To an unsuspecting anybody else the corner of Tenth and Arch was just another street corner in Chinatown. An innocent enough place—until a variety of sketchy characters began to amass. There was an assumed schedule, but the bus never arrived until a well-dressed Asian woman in faux leather high-heeled boots appeared to sell tickets. Ten minutes later the high-heeled woman would vanish as surreptitiously as she appeared—a bus from New York, eager to ping pong its way back, taking her place.

It's an odd scene in Philly, but it's absolute mayhem catching the Chinatown Express on the flipside.

In New York, the Chinatown bus picks up passengers on the corner of Forsyth and Division Streets, in the shadow of the Manhattan Bridge, where street-level stores sell noodles and dried fish and do dry cleaning all in one room. Two competing bus companies operate a shuttle service between New York and Philadelphia. Each has a team of cunning women on the sidewalk hawking tickets, yelling at passersby on the street, stealing passengers from one another. They'll stop any pedestrian and try to sell them a ticket, even if they don't want a ticket, even if they are just out for a stroll, or picking up their dry cleaning and some egg rolls. They'll stick their foam-core signs in people's faces and usher them toward the door of an awaiting bus, insisting that, yes, they do in fact want to go to Philadelphia today, *let me show you how!*

And it's not just Philly. You can catch a bus to Maryland or D.C., even Ohio or New Hampshire.

"D.C.! D.C.! Twenty dollar D.C.!"

"Philadelphia."

"You want go D.C.?"

"No. Philadelphia."

"D.C. Twenty dollar D.C."

"I need a bus to Philadelphia."

"Today you go Washington. Washington, D.C."

"No. Me go Philadelphia."

I don't doubt that you can catch a bus to Hong Kong from there.

THREE

Elise's apartment on Walnut Street was within walking distance of two mosques, an Indian grocer, a rusting supermarket, an Ethiopian restaurant with "Karaoke Thursdays," a box truck that mysteriously appeared each morning selling farm-fresh vegetables at criminally low prices, and the original American Bandstand studios. Despite the diversity and domestic conveniences (and the allure of American Bandstand nostalgia), the neighborhood never realized itself as a paradigm of peace and prosperity—the quintessential American community.

Elise's Philadelphia, leaning to the west, only loosely locked fingers with Philadelphia proper, standing solidly a river away to the east. It was as though the two were participating in an exercise of trust; one headstrong and steadfast, the other credulous and overextended, about to be betrayed—but still hanging on.

While the ubiquitous presence of Starbucks and eateries built on benchmarks set by nouveau American bistro cuisine marked the progress of Center City Philadelphia, Elise's neighborhood still struggled with the basics of urban infrastructure. For starters, no one in the surrounding flats had a doorbell, cellphone, or landline. In the absence of such, people were left to improvise.

"Bitch. You open the door now'r'else I come up there and beat you like an egg," a man would bark up from the sidewalk to an upper-floor window indistinguishable from its peers in a long line of anonymous, shoddy, row-house windows.

"You best turn your ass 'round and start walking right back to the piss hole you came from," a voice would respond. "Don't make me call the po-lice. You know they throw yo'r ass in jail. Don'tchu make me . . . "

"Bitch!"

Outside: Access was requested, access was denied. The details of financial obligations were argued. Fatherhood was disputed. Violence threatened. Any number of global issues were on the agenda in the conference room that existed between the open market that was the pavement and the hallowed holes that were the apartment windows above.

Inside: We listened to the Smiths.

"Morrissey represents a role model for men that women entirely lack," she'd say. "His disregard of traditional gender roles and his ability to be sexually ambiguous while still maintaining a masculine persona—in a *with us or against us* American day and age—"

Elise loved Morrissey. Elise loved the Smiths.

Weekend mornings, before a walk to the dog park, Elise and I would sit at her kitchen table and pore over the morning paper, suck down our first cups of coffee, cigarettes—listen to the Smiths. She'd crank "The Queen is Dead"—one of those sentimental Smiths songs would be playing, one that was sweet in a creep-ass way. *To die by your side . . . blah, blah, blah, the pleasure and the privilege is mine . . .*

"Let's make a collage."

"A wha?"

Take me anywhere—I don't care—I don't care—

"A collage."

Elise was an artist at heart. In minutes she reduced the morning paper to a shredded version of its former self. Scissors and glue sticks lay about the table like worn out tools on a cluttered jobsite. I drank more coffee and mentally arbitrated between a forlorn, if not headstrong, man on the street

164

and his belligerent Rapunzel while Elise hummed along with the lyrics. Out the window a cathedral with the tip of its spire lopped off weakly attempted to penetrate the sky.

"Really, the man has totally reinvented himself," Elise said. "He's given up that cycling-through-Manchester look and moved to L.A. to target a male Chicano audience—how brilliant is that?"

Johnny Marr's guitar chingy-chingied along while ethereal synthesizer chords wafted about like incense, partnering in a *pas de deux* with the exhaust of our cigarettes. Elise was steadfast in her collage composition, constructing a masterpiece loosely based on ransom-note aesthetics and Smiths themes:

> *if tonight this bus unexpectedly implodes along the new jersey turnpike*
> *and you think that you are about to die ALONE*
> *and in flames, covered in wontons, gasoline, and brake fluid*
> *skidding naked down the asphalt at 80 mph with your reality unrealized*
> *and your purpose in this world not yet ripe for the harvesting . . .*
> *know that you are wrong, because WE LOVE YOU!!!*

"Leave it on the seat."

"The what?"

"The seat," Elise said, the irrefutable look of *duh* in her eyes. "When you take the bus back to New York. Leave this note on the seat for the next passenger."

"For the next passenger?"

"For the next passenger that sits in your seat."

"Yo Janelle!"

"In my seat?"

"Janelle—c'mon baby open the door."

"For safe passage."

FOUR

Often on the bus there was a violent martial arts movie. At first I could go without the in-flight entertainment. I mean, a book, a snooze, that'd do the job. A kung fu film illegal in thirty-seven states I could deal without.

But it was free, so I watched. I watched even though it was in a Far Eastern language I couldn't make out. Luckily there were subtitles. Unluckily, the subtitles were always in characters representing yet another language I couldn't make out. No matter. The gore. The death. The killing. Arms breaking. Legs breaking. Crazy weapons flashing. The body count. It was universal. There was a vendetta. There was something to be avenged—

and more often than not there was a village burning in the night. Sometimes even aliens came down to Earth to take over the world—with extra appendages to kick and punch and leap and throw shiny weapons with. On rare occasions they showed American films, like *The Lion King*, but those too were dubbed in Asian tongues with characters for subtitles. I could pass on *The Lion King*, but it was hard to peel my eyes off a flashy kung fu movie.

On one bus trip to Philly I was so engrossed in a film about a gang of young boys terrorizing small villages and mortally wounding grown men with their prodigal killer dexterity, I didn't even notice the bus had been pulled over.

A state trooper boarded the bus with the backdrop of red and blue lights flashing like a rave hall light show. He was the Coast Guard and we were a small vessel full of illegal immigrants sailing to American shores.

There were some words between the trooper and the driver and some fumbling for information that clearly didn't exist—all the while men were having their arms chopped off and femurs were being snapped at awful angles on the little screens. After the driver had significantly tried the trooper's patience, it was announced that we all had to get off the bus—as two nine-year-olds used a bamboo pole to skewer four men with pointy beards and long ponytails.

The trooper revealed that the bus was neither registered nor insured. There was no inspection sticker in the window and some uncertainty as to the authenticity of the tags. The driver didn't even have a license. The trooper told the driver that the bus needed to be cleared and that he had to refund all of our money. The driver tried pulling a *me no speak English*. Damn convincing and likely true, but the trooper wasn't buying it. The dude wound up giving everyone their twelve bucks back as we got off the bus—off the bus and onto the side of the New Jersey Turnpike. Everyone was like: *Great, now what the—*

As soon as the trooper pulled away another bus pulled up. Another Chinatown Express. At the sight of this, the driver of the first bus ran from the highway, hopped a fence and kept running.

The new bus scooped us up like cat shit in a litter box.

Put on a movie.

Made us pay twelve bucks to be dumped in Philly.

FIVE

Elise never took the Chinatown bus. Elise had a car. The weekends she came to New York she drove, finding parking with shocking ease. It worked for her—but to this day I believe there was a special aspect of our relationship that she never experienced, which I am infinitely richer for having had.

Arranging a rendezvous time was tricky. The hundred-miles worth of variables that lay ahead made calling Elise from New York a pointless exercise. As an alternative she told me to call her when I saw the Philly skyline. This wasn't a hot plan either because the Philly skyline was invisible until the bus was engulfed in the maw of the city. That's not to say that Philly doesn't have a noteworthy skyline. Rather, the Chinatown Express doesn't approach the city from an angle that presents the skyline to the weary traveler from afar. Instead, the bus creeps up on the city, as if hoping to sneak in unnoticed.

I had to come up with a better landmark. Before long I realized that my timing would be flawless if I called Elise as the bus passed a Bob Evans restaurant in Cherry Hill, New Jersey. A call placed then gave Elise ample time to drive downtown and pick me up. When I'd arrive she'd often complain about traffic, being tired, stressed. Invariably, she'd say: "Sweetie—you smell like . . . *(sniff)* like . . . *(sniff-sniff)* like . . . sweet and sour duck."

The sauce changed—but I always smelled like a duck.

SIX

The night I arrived in Philadelphia not smelling like a duck was the most harrowing ride on the Chinatown Express I'd had.

I was on a bus so packed to capacity that the only seat left was one in the very last row, next to the bathroom. The door to the bathroom never stayed closed. This trip was no exception. However, what made this trip particularly memorable wasn't the bathroom door flapping back and forth like a barn door in a twister, rather, it was the fact that the toilet (not the kind that has a button that activates a jet action blast of water to rocket away unwanted waste into an airtight container far below the cabin—think Port-A-Potty bungee-corded to the back of Ken Kesey's bus) was overflowing and sluicing down the aisle.

Everyone kept their feet on the seats. No one touched the floor with any part of their person. It was like a game my little brother and I used to play when we were kids. We'd try to make our way around the house by jumping from one piece of furniture to the next—pretending the floor was quicksand, an alligator infested swamp, or a sea full of hungry sharks.

The smell was horrific.

Everyone with matches lit all their matches. The bus was full of smoke.

Someone sprayed an entire can of aerosol deodorant.

Nothing worked.

Of course, there were no operable windows on the bus. Asphyxiation seemed inevitable until some brave soul crawled on top of the seats and opened the emergency hatches on the roof of the vehicle.

That worked.

Sorta . . .

Being in the very back of the bus, I was at the source of the sluice—but also received the bulk of the incoming breeze. My hair was parted down the middle and feathered back like a 1984 sitcom heartthrob by the time we arrived in Philadelphia, but the air I was blessed to breathe throughout the ride was the finest, sweetest oxygen the Armpit of America had to offer.

"Sweetie!" Elise exclaimed when she saw me. She hugged me hello, then sniffed. "Sweetie what happened?"

SEVEN

If it wasn't a martial arts film, it was the radio. Sometimes there was the radio and a martial arts film, which could really overload the circuits if you weren't used to it. Rarely a ride on the Chinatown Express came without some form of entertainment, however unintentional.

On one ride, the bus driver was solely playing the radio. It was a thrash metal station transmitting from *"the bowels of Satan"* as the DJ put it. He was playing old Black Flag songs mixed in with punk rock renditions of show tunes. Oddly enough, he said he had movie tickets to give away. *"For the first caller who can tell me . . . "*

Before I'd landed in Philadelphia I'd won two free tickets to see a movie at the Bridge because I knew that *beaver in a blue suit* was a pejorative term for a female police officer in trucker lingo. I was on the radio, on the bus, live! Before signing off the DJ asked where I was calling from. My fellow passengers looked up in disbelief at the bus' speakers, then over to me. The DJ said: *"Dude . . . "*

Elise and I chose a Friday in September to see some weird Canadian film about a chick with glass legs filled with beer and a narcoleptic nymphomaniac who falls for the town's only American. On our way back to her apartment two college brats stopped us and asked if we knew where the pony rides the devil like the dawn into the night.

"No," we said.

"Are you *sure*?" they asked. Not like they thought we were lying—more like they thought we might actually know where the pony rides the devil like the dawn into the night if we only thought about it a little more. Like it was a math equation that needed some figuring. Like they'd asked, *"What's twelve minus three plus seven divided by four over two squared?"* I looked at Elise thinking maybe she knew where the pony rides the devil like the dawn into the night.

"No," she said.

"No," I said, an octave lower and two decibels louder.

Again they asked, "Are you sure?" and we said, "yeah," because by then, we were sure. We didn't know where the pony rides the devil like the dawn into the night. They realized this and a pallor swept their faces like someone had just dumped a Gatorade bucket full of sadness-flavored white-wash over their heads. I gave Elise my *can we take them home and feed them—just for one night* look. It was the look I gave her whenever an alley cat would pop up out of nowhere and rub its chin against our shins, or when we'd find wandering toddlers in the grocery store waddling the aisles aim-lessly, a squished loaf of bread or unidentifiable fish product trapped within their clutches.

Elise didn't share my sentiment; instead, she asked the following: "What the hell are you guys talking about?"

It hadn't occurred to me to ask that question.

The brats said they were pledging a fraternity and had until midnight to return to the frat house with three pink quarters. "Three what?" Elise asked. One of the brats held out his hand. Two quarters were in the middle of his palm, both painted pink. Elise began her query: "So these quarters were all planted somewhere within the city?" They nodded their heads. "And you were given clues to where these quarters were hidden?" They nodded their heads again—voraciously.

Elise had it figured out.

"Where did you find these two?"

They'd found one at the foot of the angel statue along the Schuylkill in Fairmont Park, the other they found in a Dunkin Donuts. Elise asked what clues they were given for those two.

"The clue for the one we found at the Angel statue was 'fairies dance in goose shit,'" they said. "And the clue for the one we found in Dunkin Donuts was 'Dunkin Donuts.'"

"*Dunkin Donuts*? That was your clue?" Elise said.

"Yeah," they said.

They'd been to twenty-seven Dunkin Donuts before they found the pink quarter at the bottom of a container of stir sticks at a Dunkin Donuts in South Philly.

"Wow!" Elise said.

"Holy fuck-bitch!" I said.

We were both impressed.

"You guys really have no idea where the pony rides the devil like the dawn into the night?" they gave one last stab.

"No," we said.

It was 11:38 p.m.

To make up for our uselessness we gave the brats cigarettes they didn't ask for and wished them good luck.

The brats said something that sounded like *thanks* and were gone. Elise and I fired up two smokes for ourselves. Just then we heard glass breaking across the street. A body fell from the second floor balcony of a frat house into the bushes below. There were cheers and laughter. The bushes shook for a moment, like they were cold, then the fallen body emerged, crawling out like a stepped-upon bug that wasn't dead yet. A second wave of cheers erupted from the gaggle of guys gathered on the balcony. The bug threw up on the lawn and collapsed.

Elise pulled my hand out of my pocket and tangled our fingers into a knot. "I want you to move to Philadelphia," she said, looking at me like I was cross-eyed. Like she was trying to decide which eye to focus on.

"Okay," I said, juggling my expression from retina to retina.

EIGHT

The money I arrived with quickly evaporated. Finding a lucrative job in the philanthropic arts proved fruitless. The best thing I had going was a possible gig as a bus boy at a Founding Fathers–themed restaurant in Old City. If I got the job I would have to wear britches, buckled shoes, and a puffy white shirt. Either that or stock shelves for the Thriftway across the street. Neither the Founding Fathers nor the grocery store called me back.

A third wave feminist theory research assistant's stipend wasn't enough to provide for the two of us—and Elise quickly tired of paying my way. (Not to mention there was something suspicious happening between Elise and a new research assistant she'd met. Some guy whose thesis argued that the cultural criticisms made by radical feminists ran parallel to recent shifts in modern urban architecture.)

A month after I moved to Philadelphia, Elise told me to fuck off.

The day it happened I jammed as much of my wardrobe as I could into a backpack and hopped a cab outside our apartment. The driver asked where to. I told him to take me somewhere I could get tanked for cheap. He took me to a Center City bar on Sansom Street that had a bobble-head doll theme. Not what I had in mind, but fuck it—

Inside, I planted myself on a stool, stuffed an arbitrary amount of money into my back pocket and put the rest of my cash on the bar with the intention of eating and drinking till it was gone. Surprisingly, the place had a delightful menu I couldn't resist. I ordered bottom-shelf bourbon to compensate for the extravagancy of crab cakes drizzled with chipotle sauce and a tuna burger served black and blue with caramelized leeks and bleu cheese.

Three Old Crows and several pints of grog later, I left the bobble-head bar and stumbled into the street. I pried out the money I'd stuffed into my back pocket.

170

Twelve dollars.

For the sake of efficiency, I decided I should spend it all in one place, all at once. Only one thing came to mind that would cost me exactly twelve dollars.

"New York. New York. New York twelve dollar. New York New York twelve dollar."

"One way."

"You want round trip?"

"One way."

"Round trip twenty dollar."

"One way."

"Twenty dollar round trip."

"Just one way, sweetie."

"Twenty dollar?"

"Twelve dollars."

"You want round trip for twenty dollar?"

"I want a one-way ticket to New York for TWELVE dollars."

"I sell you round trip twenty."

"Twelve."

"Round trip?"

"No."

"No come back?"

"No come back."

The bus was filling up with passengers carrying red plastic bags full of dried squid and litchis as I jammed my backpack into the overhead rack and sat down. With a quick series of spasms the bus started and rolled away.

Lights out, the kung fu movies began. The bus shook and rocked and rocked and shook and jerked and braked and accelerated and decelerated and shook and jolted and rolled. On each of the tiny television screens bones broke without ceremony, each cracking in a different color, in another language.

The bus shook and braked and accelerated.

There's nothing all that clean about the Chinatown Express. But perhaps the least clean element of the whole bus . . . I turned the handle to the bathroom door, stepped inside and let the door slam behind me just as my insides DECELERATE ACCELERATE BRAKE ACCELERATE moved back and forth.

Guts. ROCK/SHAKE ROCK/SHAKE

I lifted the cover of the toilet. The stench—

Out it came.

ROUND ONE: The crab cake and pints of grog, the bourbon and the tuna burger with the caramelized leeks and bleu cheese—

ROCK/SHAKE ACCELERATE BRAKE ACCELERATE ROCK/SHAKE BRAKE

ROUND TWO: I planted myself on the floor. On the floor of the Chinatown Express toilet. Fucking floor. Fucking toilet. Fucking—

. . . driving in your car—I never, never want to go home—

ROUND THREE: More beer, more bourbon. ROCK/SHAKE JOLT/ROLL ACCELERATE BRAKE Bile and bleu cheese. BRAKE SHAKE *FUCK*—

ROUND FOUR: I retched and shook and rocked and chucked into the well of blue shit. Blue shit. Not even liquid, whatever that stuff was, or was supposed to be. That stuff, it was a murky mass of excrement and puke and cigarette butts and piss and tampons and fucking shit, shit, shit THUD THUD

. . . and if a double-decker bus, crashes into us—

ROUND FIVE: A lumpy, massive thing with weight, with volume, not swishing back and forth so much as thumping from side to side. ACCELERATE DECELERATE Bourbon. Bile. Beer—

ROUND SIX: *(dry)* FUCK SHAKE

ROUND SEVEN: *(dry)* fuck—*FUCK!* DECELERATE FUCK SHAKE BRAKE—

. . . and if a ten ton truck, kills the both of us—

Elise.

SHAKE BRAKE *(dry)* Fuck! ACCELERATE That night—the night I left Elise's collage on the seat—that night I was humming. THUD-THUD THUD-THUD Humming that song all the way back to Manhattan: *hmm, hmm, hmm die . . . hmm, hmm, hmm your side . . .*

All the way from Philadelphia.

Thinking.

SHAKE/DECELERATE

ACCELERATE/BRAKE

BUMP

BRAKE

I thought of Elise and I watching all the little fuckers scoot around at the dog park, the way they all tackled and rolled and nipped at each other's heels, sniffing one another's asses and licking their sacks. I mean, you've got to see the beauty there, right? A bunch of dogs got dragged to that hole in the ground, got let off their leads, ran around, panting and sniffing butts. Christ— now that's interaction, that's freedom! That's fucking community, man. Jeez—if only there were bars like that—with Smiths songs on the jukebox!

But there weren't bars like that with Smiths songs on the jukebox.

There were bobble-head bars and buckled shoes and pink quarters and thrash metal stations and cigarette smoke dancing to the melody of street violence hovering in the air above our kitchen table where Elise cut the morning paper to shreds and then used a glue stick to turn our lazy weekends into collages for strangers.

If Philadelphia had a soundtrack it wasn't a Smiths song. There were no double-decker buses, no lights that never went out. Philadelphia was one long violent film in a foreign language with subtitles that didn't make sense— and the hum of the bus, the thump and thud of that noxious: THUD THUD THUD-THUD THUD-THUD

That was my lullaby, all twelve dollars worth—rock-shaking me to sleep.

ABOUT THE CONTRIBUTORS

PHYLLIS CAROL AGINS ("Black and White") has long found inspiration in Philadelphia. Two novels, short stories and essays, a children's book, and an architectural study of synagogues and churches along Old York Road were published during her years here. Lately, she divides her time between Center City and Nice, France, adding the Mediterranean rhythms to those of Fairmont Park.

MICHAEL ARONOVITZ ("The Big Picture") teaches twelfth-grade language arts in a Philadelphia charter school and creative writing at Rosemont College. Aronovitz has published short fiction in *Midnight Zoo*, *Slippery When Wet*, *The Leopard's Realm*, and *Crimson & Gray*. His *Twisted Campfire Tales*, a collection of novellas, was published in 2002. Aronovitz lives with his wife and son in Wynnewood, Pennsylvania.

B. J. BURTON ("Alexandra in the Middle of the Night") was born in Philadelphia. She writes fiction, plays, and poetry. She has been awarded two fellowships from Pennsylvania Council on the Arts and won the Pennsylvania Playwriting Award. Her plays have been produced in Pittsburgh, New York, and Philadelphia.

EDWARD P. CLAPP ("The Shanghai Ship to Love") taught writing at the Art Institute of Philadelphia while living in West Philly. His fiction and poetry have been included in journals and anthologies in the United States and the United Kingdom and his spoken word performances have been featured as part of the Edinburgh Festival Fringe and the Guild Hall (East Hampton, New York) Summer Writers Series. "The Shanghai Ship to Love" is excerpted from his first novel, *Paint*. Clapp lives and works in New York.

ELISE JUSKA's ("The Stoop-Sitters") short stories have appeared the *Harvard Review*, *Seattle Review*, *Berkeley Fiction Review*, *Calyx*, *Salmagundi*, *Black Warrior Review*, and *The Hudson Review*. She is the author of two novels, *The Hazards of Sleeping Alone* and *Getting Over Jack Wagner*; her third novel, *One for Sorrow, Two for Joy*, is forthcoming in Summer 2006. A Philadelphia native, Juska teaches fiction writing at the University of the Arts in Philadelphia and The New School in New York City.

TIM KEPPEL's ("Urban Renewal") stories have appeared in *Glimmer Train*, *The Literary Review*, *Mid-American Review*, and elsewhere. The Spanish translation of his collection, *Earthquake Watch*, is forthcoming from Alfaguara. During his years in Philadelphia he was a social worker with the homeless and in prisons. He currently lives in Cali, Colombia, where he teaches at the Universidad del Valle.

JAIME LEON LIN-YU ("We Are Pomegranates, We Are Apples") spent her college years riding the R5 into Philadelphia, getting late night meals at the South Street Diner, watching fireworks at Penn's Landing, seeing movies at the Ritz, eating cheese steaks at Gino's or Pat's (depending on which line was shorter), running up the art museum steps Rocky-style, and dating boys from UPenn. She has served as fiction editor for *580 Split* and written for AsianAvenue.com, *Seattle Weekly*, *MetroKids*, and *York Daily Dispatch*. She lives in New Jersey with her husband.

JOSH MCILVAIN (Editor, "Health Insurance and the Girl"), playwright, poet, musician, fiction writer, and professional man about town, grew up in Philadelphia. He moved to New York, then back to Philadelphia, gaining weight as a consequence. He actually followed the Phillies in the Shane Rawley years and feels the Eagles should have never traded Keith Jackson. The chicken cutlet with broccoli rabe and roasted peppers covered in melted sharp provolone from Pagano's under Ross's at Eighth and Market is one of his favorite sandwiches.

CHRISTOPHER MUNDEN (Editor, Layout) was born in Newcastle upon Tyne, England, and has lived in the Philadelphia area on-and-off for the last twelve years. He has written and edited non-fiction and fiction for various inconsequential publications and works as an editor in Old City. He lives in Queen Village and misses his cat, Bubbagus.

GREG NOVEMBER (Editor, "Dinnertime at 42B") came back to Philadelphia in the early 2000s after leaving when he was young. He moved from Upper Darby to a tiny closet in the slums of Rittenhouse. His short stories have been published in *Magazine Shiver* and *The Hiss Quarterly* and he was editor-in-chief of the student newspaper at Franklin & Marshall College. He considers the special at Bob and Barbara's the greatest deal in the Western World.

TRACY PARKER (Editor) grew up just outside Philadelphia and now lives in Society Hill. She was an editor for her college newspaper and has won awards for both non-fiction prose and artwork. She is a non-fiction editor and a student of art history. Regrettably, she is not related to Dorothy Parker.

C. NATALE PEDITTO ("The Veterans") was born and raised in South Jersey and lived in Philadelphia for nearly twenty years. In the early 1980s, he was actively involved in the local poetry scene, as a writer, performer, editor, and cofounder of the Open Mouth Poetry series. He currently lives in Los Angeles, where he is completing a book of fiction set in the bohemian milieu of 1970s–1980s Philadelphia, in which "The Veterans" will appear.

JON PETRUSCHKE ("Bragging About Annie") has had work published in *Poetic Hours*, *Paper Wasp*, *Waterways: Poetry in the Mainstream*, *Children, Churches and Daddies*, and the poetry anthology *In Our Own Words: Generation X Poetry*. He was born and raised in the Philadelphia area and now resides in Portland, Maine, with his wife and two cats.

RAFAEL REYNA ("Ecrasez l'infame") was born 12 August 1984 in Washington, D.C. He found inspiration for his Philly-based novel, *The Pilgrim*, behind the white veranda in Fairmount Park. He came to Philly in 2003, homeless, very much alone, and suffering from stomach problems. He now lives in Baltimore.

XAVIER RICHARDSON ("The Good Pretender") was a 2001 Pennsylvania Council on the Arts Fellow. In 2003 he was a semifinalist in the Great American Novelist Contest for an unpublished manuscript. He has taught creative writing workshops at the University City Arts League. When Xavier was in middle school, his uncle would get tickets to Phillies games from his boss and they would make the hour journey from rural South Jersey to the Vet. A job, then a social life, eased him across the bridge. University City has been his home since the early 1990s.

DAVID SANDERS ("Nothing Matters") has had his fiction published in *The Laurel Review*, *The Baltimore Review*, *The Bucks County Writer*, *Schuylkill Valley Journal*, and *Talking Stick Review*. His non-fiction has been widely published and has won awards that include four CASE Awards, two IABC Epic Awards, and the Jesse H. Neal Medal. He is the founder and director of the Writing Aloud series at InterAct Theatre Company. He lives with his wife, photography writer Nancy Brokaw, in Queen Village.

SERGE SHEA ("Invisible Predators") is a writer and photographer who spent most of his youth in Philadelphia. He is a graduate of NYU's M.F.A. program and a self-exiled cheese steak enthusiast. He lives in Brooklyn where he teaches high school and is finishing a book of short stories.

AMBER DORKO STOPPER ("The Slender Nerve") has been a fiction fellow of the Pennsylvania Council on the Arts and has been nominated for the Pushcart Prize (Best of the American Small Presses). She was the publisher and editor of the literary journal *Night Rally*. She has written the texts for three original Tarot decks, including The Eighties Tarot and Knitting Tarot. She believes she is the owner of the only iron handprinting press in the city of Philadelphia.

WALT VAIL ("The Red Truck") was the recipient of a New Jersey Council on the Arts Fellowship for his play *Angalak*. His plays have been produced by the Philadelphia Festival Theatre for New Plays, Society Hill Playhouse, Hedgerow Theatre, Theatre Catalyst, and have been published by Purdue University (in *First Stage*), and by Eldridge Play Publishers. Vail is literary manager at Hedgerow Theatre, a lifetime member of Philadelphia Dramatists Center, and a voting member of the Dramatists Guild of America.

THERON C. WARREN (Cover Art and Design) is a Philadelphia-based freelance graphic designer and illustrator. He has designed for Miskeen Originals and Meezan Art Couture, and various entertainment publications. He is working on an illustrated book of short stories for adults.

JIM ZERVANOS's ("Georgie") stories have appeared in the *Cimarron Review*, *Green Mountains Review*, *Chicago Quarterly Review*, and *Folio*, and on failbetter.com. Originally from Lancaster, he moved to Philadelphia in 1992 after graduating from Bucknell Univeristy. Since then he has attended Temple Law School, waited tables in Manayunk, interned at *Philadelphia Magazine*, and, for the last ten years, taught high school English in the suburbs. He lives with his wife in the Art Museum area.